Horror Stories to Ruin Christmas

Serenity Falls Forever

26 Best-selling Authors

The stories and art contained herein are the intellectual property of the individual authors and artists. No duplication may be made without the explicit consent of that author or artist.

Copyright © 2019 Delora Publishing

All rights reserved.

ISBN: 9781093647761

ACKNOWLEDGEMENTS

This is the product of many different people working as one; those combined efforts breathed life into a world that otherwise never would have existed. Each author has their own moment in the coming pages, so this is the time to recognize those who contributed by doing things beyond just putting words together.

Rebecca Levine and Ashley Collinge checked every word, then tied twenty-six stories into one.

Taylor Tate did thirteen illustrations and the cover art. She made this book come alive in ways that simple writing cannot.

They are invaluable denizens of Serenity Falls.

CONTENTS

	Foreword	Pg. 7
1	On the First Day of Christmas, I Lost my Innocence	Pg. 9
2	On the Second Day of Christmas, my World was Destroyed	Pg. 15
3	The Third Day of Christmas is Well-Behaved	Pg. 25
4	The Fourth Day of Christmas is Hot as Hell	Pg. 39
5	The Fifth Day of Christmas is for the Lonely	Pg. 47
6	The Sixth Day of Christmas is Pied	Pg. 53
7	The Seventh Day of Christmas is Stuffed	Pg. 57
8	On the Eighth Day of Christmas, I Encountered a Death Cult	Pg. 65
9	On the Ninth Day of Christmas, an Opportunity Presented Itself	Pg. 71
10	On the Tenth Day of Christmas, T'wasn't a Bear	Pg. 77
11	The Eleventh Day of Christmas Dug Too Deep	Pg. 85
12	The Twelfth Day of Christmas Isn't Very Funny at All	Pg. 91
13	On the Thirteenth Day of Christmas, my Luck Ran Out	Pg. 103

DISCONTENTS

14	The First Night of Christmas is for Special People	Pg. 113
15	The Second Night of Christmas is a Huge Mistake	Pg. 125
16	The Third Night of Christmas is Well-Intentioned	Pg. 129
17	The Fourth Night of Christmas is Full of Regret	Pg. 145
18	The Fifth Night of Christmas is for the Sociopath	Pg. 155
19	The Sixth Night of Christmas is for All the Sweet Boys	Pg. 161
20	The Seventh Night of Christmas is Empty	Pg. 177
21	The Eighth Night of Christmas is Clandestine	Pg. 187
22	The Ninth Night of Christmas is Like Pulling Teeth	Pg. 193
23	On the Tenth Night of Christmas, T'was Too Much to Bear	Pg. 197
24	The Eleventh Night of Christmas Keeps Bad Company	Pg. 201
25	The Twelfth Night of Christmas is Just Pretend	Pg. 207
26	The Thirteenth Night of Christmas is Merry	Pg. 215
	A Final Note	Pg. 225

*THIS BOOK IS DEDICATED
TO THE MEMORY
OF ALL THE VICTIMS
FROM SERENITY FALLS, WISCONSIN*

FOREWORD

This book is a single fallen domino in an unpredictable string of unplanned events.

A man by the name of Chris Smith made a passing comment in November 2017 that twenty-six writers should combine their efforts on the NoSleep forum of the online Reddit community.

The comment almost got overlooked. But a few people thought it was a good idea. Then a few dozen people wanted to join their project. The plan went from an online collaboration to a published book, and most of the writers got to see their names in print for the first time.

A year later, twenty-six people combined their efforts once more. The result, for better or for worse, is the book in your hands.

It wasn't the same twenty-six people, however. The most prominent absence is that of Kyle Alexander. He had developed a supportive online fan base, and he was featured in multiple books. Kyle had a young son.

Kyle died in an accident on May 31st, 2018.

Many of us had been caught up in the idea of stories leading into other stories, excited to see what the next toppled domino would set in motion. I, for one, had embraced the cocky assuredness that there would always be another page to turn.

Kyle's loss leaves a prominent gap in the chain. The unwritten stories that he would have shared create a powerful emptiness in the narrative that, by all rights, should have been filled in by him.

We've wanted to find a reason that makes the sadness go away. What we received instead was a powerful reminder that we aren't guaranteed a damn thing about tomorrow, no matter how special the path in front of us seems to be.

Our only option is to keep pushing the next domino. The hope of all writers is that their work will set in motion a chain of events that eventually takes on a life of its own.

Everyone will eventually put down their pen for the last time. Stories have a hope of immortality that the writer does not, and each storyteller is scrambling to spin the right combination of words that will connect with the rest of us after they're gone.

Kyle achieved this. And as these twenty-six dominoes tumble, please remember that they were set in motion by people who are still here, even if they're not.

-P. F. McGrail

January 2019

HORROR STORIES TO RUIN CHRISTMAS

ON THE FIRST DAY OF CHRISTMAS, I LOST MY INNOCENCE

BY TOBIAS WADE

My father was a diplomat who shook hands with the most powerful people in the world. A businessman with foreign affairs, managing an empire so vast that the sun never set upon it. He was an Army veteran in Afghanistan and a doctor in Ethiopia. In fact, he was so important that he went everywhere and did everything—except for come home, that is.

I used to love hearing stories about him when I was younger. I liked to imagine that I'd get to meet him someday, and the two of us would go everywhere I had heard about in mom's stories. It wasn't until I was eight years old that I realized how strained her voice was when she talked about him, or how selfish I was for always bringing him up. I didn't ask for any more stories after that, and mom never brought him up on her own.

She must have loved him terribly for it to still hurt after all these years. My mother once said the longer you wait for something you want, the better it is to have, like interest building up in the bank. So every day he didn't come home wasn't a punishment, it would only make their reunion that much happier when it finally did happen.

It would have been so much easier if he did come back though. I wouldn't have to walk home from school because mom would be there to pick me up. I wouldn't have to make my own dinner because mom wouldn't need a second job in the evening. Some nights I'd try to stay up until she got back, but I'd usually fall asleep on the couch watching TV and wouldn't see her until the morning when she woke me in my bed.

The older I got, the less sense my mother's stories made. Even if only one of them was true, he must have had at least one opportunity to visit by now. Army contracts are only 4 years, and if he was as rich and important as she said, then he should have been able to send a little money so mom wouldn't have to work so hard.

The only explanations I could think of were that he was either dead or lost. If he was dead, I intended to find out where he was buried so mom wouldn't have to keep waiting. If he was lost, I'd help him find his way home again. A friend suggested that my parents might have gotten divorced and just didn't love each other anymore, but I didn't think that was true. Mom wouldn't still be hurt if she didn't love him, and I didn't think it was possible for anyone not to love my mom.

So I started my search. I asked my grandparents on my mother's side, but they were tight-lipped and quick to change the subject. I spent my lunches looking for him online on the school computers, but there were hundreds of people with the same name and I only had a single grainy photo to compare it with. He might have gained weight, or grown a mustache, or even lost an arm in battle for all I knew.

The one thing I was sure about was that he never changed his name, because if he was lost then he'd want to be found again. So I started going down the list of the hundreds of people with the right name and sending each a message asking if they were my dad.

Most didn't reply. Some seemed concerned, others creepy, but I didn't let that bother me. I started out with my city, Serenity Falls, but quickly expanded my search to the whole state of Wisconsin. We'd moved around quite a bit when I was younger, but we'd never left the state so I thought that's where he must be looking for us.

At last, the day came. I messaged someone and asked if they were my father, and he replied with my mother's name, and I knew I'd found him. He was older than I expected and most of his hair was gone, but he still looked a lot like the photograph. A lot like me. And no one using the other school computers could understand why I started to cry.

He asked a bunch of questions about my mother. He asked for pictures of her and wanted me to tell him everything. I told him what city we lived in, and he promised to drive there right away even though it was over a hundred miles away. He didn't seem to mind that mom would still be at work because he was excited to meet me too.

For the first time in my life, my dad was going to pick me up from school. I couldn't focus or sit still through any of my remaining classes. When the final bell rang I exploded out of my chair so fast I knocked my whole desk over, but I didn't stay to pick it up. I was the first out of the building and made it to the parking lot within a minute. He was already waiting for me.

My dad had even less hair than his picture, but I didn't mind because he drove a red Ferrari. I asked if he really was an international businessman, and he laughed and said he did that in his spare time.

He didn't want to meet mom at home or at work because that wasn't romantic. Instead, he wanted to take me to the real Serenity Falls the town is named after. That's where they had their first date, and he wanted to surprise her. I texted mom and let her know a surprise was waiting for her there, and she promised to get off work early.

It was only about a twenty minute drive, but I felt like we really bonded in that time. Dad didn't like talking about himself and asked me a thousand questions instead. What games did I like to play? How was I doing in my classes? Who were my friends, and a thousand other nothings. His eyes would light up with even the most boring answer as though it was a miraculous revelation from on high.

I teased him for that, but he got all serious and said, "You don't understand. I didn't even know you existed until today. You aren't just telling me about yourself—you're being created from nothing right here in front of my eyes. It really is a bit like a miracle."

Serenity Falls was quiet around the holiday season. We were the only ones in the parking lot, so we got to drive all the way to the head of the trail which led to the viewpoint. The water had frozen in to snow and ice, and it wouldn't be a waterfall again until the thaw of the spring. It was still beautiful because of the long icicles lancing off the jagged rock. The light seemed trapped within the crystals, who shimmered as it faded.

We stood together in silence overlooking the falls for several minutes. I started to shiver, but he put his arm around me and drew me close, and I almost started to cry again without knowing why.

"When is your mom going to be here?" he asked at last.

"Not for at least an hour."

"Do you want to wait in the car where it's warm?" he asked.

"Why did you really leave?" I blurted out.

He withdrew his arm from around my shoulders and we stood together in silence again.

"I lied earlier," he said, still staring at the hanging ice. I counted twenty-six individual icicles before he continued. "I did know you existed before today."

"Then why did you—" I cut myself short.

"I wasn't ready. I loved your mother, but I didn't want to have a family yet. I'm sorry."

I shrugged as if it had nothing to do with me, but I couldn't look at him.

"Were you really in the Army?"

"I was."

"And a diplomat? And a doctor?"

He laughed in response. It was a warm sound, and I wasn't shivering anymore.

"But you really did love my mom?" I asked.

"I still do. More than anything," he said. "That's why I'm here. But I'm still not ready to have a kid. I don't think I ever will be."

It hadn't gotten any colder, but I started shivering again anyway. He put his arm around me again, but it didn't feel as comforting as it had before. His fingers were gripping my shoulder a little too tight.

"It's only going to be cold for a minute," he said. "After that you won't even feel it. It'll be just like drifting off to sleep."

"I want to go back to the car." I tried to pull away, but he wouldn't let go.

"Everybody wants something," he said, "but not everybody is willing to do what it takes to get it."

He slid behind me, and suddenly both of his arms were around me. I struggled and kicked, landing a solid one to his thigh before he got me fully off the ground. He grunted but didn't let go as he lifted me over the railing. I braced my feet against it and tried to push back, but he lifted me even higher until I couldn't reach it anymore.

He flung me over the ledge to tumble down the twenty-foot drop to the frozen water. I smashed straight through the ice and plunged into the numbing depths. I spun over once or twice trying to orient myself, and by the time I was able to surge upward again I couldn't find the hole I'd broken through.

All I could feel was the underside of the ice. It was thicker than it seemed when I fell through. My numb fists moved sluggishly through the water, pounding feebly. I went back to searching for the hole instead, but the freezing water stung my eyes so badly I could barely see.

I saw the vague outline of his shape through the ice though. He was standing directly over me, looking down. He watched me flail against the underside. The weight of my wet clothes was beginning to drag me down, and my chest felt like it was about to explode. Each time I surged upward it became a little harder to reach the ice, until I couldn't reach it at all and began drifting down.

I watched him turn and start climbing up the slope, and everything went black. I came to a moment later when I heard the sports car rev to life and pull away. I lurched upward again, and by blind chance one hand slipped through the hole in the ice. I couldn't feel my fingers as they latched onto the edge. Somehow the air was even colder than the water, but inch by excruciating inch I dragged myself upward until I was out of the water.

I was barely alive when my mom found me. I didn't want to tell her what happened at first, but even lies meant to protect someone can do more harm than good. I told her everything, and she promised never to let that man back into our lives again.

If my future children ever ask me about my father, I'm going to tell them the truth. That he tried to kill me, that he was never caught, and that no family is incomplete that has love.

HORROR STORIES TO RUIN CHRISTMAS

ON THE SECOND DAY OF CHRISTMAS, MY WORLD WAS DESTROYED

BY TARA A. DEVLIN

THE MAN FROM THE REAL ESTATE COMPANY GRINNED AT me from the front porch again.
"Good morning, sir! Have you perhaps reconsidered our offer yet?"
I rubbed my forehead. This guy just wouldn't quit.
"Look, I told you the first time, I'm not selling the farm. Stop coming around here, it's not going to happen." I was losing what little patience I had left. Every day for the last five days he'd appeared at my front door, flashing that creepy grin and holding out a card with "Pure Serenity Realty" emblazoned in bold letters upon the top.
"But sir, have you truly considered how lonely it gets all the way out here, away from the safety of civilization?"
I wanted nothing more than to punch that grin off his face.
"I like the isolation," I said.
He continued to hold the card out in front of him. "But sir, there is a downside to that isolation as well."
"And what's that?"
"There's nowhere to run."
I narrowed my eyes. "Get off my property." I slammed the door in the man's face, my hands shaking with rage. Was he threatening me? I turned to my wife, who was preparing breakfast in the kitchen.
"Can you believe this guy? How many times do I have to tell him, we're not gonna sell. And now he's making thinly veiled threats!"
"Well, if he doesn't get the message now, he must be thicker than a stack of bricks." She was mixing scrambled eggs for a late breakfast. She knew despite the man's tireless efforts to convince me to sell our farm, it wasn't going to happen. The farm had been in my family for generations, and my children, both grown up now, would be home that very afternoon for Christmas. I had more pressing matters to concern myself with.
"Did you clean Jack's room?" Amanda called out as she poured the eggs into the pan.
"I was planning on it later today."

"Don't forget you need to air out Syd's bedding, too."

"Yes, dear."

The kids arrived later that night and I ran to the front gate to help them with their luggage.

"Hey! It's so good to see you again. How was the ride?"

"Not bad," Jack said. "As usual, the closer we get to home, the less there is to see, but we did pass an awesome red Ferrari on the way."

Syd nodded and brushed past me toward the house, chatty as always.

"A red Ferrari, hey? Fancy." Jack and I soon followed her. "And how's school?"

"Okay. How's the farm?"

"Okay. Well, some guy keeps trying to buy it from me and he won't leave us alone."

"Did you tell him where to go?"

"Several times. He didn't seem to take the hint."

"Let me deal with him next time he's here. I'll make sure he gets the picture."

I smiled. Despite being the youngest, Jack was a head taller than myself and much broader in the shoulders as well. He was certainly more physically intimidating than my old frame.

"Let's just hope he got the message last time. Although, he's been very persistent…"

We walked into the living room and Jack stopped, mouth agape.

"What the…"

He was looking at the 26 bottles of Chartreuse lining the wall. He turned to look at me and blinked a few times, at a loss for words.

"Dad, is there something you'd like to talk about?"

I shrugged. "They were on special, the liquor store in town was having a going out of business sale. It would have been a shame to let it all go to waste."

Jack picked a bottle up and smiled. "Guess you won't miss just one then."

I motioned for him to take it. Syd was already upstairs.

"Ugh. Dad, did you even air my room out since I was here last?"

Amanda stuck her head around the corner and raised her eyebrows knowingly. I shooed her away.

"I have Chartreuse!" I called upstairs.

"I don't drink."

Jack shrugged his shoulders and took the bottle of yellow liquor and his luggage up to his room. I sighed. Jack and I were like best friends, but Syd... Syd was more like a much younger, distant cousin I only saw at family reunions every ten years, and not my first-born. She barely responded and when she did, it was with short, curt answers. She wasn't being rude, I knew that, but I wished she would open up to me more, like Jack did. She was my daughter, after all.

"You kids get comfortable and then go wash up, dinner will be ready soon! We're having your favorite, homemade lasagna!" Amanda announced from the kitchen. I smiled. It was going to be a great Christmas.

But when I woke up the next morning, I found a decapitated sheep strung up between two trees. Its head was nailed to the nearby barn door.

"Oh my god." Jack took a step back at the sight. "Who could do such a thing?"

I had an idea who.

"Fetch the axe. We need to get this down before your mother sees it."

The sheep hit the ground with a plop. Jack got to work digging a hole while I removed the head from the barn. My insides burned with fury. There was no mistaking it; it was that man from the real estate company. He was trying to scare me out of my own home.

"So," I joined Jack with a shovel of my own, "have you thought much about my offer?"

"To help you on the farm after school finishes?"

"Yeah." We were out of sight from the house, and the headless sheep with its guts torn open lay flat on the grass beside us.

"I dunno. I mean..." His voice trailed off as he scooped out another shovelful of dirt.

"Farm work isn't for you." I finished the sentence for him. He grimaced.

"It's not that, but... there's nothing here for me, you know? In Serenity Falls. I grew up here, and I love the farm, I really do, but..." He looked down at the sheep. "I wanna go somewhere new. See new places. Try new things."

I forced a smile. "It's okay, son. I understand." Truth of the matter was, I had no one to take over the farm when it was my time to move on. Retirement was still a few years off, but it was never too soon to start thinking about the future.

"Why don't you ask Syd?"

I almost laughed in his face.

"I'm sorry, Syd? Doing farm work?"

This time Jack raised an eyebrow at me.

"She's not a dainty little princess, you know, and maybe if you tried talking to her more, you'd see that."

I stopped digging and stood up straight.

"What's that supposed to mean?"

Jack continued piling dirt next to the sheep's head.

"Nothing."

We finished digging in silence, but his words weighed on my mind. I didn't treat her like a dainty princess, did I? And if I did, it was only because she was my little girl, and she would always be my little girl.

We did our best to put the gruesome discovery behind us and continue the day as normal. Christmas was coming up and the family was all together again, it was supposed to be a happy occasion. But doubt niggled at the back of my mind. About what Jack said about Syd, and about that man from the real estate company.

"Syd. Can I talk to you for a moment?" I approached my daughter after dinner as she read a magazine in the living room.

"What?"

"Uh, outside, if you don't mind."

She put her magazine down on the table and wordlessly walked outside.

"What is it?"

I closed the door behind us and looked around. The farm was dark and cold. I rubbed my hands together and blew on them a few times. I didn't know where to start, so I grabbed the first thing that came to mind.

"One of the sheep was killed today."

She raised an eyebrow. The resemblance to her brother was uncanny. "And?"

I scratched the back of my head. Jack was right. I had to stop treating her like a dainty princess. Maybe... maybe she could help.

"It was strung up between two trees. Its... its insides were torn out. And... it was missing its head."

"Okay..."

I took a deep breath. "I think someone's trying to run us out of the farm, and I think this might only be the beginning."

Syd crossed her arms and looked at me a little more seriously. "Have you been to the police?"

I shook my head. "You know we deal with matters on our own out here."

"Do you know who it is?"

"I have an idea."

"What do you want me to do?"

A scream from inside the house interrupted us.

"Mom!"

"Amanda!"

I threw the door open and rushed inside. Amanda was slumped on the kitchen floor, holding her stomach. A bloody knife lay on the tiles before her, and blood trickled through her fingers.

"Oh god…" Syd covered her mouth in shock.

"A… A man…" Amanda's voice trembled as she pointed towards the door.

Jack came pounding down the stairs. "What's wrong? What's wrong?" He took one look at his mother bleeding on the floor and his eyes shot open wide.

I froze. I didn't know what to do. My wife was bleeding out on the kitchen floor and all I could think was how strange her dress looked with that growing red stain on it.

"Dad. Dad!" The word was faint and distant. Syd grabbed my arms and shook me. "Dad!"

"W-What?"

"Who was it?"

"I'm sorry?"

"You said you suspected someone. Who?"

"O-Oh, um…" I couldn't think. My mind was a fog, and my ability to comprehend ground to a halt. "I don't remember his name… something like… Al or… Frank or… I don't know! The real estate guy!"

"The real estate guy?"

Jack was holding a tea towel to his mother's stomach, his face white as a sheet. Syd took charge.

"Jack, call an ambulance, now." She threw her phone at him. "Dad, come back to me." She slapped my cheek a few times. "I need you here right now. Mom will be okay, but only if you're here with us, okay?"

I nodded. "Y-Yeah, sure, of course. What do you need?"

"This real estate man, if it really is him, can't be far away. He's gotta be outside somewhere. He's trying to scare us, and clearly he's willing to go to any lengths to do it. But he didn't bargain on one thing."

"What's that?"

"I'm not letting anybody ruin my Christmas."

The lights suddenly turned off all at once, plunging us into darkness.

"Dad, where's your gun?"

Jack was pressing the screen on Syd's phone over and over with bloody fingers. Finally, he threw it down in disgust.

"It's not working! Dad, what are we gonna do?"

My head felt like a sledgehammer had been taken to it. I looked at Jack on the floor, holding my wife's guts in with a towel.

"We… don't get good reception out here," I said. I turned to Syd, doing everything I could to maintain my composure and not break down in front of her. "The… the gun's in the shed. I think." I didn't remember the last time I used it. There wasn't much use for it out here.

A window broke in the living room and everyone turned at the same time. Syd brushed past me before I could stop her.

"Hey, asshole! I'm not scared of you!"

I followed her and tried to grab her arm, but she shrugged me off. She grabbed one of the bottles of liquor and smashed it against the windowsill.

"You think it's fun to pick on poor farmers, huh?"

A dark figure stood outside the window. A balaclava was pulled down over his face, and his clothes were equally black. He looked at Syd, around her towards me, then disappeared into the night.

"Oh no, you don't." Syd ran for the front door, broken bottle in hand. The room smelled both spicy and sweet. It reminded me of Christmases when the children were younger. The smell of gingerbread and the fancy spice cake my wife liked to make. The kids would sit by the tree and tear open their presents, and I would kick back in my chair with a warm drink. They were good times. I missed those times.

It took me a moment to realize my daughter, in the present, was running after a potential murderer and not sitting by the tree with her presents.

"Syd, wait! No!"

I ran out the door after her. She was running towards the shed, and by the time I reached her, she had already yanked the doors open.

"Where's your gun, Dad?"

"Sweetie, we need to get out of here. We need to get your mother to a hospital."

"You go and take Jack. Go. I'll take care of this asshole."

She turned the barn light on and we both froze. The man was standing there, and he had my gun in his hands.

"Get down!"

A bang echoed throughout the barn, followed by the tinkling of glass falling. The silhouette of the man standing on the other side of the barn burned into my eyes before all illumination disappeared. He'd only shot the light, like a specter toying with its prey. We were alive and unharmed, but if we didn't do something, we wouldn't be for much longer.

I dragged Syd out of the building and ran down the side.

"Dad! Let me go! What are you doing?"

The shovels. They wouldn't be much good in a gunfight, but they would be better than nothing. Both were laying on the ground next to the sheep's grave. I picked one up when we got there and handed it to Syd. She looked at it like I just handed her an alien baby.

"It's got a little more reach than your broken bottle there," I said.

She held the bottle up close to my face, and I took a step back before I could stop myself. "Yeah, but my broken bottle can at least cut a man."

There was another shot in the distance. We fled into the trees.

"Shoulda just sold the farm!" A voice bellowed from the darkness. "I didn't want it to come to this!" Another shot. I indicated with my head and we crawled back toward the barn. He was still standing in the doorway, scanning the area. Before I could stop her, Syd ran out and screamed, thrusting her broken bottle toward the man's face. They fell to the ground and tussled. Jack's words echoed in my mind.

"She's not a dainty little princess, you know."

No, she most certainly wasn't.

It took a few moments to realize my only daughter was wrestling with a crazed murderer. The man who had attempted to cut my wife's insides out. I ran over and, with a scream, brought the shovel down hard on his side. The gun went off. I shielded my eyes and my ears rang. I couldn't see or hear anything.

"Syd! Syd!" I could barely hear my own voice over the echo in my head. I groped around on the dirt and felt a warm body. It was covered in sticky liquid.

"No. No!"

I opened my eyes and squinted into the darkness. A figure was taking off in the distance. Syd was lying in the dirt in front of the barn, a giant hole in her side.

"No, no, no, no."

The man was getting away. It wouldn't be long before he disappeared into the trees, and then I'd never be able to find him; not in this darkness.

"Mom! Mom, wake up!"

Jack's screams reached my ears on the wind. The cold, numbing wind. I put my fingers to Syd's neck and waited. Nothing. The farm filled with the sounds of Jack's cries and little else. I fumbled around in the darkness for the gun, but it was gone. The man took it with him. I laughed, but the laughter soon turned into tears.

"Shoulda just sold the farm!"

I picked my lifeless daughter up and stumbled towards the house. I didn't want to see what I knew was waiting for me there.

There would be no Merry Christmas. Not anymore.

HORROR STORIES TO RUIN CHRISTMAS

THE THIRD DAY OF CHRISTMAS IS WELL-BEHAVED

BY JACK T. ANDERSON

THEY ARRIVED QUIETLY, UNANNOUNCED AND understated, hanging patiently from the common hackberry trees of Serenity Falls. No one knew who put them up, or when, for that matter. So subtle was their appearance that by the time anybody noticed the strange posters on Wilt Avenue, the low quality printer paper had already become waterlogged, black ink bleeding into empty space like fungus on a branch, and a green-orange bloom of rust had formed across the cheap thumbtacks which pinned each notice to its tree.

I wish they'd never received the attention they did. I wish we'd all simply passed them by, until the rain and snow soaked the stock into shreds of wadded tissue, smudging the text into pools of gray mush, degrading its structure until they slipped from their pins and fell to the ground. Harmless mulch. Dead words decomposing on a wet sidewalk.

Suffice it to say, that isn't how this story ends.

It was earlier in the month, November 3rd, I think, when someone first passed by the modest black and white posters and circulated a grainy picture on one of the town's message boards. Our ever dwindling online community is propped up on the industry of small business owners, farmers, yard sale enthusiasts, and bored parents, the latter of whom started sharing the picture around almost immediately.

Which one of you thought of this?

On Shetland St too. Took a flyer in front of Archie this morning!

New Elf on the Shelf?

Someone should take these down.

I didn't comment, personally. I'm a long way from being a parent—I'm actually not sure I want kids all that much—but I still spend a lot of time on these parenting forums. I've been babysitting other people's children for a few years now; it's pretty chill, gives me time to do homework and writing, and it's one of the rare jobs available for 11–16 year olds in Serenity Falls. As someone on the more senior end of that spectrum, I've had a few years to make a name for myself: Sarah Jennings, babysitter extraordinaire; more reliable than an older sibling, easier to kick out than a mother-in-law.

I was halfway through posting my availability in the odd jobs section, looking to land a few gigs in the lead up to the holiday season, when my egregiously short attention span deflected me towards the aforementioned post. It was easily the busiest chain on an otherwise deserted message board. 998 comments, 74% liked, a range of opinions roughly 70/30 in favor of these strange black and white posters.

The unexpanded image was kinda shitty, and I didn't care enough to open it up at the time. Briefly scanning over it as I made my way back to the other tab, I was able to make out the ad's key phrase at the very top, scrawled in black sharpie, much larger than anything around it:

Bad Man's Home

A few days later, I got to see the notice in person.

I was heading to a regular babysitting job, the Sullivan household on Wilt Avenue. Mr. Sullivan is one of the few adults who has my number in his phone, largely due to the fact that he's a recently single father whose place of work is prone to late night meltdowns.

Mr. Sullivan's kid, a seven year old named Charlie, is super cute but undoubtedly a handful. Where a lot of kids nowadays can sink themselves into a tablet for three or four hours without coming up for air, Charlie would probably end up using it as a frisbee. He spends every waking moment running through the house, jumping down the stairs, crawling under tables, wielding an imaginary sword to save an imaginary friend from an imaginary foe. My job is to watch him bounce off the walls until he tires himself out, keep him off the furniture, and make sure he doesn't get near the knives.

I was actually looking forward to seeing him as I walked down Wilt Avenue, awkwardly fishing some headphones out of my backpack. When I was about three houses down, I saw a white rectangle of weathered paper hanging against the trunk of one of Serenity Fall's hackberry trees, the last tree before Mr. Sullivan's house.

Immediately recalling the rather hysterical forum post from a few days before, I kept my eyes on it as I drew closer, the words "Bad Man's Home" coming quickly into view.

After approaching a little further, I stopped walking, and examined the poster in full view.

Bad Man's Home

He has come. Here Winter Long. To take Misbehaved & Cruel.

Take A Number. Call If Boys & Girls:

Is Bad

Is Cruel

Breaks

or Hits.

No Tree For Presents. No Chimney For Toys.

No returns once took. Boys & Girls Kept.

The bottom of the sign had been cut into little strips of paper. Each one had the same cell phone number scrawled messily along it, ending in 0026.

That was it. Nothing special, nothing world ending. Just some Babadook-y, Krampus-y boogeyman that a random parent had concocted in the lead up to Christmas. Whoever had done it had made the flyer look like it was written by some kind of monster, jagged, uneven letters, and the stilted syntax of something with only a vague grasp of human language.

I had to admit it wasn't bad work.

I could imagine the strips at the bottom being torn from the sheets around town, brandished by impatient mothers at their misbehaving children, the number half-dialed by beleaguered fathers in a bid to quell their kid's tantrums.

On this poster alone, four strips had already been torn off.

I wasn't so sure if it sat well with me as I knocked on Mr. Sullivan's door and heard his footsteps from the hall. But, then again, I only have these kids for an evening a week. Parenting is a full time job, and I'd learned early on that I was in no position to judge. A Santa here, a boogeyman there. I guess these things exist for a reason.

"Hey Sarah, thanks for coming, I know it's short notice." Mr. Sullivan appeared at the door quickly, putting his jacket on as soon as it opened. "Charlie's in the living room, and there's money for you to order food on the table."

"No worries at all, thank you."

"Okay, I'll be back around the normal time, and I'll give you a call when I'm on my way." He smiled as we changed places, calling back through the door as he rushed down the steps. "Charlie, be good for Sarah, okay?"

Curiously, Charlie didn't reply. In fact, the house was unusually silent, no hammering footsteps on hardwood, no unintelligible battle cries from down the hall. I noticed a flicker of concern on Mr. Sullivan's face as he crossed the sidewalk and climbed into his car.

As I walked into the living room, the faint sound of some kids TV show rose through the silence. A team of superheroes were fighting across Mr. Sullivan's 4K setup, each member sporting a primary color and battling for planet Earth in the middle of a quarry. Charlie was sitting on the opposite sofa, bathed in the glow of the screen. Despite it being his favorite type of show, he didn't look at it once. His eyes were staring off into one dark corner of the room.

Something was up.

By this point, on any normal day, Charlie would have already greeted me with a hug and been sprinting up the stairs on all fours, intent on fighting evil on every piece of furniture he could find. The Charlie before me wasn't just still, he was *keeping* still. A conscious lack of movement, the kind that takes effort to maintain. Instead of letting his feet dangle down from the sofa, kicking rhythmically against the leather like normal, his knees were tucked up against his chest, his arms wrapped tightly around his legs.

His guard was up, and whatever shadowy force he feared, it was clearly too powerful for his sword and shield to handle.

"Hey Charlie, are you okay?"

He didn't answer. Instead, he looked up at me silently, then back to the corner of the dark room with a sense of fearful vigilance. As soon as I sat down, he immediately latched on to me, tightly and wordlessly, as if I were the last rock before the waterfall. His eyes never wavered however, remaining fixed on that dark point in space, paying it his unflinching attention.

Once my eyes were able to adjust, I saw what he was staring at: a small side table and, resting on top of it, a cordless landline phone.

We sat there for almost an hour. Any questions I asked ran into a wall of silence, struggling uselessly to get any purchase on his mumbled, one word answers.

I'd almost given up entirely when, in the dancing light of the TV, he turned his attention away from the phone and, for the first time, towards me.

"Sarah... what's... a femur?" He asked quietly under his breath, as if he didn't want anyone else to hear.

"Where did you hear that?"

Again, no answer.

"It's a bone in your leg. It's the thigh bone." I replied, lifting one of my legs up on the couch, and pointing.

Charlie held in place for a moment, pulling back into himself in the same way an ocean recedes before a tidal wave wrecks the shore. Seconds later, the steadily crescendoing air raid siren of a child's cry filled the room, an unchecked river of tears streaming from Charlie's eyes.

I felt his grip tighten, latching onto me even harder, as if he were scared that letting go would cause him to fall sideways into the dark corner of the living room, never to be heard from again.

He didn't say anything else for the rest of the night, but he kept me by his side the entire time, his hand only letting go of mine when he finally drifted off to sleep later in the evening.

I never learned why he'd asked that question, or what he'd heard to make my answer so deeply distressing to him.

I had to admit though, the kid was better behaved than I'd ever seen him, and in some ways, that's what concerned me the most.

A week later, new posters went up.

I'd already heard about it as I made my way down Wilt Avenue to the Sullivan house. The reaction to the signs was decidedly cooler than it had been a week prior, but it was still a definite talking point among the parenting community, of whom a small handful had, in one form or another, employed them with their children.

Tbf they're being suuuuper well behaved now

Did other people try? Didn't expect the call to go through.

I never called it. Don't know why anyone would

I think this is worth telling Sergeant Weis about.

I'm taking them down wherever I see them. This is not funny.

The next time I visited Mr. Sullivan's house, I made a point to check out the latest edition. The poster was only about three days old this time, not nearly as worn as its predecessor.

Bad Man's Home

He is choosing. Expect Him and Behave.

Answer His Call.

No Doors here. No Windows. No running on broken things.

The vague sense of threat was elevated now, or perhaps the opposite, more grounded. The statements made across these new flyers seemed less like the ramblings of a fairy tale monster and more like the threats of a deeply disturbed individual.

Suffice it to say, no one had taken a number this time.

When Mr. Sullivan answered the door, I could tell he looked worried. He greeted me distractedly, making idle small talk as he made his way out the door. Stepping quickly down onto the sidewalk, he briefly turned back to me.

"If anyone, um… if anyone…" He searched to find the words, but decided to call it off halfway through. Instead, he just looked at me, a pained expression on his face, and simply said "Thank you for looking after him tonight."

I smiled, nodded, and shut the door. Turning around, I was greeted to a vision of Charlie sitting quietly on the stairs waiting for me.

Not much happened for the first half of the night. We brought the big box of Legos up to his bedroom and started building space ships. There was a powerful quiet to his demeanor. Even when he managed to say more than a single word, it was always under his breath, solemnly, while looking down at his creations.

"Mine doesn't look very aerodynamic," I said, holding the intentionally shitty Lego ship in front of him after an hour or so of building. "Can you help me make it better?"

"It's okay. They're getting built in space." Charlie mumbled, going back to his work.

"Oh okay, then maybe I'll add some—"

A noise cut across the silence, barreling up the stairs from the living room and piercing through the door. As soon as it reached our ears, Charlie finally looked up, his eyes awash with total, mind-gripping fear.

Someone was calling the landline.

After a few rings, Charlie sprang to his feet and bolted towards the door. I caught him as he went, stopping him as gently as possible, but I could immediately feel him starting to struggle against me, increasingly distressed with every passing moment.

"Charlie, what's wrong?"

"We have to pick up the phone! Sarah, we have to pick up the phone, we need to!"

"Hey, hey, hey. It's okay. It's okay. Let's just see who it is. We'll go together, okay?"

I took Charlie's hand as he pulled me all the way down the stairs and into the living room.

By the time we reached the phone, the call had ended.

Just as I was about to turn away, the blue screen of the phone lit up, and the ringing began once more. I felt Charlie's hand clench my fist as I read the incoming number. It was from a cell ending in 0026.

I didn't want to answer, but the phone just kept ringing. Again, and again, and again. Every time it stopped, we had only a brief moment to wait before the ringing filled the room once more. In the same way that a word you've said too often starts to lose its meaning, the ring almost seemed to change as we listened to it loop over and over. Its banal tone faded away, replaced by something eerie and sinister, the constant wailing whine of an uninvited guest; *let me in, let me in, let me in, let me in.*

"You have to answer or it won't stop!" Charlie whimpered after the number called a seventh time.

"Has this number called before?" I looked down at him, the phone hailing us with sickening patience.

"Dad called it and… and then they called back and… and he talked on the phone and yelled but they… they didn't say who they were and, and they said they were going to…"

He spoke quickly, a runaway train of thought that had dropped back into his mind when he could no longer bring himself to say the words out loud. Even as he stopped talking, I could tell the thought was continuing on, running through his brain, prompting a fresh bout of tears to escape.

Through it all, the phone kept ringing.

Turning away from Charlie, gripping his hand tightly, I snatched up the receiver and answered the call.

For a moment, when I put it to my ear, all I could hear was deep, low breathing.

"The boy."

The voice was unimaginably low, grating and deep, as if the words were being dragged over gravel on their way toward me. The two words were spoken with a bristling anger, an impatient demand. If Charlie had heard this voice before, then it was no wonder he'd been terrified of the phones in this house.

"No, you're talking to me." I squeezed Charlie's hand, hoping to project confidence I didn't feel. "I want you to stop calling. I don't want you to call this house again."

The line went silent for just a moment.

"A choice has been made. No toys. No running. The misbehaved come home."

"Fuck you."

Using the momentum of my own anger, I slammed the phone down, hanging up the call.

It didn't ring again.

Even though the line was dead, the voice's presence remained in the room, hanging over us both. I put Charlie on the couch and marched over to the windows, drawing the curtains.

"What did it say?" Charlie asked, his voice quivering.

"Nothing," I responded, walking back over to the couch.

The night went by uneasily. I tried to comfort Charlie as much as I could, but I think he knew how deeply disturbed I'd been by the incident. I think he saw that I was as worried as him.

I waited in the kitchen even after Mr. Sullivan came back. Caught between a strong reluctance to walk home alone, and a complete refusal to leave Charlie in the house without me or his father, I'd called my parents for company on the way back.

"Did you eat dinner?" Mr. Sullivan asked, concerned.

"No."

"Do you want anything before your parents get here?"

"Mr. Sullivan, did you call the number on... those flyers outside?"

I didn't know if it was because of the latent anger in my voice, or simply the complete left-field nature of my inquiry, but I saw Mr.

Sullivan's eyes darken.

"Did someone call?"

I let my silence answer his question, and waited for him to answer mine.

Mr. Sullivan took a pained, reluctant breath.

"He kept running off all day, at the store, on the way home. I couldn't keep up with him, I... I had work to do. I'd seen the posters around so I took a flyer just to... I thought some parent put them up, you know? Some spooky morality tale before Christmas. The next day he was climbing on the furniture and I... I pretended to dial the number and..."

He looked embarrassed, but I didn't have time for him to wallow. My mom was only a few streets away and I still didn't understand what was happening.

"Pretended?"

"Yeah, that's the thing." Mr. Sullivan looked at me, fear in his eyes. Reluctant as he sounded, he also spoke as if it had been torture keeping all this to himself. "I have never called that number. I didn't even dial, I just... held the phone to my ear and..."

Mr. Sullivan looked down, dreading the question he was about to ask.

"What did he say?"

I could see the fear in his eyes. He was worried for his son, terrified. I didn't want to tell him what the man on the phone said to me; the idea of reciting the insidious threat felt physically repulsive.

"He said a choice has been made. He said the... the misbehaved come home."

Mr. Sullivan stayed silent for a moment, before muttering, "I never meant for—"

The doorbell rang, making me jump a little, and causing him to stop mid-sentence. I had a feeling he was grateful for the interruption.

My mom had arrived to walk me home.

I left Mr. Sullivan behind, unsure what I could say to the man to make him feel better.

As soon as I made it down the front steps and onto the street to where my mother was waiting to collect me, I remember feeling a distinct chill running across the back of my neck, a shiver that cooled my very being as we made our way back down the darkened street. I told myself it was merely a by-product of the biting winter wind that had drifted into town that night but as we turned the corner from Wilt Avenue and the Sullivan house fell out of view, I distinctly felt the sensation ebb away.

It was something else then, a subtle mix of paranoid anxiety and fear which traveled with me along that street, and that street alone.

Deep down, I knew exactly why I'd felt that way.

When I'd picked up the phone earlier that night and held it to my ear, the figure on the other end had demanded to talk to "the boy." Those two sharp syllables kept ringing in my mind, even after Charlie had passed into some uneasy semblance of sleep, and I'd finally left Wilt Avenue behind.

The thing on the phone had been the first one to speak. It had no way of knowing that the call hadn't been picked up by Charlie, that I'd intercepted it instead.

Unless something could see us.

Unless something was watching the Sullivan house.

Ok whoever's behind this, you need to stop.

This has gone beyond a joke, our girl is terrified.

I'm calling Sergeant Weis when I get home from work

Please someone stop this.

It's a prank. Just don't answer when they call...

I didn't see Charlie before the posters changed again. I'd taken a bit of a break from babysitting after the events of the previous week. Mr. Sullivan triggered that particular decision when he called me up a few days later, cancelling my next two jobs with him.

"I, uh… I think I'm going to just work from home for a week or two," he said soberly down the line. "I'm sorry, I just want to… keep an eye on things."

I could understand why. The forum post was slowly thinning down, now solely populated by the two or three sets of parents who had actually acted on the sinister notices. However, as those without a stake in the game drifted from the conversation, the remaining comments grew more hysterical than ever.

They spoke about receiving calls at all hours of the night, feeling like they were being watched as they walked their children to school, hearing someone move around outside their homes, knocking on doors, passing by windows.

Whatever this was, it had moved far beyond a joke.

The final few parents left on the comment thread started to discuss using their sick days. Staying home with their kids, or passing them off to grandparents who lived out of town.

I don't know whether they followed through with their ideas. I dropped off the message board shortly after, believing my part in the whole ordeal was over.

Last night I discovered otherwise.

It was 11:03. I was in bed, trying to pull myself away from the harsh, hypnotic glow of my phone screen and chase an elusive, uneasy sleep.

Suddenly everything went dark, the backlight of my phone turning black except for two expectant circles, one red, one green, and the number of an incoming caller.

A number ending in 0026.

I felt my throat drop into the pit of my stomach. I stared at the number for almost a minute, my heartbeat quickly outpacing the phone's rhythmic shuddering before I realized it wasn't going to stop.

So far, my involvement with these strange events had been indirect, partial, merely the result of my being in the wrong place in the presence of those at the center of the being's dark lens.

Now, I was at home, alone... and the call was meant for me.

With a quivering hand, I reached out and slowly led the green circle to the other side of the screen.

That same deep breathing, a noise I hoped I'd never have to hear again, drifted through the phone.

"What... what do you want?" I asked, anxious for the answer, yet treasuring every second that the voice chose not to reply.

When it finally answered, it said only two words.

"He's home."

After that, the line went dead.

For the briefest moment I lay paralyzed, held firm by that dark, dreadful admission.

The next moment, I was up, throwing the covers aside, switching out my thermal pajamas for a pair of jeans and an old jacket. As I burst out of my room into the dark corridor, I screamed for my mom to wake up. My voice broke and shook as I spoke, a pressurized cry of worry and terror erupting from within me in one desperate syllable.

I could tell she'd heard it in my voice. I could hear her rushing out of bed and up to the door.

"Sarah, what is it? What's wrong?" She half-whispered as she emerged from the dark bedroom, pulled from the edge of sleep into a dark hallway, needing a moment to adjust to the waking world.

I didn't know what to say in response. I didn't have a plan, or the time to explain myself. Instead all I could bring myself to say was:

"I need a ride to the Sullivan's."

I told her everything I knew on the drive over. As strange as the chain of events sounded, she seemed to believe me. I guess she'd noticed I hadn't been myself lately. Halfway through the story, she pulled her work phone from the glove box and handed it over, telling me to call the cops.

We got there about five minutes later. Wilt Avenue was lit up for Christmas, red and blue dancing across the street as we made our way toward the Sullivan household. I felt a sensation vaguely resembling relief upon seeing that the cops had gotten there before us.

We crept to a stop a little further down the street, our view of the Sullivan house obscured by a slowly gathering crowd of concerned neighbors. As soon as the wheels ground to a halt, I threw open the door and started to climb out. My mom briefly tried to stop me, a single look between us causing her to leave me be. As I stepped out and began to storm down the sidewalk, I heard the driver's side door open and shut behind me, my mom quickly following in my wake.

Forcing my way towards the gathering crowd, my heart in my throat, I found myself marching in the direction of the hackberry, its dark trunk mockingly displaying one of the latest posters, the words obscured by an alternation of dark shadow and the disorienting lights of the idling cop car.

I tore the crisp white page from its shiny new thumbtack without breaking stride, crumpling it up as I pushed through the crowd and stepped up towards the house.

The door was ajar, the lock broken. All of the lights in the house were off. The only cop present was at the bottom of the steps, facing away from me, squatting down as if examining some evidence on the ground.

I called out to her as soon as I was in earshot.

"Where's Charlie... where's Charlie Sullivan?" I cast the question desperately into the air, terrified of the fresh nightmare its response might bring.

"Sarah?"

The cop turned around at my question, but she wasn't the one who responded.

As she turned to face me, rising back to her feet, the small figure of Charlie Sullivan pushed past and started running toward me, tears that had become all too familiar streaming freely down his cheeks. I dropped down to the ground to meet him as he collapsed immediately into my arms, grasping me close and pressing his head into my shoulder.

"I thought…" I begin to say, overwhelmed by relief, as I heard my mother arrive behind me, waiting patiently alongside the still gathering crowd.

"It… came… came inside and it took… it…"

Charlie whimpered and erupted into a wail, his little arms squeezing me tighter.

"Charlie?" I asked, as I stared past the cop and over to the empty house. "Charlie, where's your father?"

Charlie didn't answer, he just kept screaming into the cold November night, trapped in a horrible new world he didn't understand.

As I wrapped one arm firmly around him, I used my free hand to uncrumple the newest poster, holding it close, reading the words that had been left for us.

Bad Man's Home.

No windows. No doors. No light.
You called for bad people. Were cruel. Misbehaved.
Bad people are coming.
No returns once took. Boys & Girls Kept.

I dropped the paper to the cold, damp ground, putting both my arms around Charlie as I watched the cop walk back to her car.

She reached in and brought the receiver up to her mouth.

"Hey, it's Hatch, can you spare anyone for Wilt Avenue? Yeah. Well… looks like we got a third one… Yeah, same as the others…"

It was only then, as my blinding focus ebbed away and I started to become aware of my surroundings, that I noticed the distant noise of sirens a few streets over, emanating from two separate directions.

As the minutes passed, the sirens only grew quieter, their tragic song drowned out by a child's unending cries.

THE FOURTH DAY OF CHRISTMAS IS HOT AS HELL

BY S. F. BARKLEY

MY NAME IS JULIA HATCH. I'M A DEPUTY WITH THE Waushara County Police Department stationed in Serenity Falls, Wisconsin. I always knew I wanted to be a cop and I was prepared for both the good and the bad. The "bad" just so happens to include lying here in this hospital bed with my leg propped up in a cast. I actually asked to be assigned to Serenity Falls when a position opened up, because I like the sense of community that comes with small town beats. I understood that working in such a rural area would mean that I wouldn't always have ample backup, and until last night I'd never had any reason to regret it.

Serenity Falls is a quiet town. With a population of less than 2,000 residents, the majority of the calls that we receive have more to do with drunk drivers on tractors and nuisance dog barking complaints than what you'd call "real emergencies." Despite the usual calmness of this town, I'd have to say that I just survived the week from Hell. The other night I spent fourteen hours straight working an actual murder case and then the next day I dealt with a handful of reports for missing adults who left their children home alone. Even with all that chaos, it was my shift last night that really put me over the edge. I got dispatched to a call I'll never be able to forget. Even if I could momentarily forget the nightmare I experienced, the physical scars and a titanium rod with six screws will still serve as a sharp reminder of the worst night of my life.

Around 0200 hours, Dispatch got on the air. "Dispatch to 26 alpha." Leanne was always one of my favorite dispatchers. She has one of the best, clearest, radio voices.

"26 alpha, go ahead."

"Please respond to [address redacted]. Caller stated that they witnessed someone enter the abandoned residence and could see them using a flashlight throughout the house."

"10-4. Does the caller want to be seen?"

"Negative. Caller was anonymous."

I headed towards the residence. It didn't take long to find the place—just fifteen minutes outside the edge of town. I turned left down a narrow lane. I passed two other houses before I approached the last house on the right. I parked my cruiser a safe distance away and waited, watching. Nothing looked particularly out of the ordinary; it was tall and imposing, reminding me of all the reasons I lived in a single-story ranch, but it was typical for the area. As an older building, it had probably been here since the town was built, and given the size of it—three stories and probably more square footage than Beverly's Bed and Breakfast on Elm—it was no doubt the product of a wealthy family's century-old vision, but its glory days were long since past. Now it stood abandoned and dark.

As I made my way nearer the house, I didn't see any flashlights inside. I gave it a good once-over, imagining what it must have looked like new while simultaneously searching for signs of intrusion. The white painted siding was chipping and the shutters were pulling away from the windows. The wrap-around porch looked as though it would collapse if I didn't tread lightly enough, but nothing looked recently disturbed.

Right as I raised my hand to try the door, I saw a slice of light through the first-floor window.

Someone was inside.

I reached down, grabbed the handle, and opened the door.

"Waushara County Police Department!"

A flash of light rebounded off the walls, and I heard heavy footsteps receding in the dark. I drew my gun and kept it at low-ready. The house was pitch black, so I took out my flashlight with my left hand to shine a path. I didn't want the suspect to be able to see me, so I only used my light in quick bursts every few seconds to search the place.

Flash.

I was in an empty family room. I stood facing peeling wallpaper and continued to move forward into the stale, rotting dark about ten steps. I paused to use my light again.

Flash.

There was a hallway to my right.

I continued down the hallway, staying as close to the wall as I dared in an attempt to reduce the amount of noise the moldering old house made around me. When I reached a stairwell, I aimed my light upward.

Flash.

There was someone standing at the top of the stairs.

I quickly stepped to the side of the staircase as soon as I was in the dark before turning my flashlight on again, ready to react to any move they made. Nobody was there.

My heart was beating through my chest as my breaths grew shorter and louder. Someone was in this house with me and they wanted me to follow them.

I turned my flashlight back off and cautiously continued up the stairs. Once I was at the top, I made a button hook, stepping quickly against the wall to stay clear of the fatal funnel of the center, and headed down the hallway. The first door on my right was wide open. I slowly peered around the doorway, carefully moving from one side of the threshold to the other to get a good look inside the room. I took one squeaking step to my left and *flash*.

Someone was standing in the room.

I turned my flashlight back on, and raised my gun.

"Police! Don't move!"

I growled softly as the steady light revealed an empty room. I ran towards the closet they had been standing next to and slowly opened the door. It wasn't a closet. It was a staircase to the attic on the third floor.

"Fuck," I swore under my breath.

The suspect had no way out except to the attic, which meant that was where I was going, too. Avoiding the window and the dizzying view it offered, I clicked off my light and slowly climbed the crumbling stairs, pushing the thought of how far up I was to the back of my mind; a fear of heights was no help when attempting to safely corner a suspect.

Once at the top, I flashed my light to my right.

Nothing.

I took a few hesitant steps across the brittle floor and flashed my light to my left.

Nothing.

Where was my suspect?

I turned my flashlight back on and shined it the entire way around the attic. It stretched from one end of the house to the other, one single, empty room with a window at either end.

I was alone.

As my mind began turning through different scenarios of where my suspect could have fled, I was hit with the cold November breeze washing in through the open attic window. The octagonal window was approximately three feet wide, and opened on hinges, much like a door.

Did my suspect jump?

I made my way towards the window as the floorboards squeaked under my boots with every step. I took a deep, steadying breath as I reached the threshold. I leaned over to look outside. My heart was racing and my palms were sweating, but I had to cover every possible option.

As my weight shifted, I heard a loud *snap*. At the same time, my right leg fell through the floorboards. I lost my balance and tipped forward. Half of my body hung out of the window as I braced myself against the splintery sill.

Nausea punched me in the gut, and I felt my stomach turn upside down. The ground was too far away. It spun and pulsed, throbbing in time with my panicked heart as my vision blurred. I tried to grab at the window sill to hoist myself back up, but with a gun in one hand and a flashlight in the other I had no grip.

Stop it, Julia.

I forced myself to close my eyes and take a long, shuddering breath.

I braced myself against the window's edge, careful to keep my pointer finger off the trigger. I pushed back, using my palm, sliding myself back into the attic with a combination of abdominal muscles and sheer stubborn will. I sat on the floor, panting and shaking as I gently pried my right foot out from the broken floorboards.

A scent trailed behind my foot as I freed it from the floorboards.

What is that?

I could smell the dry rot and stale musk of the house mixed with… smoke. Where was the smoke coming from?

I shot up from the floor, wincing as I dashed back down the stairs and into the bedroom.

The smell grew stronger.

I ran out of the bedroom and felt a wave of heat; the entire first floor was engulfed in flames. I got on my police radio but received the low-pitch buzz sound when I pressed the mic button that meant that I had no reception.

I ran to the closest window, ignoring the memory of nearly falling from the attic, and unlocked the latch before thrusting my palms against the frame to push it up.

It wouldn't move.

I double-checked that it was unlocked and tried again, but it was stuck. I ran into the next bedroom and tried that window, but it wouldn't move either. It was as if all of the windows were glued shut. By then, the smoke had grown thicker and I used my arm to cover my face as a filter.

I'd fumbled the flashlight back into my belt and reached for my ASP baton to shatter the window when I heard it.

The fire roared up the stairs, bright orange flames filling the hall behind me, and I could feel it coming closer. I was running out of time.

It's common knowledge that fires are hot and the smoke is thick, but nobody ever tells you how loud they are. The roar was everything in that moment. Beneath the ferocity of the fire's angry howl, I could hear the house popping, crackling, and collapsing in chunks. I could barely make out the sound of myself choking on the smoke as I rushed back across the hall to the room with the attic stairs. Soaked with my own sweat and covered in soot and ash, I stumbled back up to the attic and faced the window.

My stomach turned again as my heart raced. Was I really considering this option? Even though the fire's roar was less up there, it filled the house. Yet, despite this, I could hear my pulse thundering over the sounds of the flames chewing through the house.

I felt my hands tingle as I looked through the window and leaned in closer.

I had to jump.

I tried my radio once more, desperate to call Dispatch for help, but this time I didn't even get the tone. My radio was dead.

The fire was consuming the house. Black smoke swirled and billowed up the stairs behind me, flooding out the open window. I didn't have any more time to think. I had to get out immediately.

In one swift motion, I grabbed the window sill, threw both of my legs out onto the shallow ledge, and jumped.

My stomach turned summersaults as I tried to remember everything I'd ever learned about how to safely land from a fall. I did my best to bend my legs to soften the landing, but it wasn't enough. It was three stories high and I snapped my left leg. The pain was excruciating and I screamed louder than I knew my vocal chords could even manage.

I don't remember what happened next. Hell, I don't even remember anyone finding me. I suspect a neighbor called 911 when they saw the flames.

The next thing I knew, I was in the hospital with a bunch of metal in my leg and a nurse telling me I wasn't allowed to leave.

When Sergeant Weis came by to check on me, I asked if they had found anyone else in the house. He told me I was the only one on the premises. The suspect must have escaped after setting the fire.

I never knew fires could grow so rapidly. They haven't told me yet what caused it, but I think someone intentionally lured me into that house and set it on fire.

Later, as I was arguing with a nurse about returning my personal items so I could get ready to leave the hospital, my Sergeant stopped by again.

"Hey Julia, how you feeling?" Weis asked as the angry nurse left.

"I'll be better when they give me back my things and let me out of this damn bed, but I'm hanging in there."

"No surprise there," he smiled. "You're tough. But, you know, I have to ask why you told Dispatch there was no fire."

Confusion washed over me. "What are you talking about?"

"Last night—er, well, this morning. You know what I mean. While you were at the house, Leanne received a call from a neighbor saying they saw flames coming from the house. You got on the radio and said to disregard that and that there was no fire. Then, sure as shit, a flood of calls came in from more and more neighbors that there was a fire. Why the hell did you tell Leanne there was no fire?"

"That wasn't me..."

HORROR STORIES TO RUIN CHRISTMAS

THE FIFTH DAY OF CHRISTMAS IS FOR THE LONELY

BY MATT RICHARDSEN

I'VE NEVER BEEN THE TYPE TO REACH OUT AND GRAB THE girl. I've never been the type to kiss her on command. Call it a shortage of self-assurance. Call it social anxiety. Call it depression, or lack of confidence, or any fucked up term you might find in this coddled crazy new century. Call it whatever you will. I just know I never had it.

I certainly tried though. Throughout my adolescence, I hid the panic bubbling under the surface with a mask comprised of awkward smiles and bad jokes. Most people fell for that. In fact, my shell became so thick that not even my own mother could crack it. The mask started to slip in college, so I learned how to self-medicate, and then it stayed properly fixed until after graduation. By that time, my friends moved on to big jobs and better wives. I found myself always at home, always alone, and without much of a life.

And so it surprised absolutely nobody when I fell in love online.

From the moment Ally entered my life, it amazed me how the pieces fit together so seamlessly. Suddenly, it didn't feel like such a struggle to wake up in the morning and get dressed. Suddenly, my problems seemed small and stupid. Because, ultimately, at the start of the day, Ally would always have a message for me. And it would always say the same thing:

Where are you now?

Sometimes that message would come in a text. Sometimes a voice mail. Sometimes I would wake up an hour early just to hear her voice for a bit before I had to go to work. After two months of this back and forth, I started to get obsessed. She ruled my life. Ally quickly became the only thing that seemed worth living for.

That wasn't a bad thing. My dad was happy. My friends were happy. Most importantly, *I* was happy. There was only one problem. Ally lived in the small town of Serenity Falls, Wisconsin, which made her a twenty hour drive away.

We tried our best to make the long distance work. Sometimes, she would text me at funny times of the day. We would video chat every night. We used all of the modern technology that was afforded to us with a plan to someday, one day, meet up on one of our corners of the country. Sometimes it felt futile, but we fought through that, and the opportunity to meet came sooner than either of us expected.

I got fired.

Well, not exactly. One day, my boss informed me that our satellite office would be closed. All existing employees would be required to work from home, effective immediately. Long story short... it no longer matter where I lived, as long as it had an internet connection.

I can still remember the day I broke the news to Ally. I left the office and pulled out my phone to see one of her favorite questions in my notifications. Those messages have since been turned over to the Serenity Falls police department.

Where are you now?

Leaving the office. What you doin?

Leaving the dollar store in town. Why is nothing actually a dollar anymore?

I have some news.

Oh?
Okay.
What is it?
Are you okay?

I got a new job.

She did not answer for a few minutes. I thought she might be driving home. I got ready to do the same myself before a one word text buzzed my phone happily.

Where?

Anywhere. Absolutely anywhere! How does Serenity Falls sound? I'm coming, baby!

I sat back in my car and waited anxiously. When Ally didn't answer, I chalked it up to bad service and started my long drive home. The commute took an hour. I eyed my cell angrily the whole time, but no reply ever came.

I arrived at my shitty apartment just after six in the evening and immediately concocted a plan to surprise my online girlfriend. I know that sounds weird, but we talked about it often. I even had her address. I often promised to drop by Wisconsin and visit sometime, but I'd never followed through. Work always made it too difficult. This time, I called my landlord and cancelled the lease. I booked plane tickets that night. I had never lived in luxury. Everything I owned, other than the furniture, could fit inside a black travel bag. The rest could be arranged later. I needed to see Ally. I needed to start my real life for the first time.

I told myself it would be some dramatic, romantic surprise.

The flight felt like it took an eternity but I stayed awake the whole time. Snoring passengers aggravated me. Movies failed to entertain me. Perhaps I'm not explaining this properly, but every essence of how I defined my life at that point centered around Ally. Meeting her for the first time set my social anxiety on fire. Nothing could distract me from my mind.

The plane touched down in Madison sometime around mid-morning. I disembarked with a strategy to take a bus to Serenity Falls around noon, and finally passed out of sheer exhaustion soon after. My ride arrived in Serenity Falls at exactly 2:00. I nearly missed the place. Nobody else on the bus got off at that spot, and I had to ring the bell just to make sure they stopped. When they did, the driver wished me good luck, and closed the door in my face unceremoniously.

I took in the cool air and allowed myself to smile at last. The town felt foreign and familiar at the same time, and the landmarks jumped out like the pieces of a puzzle. I immediately recognized the diner at the heart of Main Street. The cobbler that probably should have been out of business years ago. The liquor store on its way out now. The dollar store that my mystery woman visited only a day ago. I crossed the street to Prospect Ave and kept going until the numbers reached 26. I recognized the cracked pavement in front of her porch. The same place she had sat and sent me hundreds of Snapchats in the dusky autumn afternoon.

I walked up the steps and knocked confidently, absurdly, like a forgotten stranger returning home for the first time in years. A middle aged woman with hazel eyes and curly brown hair opened the door. She wore a striped blue shirt and a look of concern mixed with mild familiarity.

"Can I help you?"

"Yes ma'am, my name is Matt. I'm a friend of Ally's. Is she home?"

I expected her mother to burst out laughing. I expected a giant hug. Ally had told her about me. She had seen my picture, and my social media, and everything that goes with it. She even joked that we had the same taste in TV. But the woman returned none of those same warm feelings.

"I thought she was with you."

The frigid Wisconsin air suddenly started to feel even cooler.

"No... no, ma'am, my bus just arrived a few minutes ago. I wanted to surprise her."

The woman's kind hazel eyes grew wide as she stepped outside and closed the door behind her. She began to look down the block, as if expecting Ally to jump out and scare her. Then she looked at me accusingly.

"Then who was the other fella?"

My blood started to grow cold as the hairs on the back of my neck stood up. Ally couldn't be seeing another man. We talked all the time. The logistics alone would be impossible.

"Other fella?"

"Yes. You're Matt, right?"

"Yes, ma'am."

"Well then, Ally left to meet *you* at the crack of dawn. Six AM, sometime, she got a call on her mobile."

I stared stupidly.

"She said you sounded different. Like you had a cold."

I continued to stare. My confidence was quickly replaced by an overwhelming anxiety that something had to be very seriously wrong.

"Well, if that wasn't fucking you, son, who was it?"

"Ma'am, she has not answered me since yesterday."

"Shit. Were you hacked? What the hell happened? We need to get down to the falls right now."

I nodded stupidly. Hearing a middle aged woman curse did not do much to assuage my fears, but I followed her to the RAV4 sitting in the driveway and plopped my panicked self into the passenger seat. She turned over the engine and gunned us right back down Prospect Street. Past the fire house. Past the church where Ally was baptized. Past the cemetery where her dad was buried.

We made it to the falls in less than five minutes.

There is a banister there that protects people from slipping and falling into the water and jagged rocks below. I rushed up to it and immediately looked over the edge. Because that was my first instinct, you know? If somebody wanted to kill the one and only love of my life, they could have just thrown her off the ledge. As I searched the ice below, her mother's heart-ripping screams alerted me to something behind the trees. I followed her into the woods and looked around stupidly once more. Then she pointed up.

Hanging by her neck, tied to a tree approximately thirty feet in the air, was the most beautiful dead girl I have ever seen.

A moment later, a text popped up on my phone's screen.

"Where are you now?"

THE SIXTH DAY OF CHRISTMAS IS PIED

BY J. SPEZIALE

I HAVE ALWAYS BEEN THE RECIPIENT OF JUDGMENTAL EYES and hushed whispers—ever since I went to college and came back with a son. Single parents are uncommon in Serenity Falls, especially unmarried fathers in their twenties.

Carter is named after my father, a great man who left this earth well before his time. Carter's mother stuck around for an entire month after his birth, before leaving us both without a trace. Life has been pretty quiet for us at the end of Edd Road on the outskirts of town—that is, until the ice cream truck started coming by.

It was only a few days ago when I first heard the faint, crackling tune of "Yankee Doodle," and the low rumble of an old diesel engine. As the sounds grew louder, the warm glow of headlights spilled into my living room. I looked at the clock, 12:26 AM. The box truck came to a dead stop in the middle of our gravel drive and stared out at the house like a menacing beast with huge amber eyes.

I initially assumed the driver was lost, and was trying to re-route their GPS or make a phone call, but after 10 minutes it hadn't moved. The jingle melody grew louder as it spilled out of the old speaker on the roof of the truck.

Carter walked downstairs and stood next to me. Rubbing his eyes, he sleepily asked, "Daddy, who is that outside?"

"Go back to bed, buddy. I think they're lost. I'm gonna go outside and see if they need any help. You need to stay inside, okay?" I said sternly.

"Why is it playing that music?" He asked as his interest grew.

"It's late son, go back to bed."

Carter slowly trudged up the stairs as I walked to the hall closet. I put on my coat and slipped the Ruger revolver I kept on the top shelf into my pocket. I walked back into the living room and peered up the stairs to make sure Carter wasn't sitting at the top.

I flipped on the flood lights, stepped outside, and walked into the cold night. The truck didn't move. As I got closer I could make out the faded, multi-colored text on the side of the truck painted just below a cartoon drawing of a cow wearing a milkman's hat.

"Piper's Ice Cream"

I'd never seen an ice cream truck in Serenity Falls, but I was pretty certain that peddling their frozen treats at midnight was uncommon.

I walked a bit closer, trying to get a view of the driver. "Yankee Doodle" rang in my ears. The heavily tinted windows and glow of the headlights made it nearly impossible to see inside. As I got within a few yards of the driver door, the truck shifted into gear. I took a quick step backwards in surprise, and gripped the pistol concealed within my coat.

Before I took another step, the truck peeled away in reverse, spun, and sped back down Edd road out of sight. I stood motionless for a few moments before heading back inside for the night.

Although the experience was strange, I didn't think too much of it—until the following day. I walked to the school bus stop, as I do every afternoon, to meet Carter. After we walked home together, we drove to the bank and then to the market. We couldn't have been gone more than an hour, but someone had come to the house while we were gone.

There were fresh tracks in the snow leading up to and away from the porch. They disappeared into the woods that bordered our property. Something had been placed on the welcome mat and Carter saw it too.

"What is that, daddy?" He asked.

I told him to stay put and let me check. As I got closer, I looked down and immediately felt sick upon realizing what it was. A large white bowl filled with scoops of assorted ice cream—unmelted in the cold winter air. Next to the bowl was a piece of paper that read:

For Carter,
A sweet treat for a sweet boy.

His eyes lit up when he saw the bowl, and he asked if he could have it. With a shaking voice, I reminded him, "We never eat food that strangers give us, that's the rule, son."

Carter started to pout before I reassured him that we had plenty of ice cream in the house. I took the bowl and the note and threw it away. In the distance, I thought I heard the faint tune of "Yankee Doodle."

It was harder to sleep that night, waking up at the sound of every little noise. I decided I would talk with Sheriff Mueller in the morning while Carter was at school. I barely slept that night.

The next morning I walked Carter to the bus stop, watched him climb on, and waved goodbye. The sun burst through the morning clouds in a radiant display of orange, red, yellow, and pink. I went home and worked in my office for a few hours before getting in my truck and driving to the police station to inform the sheriff of the strange events.

The minute I pulled into the lot, my phone rang and the school principal's anxious voice filled my ear. Carter and another boy had run away during recess when the teacher's back was turned. The other kids said Carter mentioned something about seeing the ice cream man before disappearing into the woods, and out of sight.

THE SEVENTH DAY OF CHRISTMAS IS STUFFED

BY KYLE BURTON

I FLIPPED THE BAGGED CELLPHONE AROUND IN MY HANDS as I stepped out of the crisp pre-dawn air and into Mel's Place. The evidence, Sergeant Daniel Weis' flippant, "Have fun with that video, it's the most recent bit," and a shaking ear-muffed head was all I got to start my shift this morning. I queried Daniel's back, "Just the video?" and got a thumbs-up that slowly turned into a thumbs-down before I turned and opened the door. Whatever that meant. I noticed Ted and Dan immediately. Sitting with their backs turned to me, two of the other bulky men in blue I worked with looked like they were sharing the morning paper. Did they know what we were here to review? I sure didn't. Thanks, Weis.

Melissa greeted me with a wry smile that said she knew to bring me my usual order. They did one thing well here, and that's what I stuck with. I walked up behind Sheriff Dan Mueller and Officer Ted Jaeger and noticed that both of them were very engrossed in the Help Wanted section. I slid in opposite them and sat close against the window, spinning the bagged phone over a third page headline declaring **First Serenity Falls Homicides in 105 Years Appear Unrelated.** Dan grunted as Ted folded up the newspaper and stowed it in the booth behind him.

"Hey Ted, got your earbuds? We're watching something." I nodded towards his coat pockets. Ted pulled out a pair of Bluetooth earbuds and handed one to me as Dan cleared his throat and choked out, "Timothy Poole, the dentist, has been acting erratically and finally flipped his lid. Got into a couple of fights two nights ago then went missing. This is his phone, unlocked, found in the snow out behind the diner about five and a half hours ago, roughly two."

I shook my wet hair down from its bun just as Melissa brought me a cup of hot coffee and a bowl of their mixed raisin rice pudding. "So?" I slipped the right earbud in and looked out the frosted glass of the diner. The sun was about to rise. It would be a clear day today. Clear, but with a bitterly cold wind blowing snowy white powder around fiercely. I sipped my coffee and eyed the pudding. A golden raisin was peeking out of the top, dusted with granules of brown sugar.

"So there are no extraneous prints, and Sergeant Weis was supposed to fill us in on what we'd be looking for on here. It's a missing person issue at this point." "Oh." I paused and pursed my lips for a second, then motioned for Dan to insert his earbud. "We're watching a movie this morning. Let's see what Mr. Poole has been up to." Ted twisted and stood suddenly upright to allow Dan to move into the opposite side of the booth next to me. I took two greedy mouthfuls of rice pudding and a long, drawn-out sip of coffee as Dan settled in. Ted sat, then motioned wildly at Melissa, who interpreted that as a cheese omelette with extra crispy hash browns and white toast.

I synced our earbuds as I opened the photo application and skimmed the last few entries. The last one was a twenty-six minute video. That's it. Sheriff Dan gave me a nod, and I pressed play. The screen was immediately filled by a gaunt clean-shaven face bearing bruises, lacerations, and missing significant features. Missing as in removed. Surgically. It was filmed at night, and it looked like the man recording himself was hiding from someone or something outside. A street light was visible a dozen yards behind him. His breath fogged the screen in the few seconds before he began speaking, as the camera struggled to focus on his face. I slowly rolled a raisin around in my mouth before popping it between my molars. The warm and wet of raisin was quickly followed by the hot and bitter of coffee.

Dan paused the screen just as it captured the 'star's' face. The pale skin was stretched taut across high cheekbones, revealing a mouth missing a random assortment of teeth. Whoever removed them seemed to have done so haphazardly. "That's our man, Timothy Poole." grunted Dan. "His problems seem to have started a week ago, when one of his patients had to be airlifted to the hospital outside of Stanley when one of her teeth became lodged in her throat during a routine cleaning, as he called it. One emergency tracheotomy later and bam, it wasn't one of her teeth that got stuck in her throat." I bit down a bit too hard on a raisin and my front teeth clacked together. I glanced outside, the sun was up, and the wind was quick.

I nodded slowly and looked back at the paused video. Circular black glasses frames slipped to the tip of his nose which was missing the piece of flesh that defined his right nostril. His right eye focused directly at the camera, and his left eye seemed to have gone completely milky white. There was no indication that it wasn't a cheap glass eyeball within the socket. I pursed my lips and blew steam off of my coffee.

His haggard breaths indicated that he'd just been running, and the way his head darted around suggested he thought he was being followed. His initial statement confirmed both of my suspicions. "I don't think they're going to find me here... yet. I don't know how much more time I have." He brought his left hand up to his forehead to mop away sweat with the crude, blood-encrusted bandage which belied a missing index finger.

"I have to tell someone what's been happening to me because if I don't tell anyone people are going to think I'm a monster. I can't tell anyone in person because at this point nobody will believe that it's not my fault." He visibly tongued the gaps where there should have been teeth before his head jerked up and around and the phone screen went black, now pressed close to his chest.

After a half minute of darkness, a distant shout is heard and Timothy takes off in a sprint. The next five minutes are of the victim breathlessly running through darkness. He seemed to be taking an erratic path as opposed to just cutting directly across private properties, apparently avoiding illumination. He didn't want to be seen. The sun's angle cast a glare on the screen and I adjusted Dan's grip on the phone.

No definable landmarks are visible until all of a sudden the phone is held at arm's length directly in front of Timothy. He was bathed in light from this diner's sign. For a brief moment I could see that there were only two patrons inside before the view started spinning. He held the phone with his left hand and again tried to wipe away sweat from his forehead with his bandaged hand before the phone focused on the town auto-shop behind him. I paused the video and rewound to the patrons. "Ted, put down that omelette and take notes for us." Ted wrote down my description of the patrons with one hand while continuing to shovel hash browns into his mouth with the other. Dan noticed my eyes narrowing and nudged my coffee towards me. I took his unspoken advice and nursed it before pressing play again.

Ten seconds later, at arm's length in a well-lit area, I could see that Timothy Poole is missing a finger, an ear, a portion of his nose, too many teeth, and his breath. His left eye looked normal now. What had happened to it before? "This is where I met Clara for the first time." A low rattling moan escaped through ragged lips. "ooooOOAAAHHHH I fed her a part of ME me me... me... I didn't know... I couldn't stop mys—" Another shout is heard in the distance and the wounded dentist again takes off running for three and a half minutes.

He pretty clearly was in the downtown area of Serenity Falls, cutting through alleyways, trying to shrug off his pursuer or pursuers, before he was almost run down by a car. *Whoa.* I paused the video and rewound thirty seconds. Four seconds of frantic running then… THERE. A Lincoln Zephyr, from 1939. A brilliant antifreeze green, too. I've always wanted one of them. I frowned intently as both Dan and Ted glanced askance at me. "Nothing," I muttered as I pressed play again. Girls weren't supposed to like cars. The car sped off. Hit and run. It looked like the phone was on the ground facing up at the sky. We listened as Timothy retched and moaned a short distance away.

A minute of scarcely heard heavy breathing and the camera trying vainly to focus on the clear night sky. The moon began to edge into frame as the phone was again scooped up and Timothy's face came into view for a moment before being shrouded entirely in darkness. He ducked between two buildings and began speaking, low and slow.

"I think I removed a kidney. I know I fed something to Clara, something of mine and I think… I think it was my kidney. I… I found where I did it, but I don't remember doing it. Mirrors… set up everywhere. Antiseptic, at least." A low chuckle. "And anesthetic. That's why I didn't feel anything while I was doing it. Local and regional. Oh man, I need some global. Maybe if I just don't wake up, then this nightmare will be over." Labored breathing for a minute, the screen still entirely dark. I paused the video again.

"Who?" I glared at Officer Jaeger for the question and filled him in tersely. "Clara Davis, primary school teacher. Timothy had started dating her recently." I sat silently for a moment.

"She's not the only person we haven't been able to get a hold of. We're a small precinct covering some nasty stuff, which is why you're both here right now." came Dan's flippant response. I took another bite of rice pudding and motioned to Melissa for another.

I turned the video back on. Immediately the screen was filled by a dimly lit, milky-white-gray eyeball, with eyelids missing eyelashes. "I can't see out of this eye and my other eye isn't telling me what's happening here." The screen goes dark again, presumably being pulled further away from Timothy's face. The sounds of him limping through frosted grass are all that's heard for two minutes before he steps back out into light. Melissa brought my new pudding and I took a big spoonful, savoring the warmth and brown sugar.

The camera is spun around to reveal a house with every room lit up. "Shit, did they…" came from behind the camera. The view slowly, shakily approaches the house then creeps around the back to an unlit sunroom. The camera suddenly falls to the ground and the sound of a handle rattling is heard. In a tiny corner of the screen, a door opens before silently swinging shut. The moon crept into view in the four minutes of stillness, broken only by Sheriff Mueller mumbling, "What's he doing in there?" He coughed once. "That's Poole's house, by the way. Looked like there was company he wasn't expecting, right?" I only glanced at the sheriff, keeping my focus on the phone on the table before us.

Suddenly the screen goes black as something soft and filled with metal and glass plops down on top of it. A second later the view radically shifts and swings around showing—I lunged forward and paused the video, then rewound a handful of frames. Timothy Poole now bore a large dark bandage over his left eye, and his shirt was soaked with blood. In my line of work, it's not often that implications can make me shudder but the chill that ran down my spine was even evident to Ted from across the table. I choked down my mouthful of pudding.

I unpaused the video for the final time. The camera swung back around, facing away from Timothy Poole's scarred face. A muffled, "Who gets to eat you, I wonder" followed by more limping footsteps crunching on the frost-covered grass. "Where am I going?" The camera swung back around to show Timothy staring skyward, his head cocked at an uncomfortable angle. He seemed to be listening to something.

Something unheard clearly startled him as he dropped both the phone and what was revealed to be a little black duffel bag. It clattered and clanged as it hit the ground. "Did you like the taste of my finger, bitch?" The angle that the camera fell at revealed the legs of someone stepping out of the shadows cast by Timothy's neighbor's house. "It's Birch, you freak. I'm going to make you eat SHIT cause you made me bite it off and then swallow, you fucking FREAK!" Two warm, gooey raisins burst between my molars.

It sounded like Timothy took a step or two back, then the sound of a pistol cocking is heard. The slow advance of Birch halted. "Huhhhhrng, want a piece of me?" Hesitant silence. "Please?" pitifully rang Timothy Poole's last recorded word. "This isn't over, freak. Imma ruin you, FREAK!" came Birch's rejoinder as he slunk back into the shadows. The moment his feet were darkened, the bag and phone were scooped up and Timothy began running frantically again. The screen was blurred and shaky and the only thing that could be heard was the labored breathing and pounding of feet.

Another minute of frantic running. *Timothy Poole, you didn't care about being seen now, did you? You're running right down Main street, straight towards downtown.* Timothy skidded to a stop and breathlessly murmured "Here" several times. The camera focused closely on his scarred face, steam wicking off in the cold Wisconsin air. I spooned one of my last mouthfuls of pudding up and in, savoring the pleasant sweetness. He jerked his head up again, then stepped inside the building he'd been hiding behind.

Into a kitchen. The kitchen of the diner I'm sitting in right now. Timothy set the phone down on a cold metal prep table, pointed at the walk-in freezer, then steps fully into view. His bandaged hand ruffled around in the black duffel before withdrawing a pair of pliers. The duffel clanked as he dropped it and made his way into the freezer.

The frame was still and nothing was heard for a few dozen seconds. My heart started pounding in my ears as I scraped up the last scoop of pudding from my bowl, barely glancing at the dark raisins within. I felt something sharp and hard in my mouth as I bit down. Timothy emerged from the freezer, both hands bandaged and weeping dark blood. As he walked up to the phone and ended the video, I spat something hard, sharp, and bitter into the bowl in front of me. My eyes immediately bulged and I retched, shoving Dan out of my way as I barreled towards the diner's kitchen. Ted eyed what was later found to be Timothy Poole's index fingernail sitting in my empty pudding bowl.

HORROR STORIES TO RUIN CHRISTMAS

HORROR STORIES TO RUIN CHRISTMAS

ON THE EIGHTH DAY OF CHRISTMAS, I ENCOUNTERED A DEATH CULT

BY RYAN COOK

"BUSINESS IS GOOD. UNFORTUNATELY."

I've said those words many, many times over the years. How else are you supposed to answer the question "How's business" when you run the town's funeral home/cemetery? What are you supposed to say? "Yeah, business is great. Thankfully that heat wave knocked off half a dozen senior citizens." Or maybe, "Business is down. Where are some good old-fashioned cancer deaths when you need them?"

It's the unpleasant reality of running a funeral home. My economic well-being is based entirely on the death and misery of others, so discussing the business side of things is a delicate process. So, "Business is good. Unfortunately." is what I say to people when they ask me about money. It seems to cover all the bases.

And business in Serenity Falls *has* been good recently. Very good. We buried *two* women on Sunday who were murdered at their family farm last week. Tomorrow we bury another young woman named Ally who got caught up with the wrong person. And soon we'll bury a little boy named Carter. That one hurt the most. I met with his father yesterday and he was inconsolable. He was most certainly in the "anger" stage of grief when I was with him, shouting, swearing, and punching the wall. By the end he was curled up on the ground, hands held up to his face as he cried and shook. It took him almost 20 minutes to compose himself. How else do you react to your little boy being murdered, by the ice cream man of all people?

And that's what the general populace doesn't understand. All of this death. Everything happening in tiny little Serenity Falls… it affects the people here more than you'd imagine. And it's always harder during the holidays. Everyone's delightful plans with their families get ripped apart and forever destroyed. They won't be enjoying Christmas this year, and it will be tainted every year hereafter.

Let's also remember the people who've gone missing around town. The number is so large I've lost count. And there are fires being spread in abandoned buildings. Murder. Arson. Kidnappings. Disappearances. Ice cream men. I mean, what the hell is happening in this town?

So yes, there most certainly is a lot of business at the Serenity Falls Funeral Home and Cemetery. And there are most certainly a lot of strange things happening around town. A *lot* of strange things.

Which is why I should have been more careful late last night when I saw some movement deep within the cemetery. It was long past closing and the gate was locked shut. Nobody should have been in there. I know now that they were *trying* to get my attention and draw me out there, but I didn't see it at the time. I probably should have called the police. I know that now. But instead, I went out there to investigate.

I would like to say that you get used to walking alone in the dark amongst the graves and tombstones, but you don't. It's always creepy. The cemetery is outside of the town center and the adjacent road has almost no traffic this time of night. Your mind plays tricks on you and your imagination runs wild. Which is why, as my flashlight shone ahead of me, I didn't even believe what I saw at first. The shadow of a man wearing a large black hooded robe, 20 feet or so in front of me.

"Welcome." His voice was monotone. There were strange relics and ornaments hanging from the trees and tombstones around him.

This was too weird for me. I decided to turn and run back to the funeral home, but before I could, someone stepped out from behind me and held a knife up to the center of my back. I remember feeling its sharp edge gently push against me. "Turn the flashlight off," the person said quietly. A woman's voice. I complied.

The man in the robe started chanting in some foreign language.

It was difficult to see in the darkness of the cemetery, but I looked around to try and gather my bearings. I think there were only the two people. Everything I saw disturbed me more than a little. I thought then, and still believe, that this was some sort of cult. There was some form of a pier in the center, and below it was what I think was a ceremonial dagger. And then I saw what worried me most of all. A hole dug in the ground. A grave. I have no idea how they dug it so quickly and discreetly, but it was definitely a grave, and I was starting to figure out who it was for.

The man in the robe spoke to me then. "How's business?" It was too dark to see clearly, but I knew his face was still emotionless. He barely even sounded human. "I imagine your business is going quite well recently." He paused before talking again. This time his speech was slow and deliberate. "*Fortunately*."

So he knew who I was. Or at the very least, someone had told him about me.

He continued speaking. "Yes, Nathan. I know who you are. And I must ask... do you know what has befallen this town? Do you think all the deaths and disappearances are mere coincidence? Do you know what we must do to you?" He paused for a moment. "During the ceremony itself, you will experience more pain than you ever thought imaginable. But you'll still be *alive* when we bury you. We'll be sure of that." He began chanting something incomprehensible again.

By this time I had finally gathered the courage to speak. "Do I know you? Why are you doing this? What is it that's befallen this town?" I thought about making a quick move and running for it... but then I felt the cult member behind me press the knife a bit more firmly against my back, almost as though she had read my thoughts.

The man in front spoke again. His tone was still completely devoid of emotion. "We're not so different Nathan, you and I. We both prosper over the death of others." He paused briefly to slowly wave his arm, hand up, around the ceremonial site. "This is all for you. You've become apathetic to pain and suffering. Allow us to remind you of it."

The man picked up some rope that I assumed was going to be used to tie me up, rendering me defenseless. "We're about to begin." He announced, taking a step towards me.

And I thought that would be it. For the first time, I thought about what it would be like. How awful and excruciating this death would be. Of being buried deep in the hole, in agony, in the pitch darkness, while slowly running out of oxygen. I guess I was supposed to fear the actual *dying* part. To be afraid that I'll never see my loved ones again. But that's not what had me panic-stricken, no. It was the *pain* that I feared most, the torture they would put me through first. I could already feel myself *wishing* for death. And maybe that's what this cult was all about.

But before he got to me, at a moment where I had completely given up hope, the voice from behind whispered in my ear. "Run for it. But make it look real."

It was a chance.

I reached my arm up and quickly elbowed the woman behind me in the temple. It wasn't very hard, but she embellished it for show. "SHIT!" she screamed.

I took off running. I don't think I've ever run so fast in my life. I imagined the cloaked man one step behind me, dagger and rope in hand. But the truth is, I don't think he took even a single step in chase of me. As I reached the gate of the cemetery, I heard him yell from far behind, still emotionless, "We'll see you again one day soon, Nathan."

I called the police, of course, and told them everything I know. You would think an attempted murder from a cult at the town cemetery would be a bigger deal to them. But I guess there is just too much on their plate with everything else going on in town. The police force is not nearly big enough to handle all of this. They barely even asked any questions. I don't know who that cult was, or why they were so intent on killing me, or why that woman saved me. But they did say something terrible has befallen this town, and I believe them. I don't think we've seen the last of that cult.

That man in the robe also said that he'll see me again someday soon. I suppose it would be safest for me to take a long vacation as far away from this place as possible and to enjoy Christmas somewhere nice and warm.

But that's not what I'm going to do.

Because business is good right now in Serenity Falls. Business is *really* good.

Unfortunately.

HORROR STORIES TO RUIN CHRISTMAS

ON THE NINTH DAY OF CHRISTMAS, AN OPPORTUNITY PRESENTED ITSELF

BY RHYS SCHWARZMAN

"Have you seen those posters, Pops?"
I ignored the question. I had seen them. *Everyone* had seen them.
"*Dad.*"
"Yes, bud. I have." I answered, frustrated. "Haven't I told you before that when I'm with a patient that you have to—"
"—write down any questions and ask them later." We said in unison. Liam rolled his eyes.

"But dad, people are talking about them!" Liam was excited at the mystery despite not fully understanding what our little town of Serenity Falls was going through. It had been a long, long time since we'd had to deal with any mysteries. I've heard the grumbles and the rumors. Our town is small. We only have a couple thousand people that live here, and that's being generous. Things don't happen here and stay quiet.

"Liam. Listen, buddy. Mrs. Hatch here might be unconscious, but I'm still not comfortable with having a conversation while my hands are in her mouth. Can we *please* save this for a bit later?" I said sternly, with a gracious side of pleading for my sanity.

"Fiiiiiine." Liam's face was bursting with impatience.

"Hey, I'll tell you what." I stood from my chair and walked towards the window in my office. "The news said that someone put those flyers all over Wilt Avenue. Go get your sister from kindergarten, then I'll give you and Michaela each a dollar for every poster you take down and bring to me."

"Really?!" Liam jumped in place.

"Yeah, go get 'em!"

Liam grabbed his purple sweater and dashed out of the building like there were free Pokemon cards at the corner store. I watched him dart down the street, stopping at telephone poles and newspaper boxes as he went.

"Huh." A red Ferrari drove down the street as Liam went out of sight. "A bit fancy for this town, pal."

I resumed my work on Mrs. Hatch. She came in to get an extraction.

Routine procedure that now took longer than it needed to thanks to my *lovely* boy. My appointments had to be moved back. In the dental industry, every minute is money. Cancellations, unfilled slots, and delays all take money out of my pocket. My practice is small, but I'm the only oral surgeon in Serenity Falls so business stays steady.

"Abigail," I called to my receptionist, "can you let my next patient know it's going to be about another twenty-six minutes?"

No response.

"Abigail?" I called again. Silence.

Although I've never been a fan of leaving patients during their examinations, Abigail's lack of response was peculiar. I hired her a few years back when she was a cashier at Martin's Wine and Spirits. As much as I hated to admit it, I had become somewhat of a regular there in the months after my wife passed. No matter how down I was, though, Abigail always managed to find some way to pick me back up.

On the first anniversary of my wife's death, I went to Martin's and loaded up a basket with whatever looked even remotely appealing. Grey Goose, Tito's, some craft beer from a place by Kenosha… anything to make the pain go away. When I went up to the counter, Abigail looked different. She was still her usual pleasant self but she carried a look in her eyes. It was determination. Her aura was strong.

"Hugh," she stated, "you aren't drinking anymore. I'm not selling to you."

"Abby, please. You don't know what today is. I-I need it today."

"I know *exactly* what today is, Hugh. The Serenity Scene only has, like, five news stories a week. I remembered, but even if I didn't I wouldn't have had to look far."

She held up a small newspaper that was already folded to a page featuring a picture of the front of my house with caution tape around the outside. I broke down. Abigail came from behind the counter and held me as I wept.

"She wouldn't have wanted this." She whispered as she placed her chin on my head. "You're going to be better."

Not even a few days later, I offered Abigail the job and we've been partners ever since. She has always been astoundingly attentive to patients and the needs of the business. I haven't had to worry about a single problem since she joined me.

Not getting a response from her meant that there was a problem. She's never *not* responded.

I cautiously walked out to the reception area where I saw her head laid down on her desk. I rushed to her.

"Calm yourself, she's asleep." A man's voice came from the other side of the glass. I fell backwards.

"Nerve agent. Non-lethal. Nothing to worry about. She won't even remember it happened." The man was wearing a black suit with a black shirt and tie.

"Can I help you," I said dryly attempting to hold back emotions, "or can the police help you?"

The man snickered.

"Hugh, let me help you up," he outstretched his hand and I rose to my feet. "I'm in the business of helping. What if I told you that I can help you expand your business? Take this small family practice and build an empire in all of Wisconsin! Get yourself out of this little town and be somebody."

"I'd politely decline," I said.

"And why is that?"

"Well, for one, I don't fucking know you. I've never even seen you in town. Secondly, I'm perfectly happy here in the Falls. I don't need to go anywhere else, or expand, or whatever bullshit you're offering me. Now, if you don't turn and leave, I will be forced to call the police, Mister…?"

The suited man held up a hand. "Names aren't important right now."

I reached for the phone on Abigail's desk.

"Disconnected."

I reached in my pocket for my cell, but it had slipped out onto the floor when I was startled. The man sighed and reached into his jacket, pulling out his own phone.

"I have to say, I'm offended that you weren't even willing to listen to our offer." He scrolled through something on the screen. "Here's our proposal."

He handed me his phone. On it was a picture of Liam and Michaela on the ground near some icy waters in the park. I cried out, but I couldn't make words.

"We can dump them down there, Hugh. Right into those waters. They'll get trapped under the ice and we'll make it look like an accident. Don't believe me? I had my guy include the flyers in the picture. I'm somewhat of an Instagram professional." He chuckled.

"What do you want?" I composed myself as best I could.

"Teeth. Well, we don't *want* the teeth. We want you to make the teeth disappear."

I felt my stomach start to get upset. There's only one reason a person would want teeth gone.

"Dental records." I said to him, confused.

"Precisely. I'll make it simple for you. *We* provide the people whose teeth need removal. *You* dispose of the teeth. We have a very secluded area at a farm not too far from here. There, you'll find a sophisticated dental setup. It has every tool you could need to take care of business. You don't even need to move the bodies."

"Bodies!" I yelled. "What do you mean *bodies?*"

"Dead people, Hugh." He responded with a grin. "Listen. I'm not going to waste either of our times pretending you have a choice in this. We *will* kill your children. We *will* kill this young lady right here. You *are* going to work with us. Be there tomorrow morning at 7."

The next morning I awoke before the sun rose up. I took a shower, got dressed, and got into my car. I drove to the farm. In an area I can't discuss, there was a dental chair fully set with all of the tools surrounding it, already occupied by a body covered with a sheet. I put on my gloves, pulled up the chair, and removed the sheet.

"Liam..." I gasped.

HORROR STORIES TO RUIN CHRISTMAS

HORROR STORIES TO RUIN CHRISTMAS

DAY 10

ON THE TENTH DAY OF CHRISTMAS, T'WASN'T A BEAR

BY P. OXFORD

MOVING TO SERENITY FALLS BECAUSE I LIKED THE NAME seemed like a good idea at the time, but it really wasn't. Big city woman in a small town, living the good life—it was supposed to be nice. The sleazy realtor from Pure Serenity Realty even promised me the town lived up to the name, but I can tell you for a fact that is not true. Yesterday, I had two small reasons. First, it was the curious case of the never-ending eggs. I keep using them, but I never seem to run out. They don't go bad either. I wasn't sure if I was just forgetful or slowly going crazy, but it was weird. The second issue, a bit more tangible, was the fucking bear that kept waking me up every night.

Twenty-four hours later I only had one issue.

When I heard the bear in the backyard again last night, I was almost more excited than annoyed. It was the 26th time it had knocked over the trash can—yes, I'm keeping count—and the third time this week. I had been tired and cranky for too long, and this night would be the first step in my plan to take that bear down.

I threw the duvet to the side and winced as my warm feet hit the cold wooden floor of my bedroom. I felt around for my slippers, slipped them on, and grabbed my camera. While I was more than willing to blast that fucker full of lead, I didn't have a hunting license, and it wasn't bear hunting season. I was already a newcomer from the big city in a small town, I didn't need to get in trouble for bear-poaching.

Calling the police had been fruitless. "Sweetie," the condescending lady that answered the police station phone said. "It's winter, right? Didn't you learn that bears hibernate in elementary school? Well, if you didn't, I'll tell you now for free. Bears hibernate."

I had tried to explain that there'd been paw prints in the light snow last week. Big paw prints.

"I don't know if you have raccoons, rats, or an overactive imagination, but honey, that's not a bear."

The other town folk weren't any more helpful. I chatted with some old farmer—Bud? Sid? I can't recall—and when I mentioned my bear problem and the unhelpful police, he looked at me like I was an idiot.

"First, that's no bear. It's winter, sweetheart. Second, if it is a bear, you go get yourself a gun and shoot that sumbitch yourself. You're in Serenity Falls now. We handle our problems."

Thanks Hoss, I'll tell the police you said that when they arrest me.

The next time the paw prints appeared, I took pictures. The police remained unimpressed.

"Those don't even look like real bear prints. Honestly, honey, it looks like someone tried to make bear prints. I don't know what your game is, but please do not bother us with this bear story again. We have our hands full with real crimes, okay? People are missing, people are dead, we're stretched thin, and you come here and try to get us to drop everything because you think a raccoon is a bear. Just keep your food out of the trash on non-collection days like the rest of us. If you want attention, put on a short dress and head down to Willie's. We're here for real problems."

So the tracks looked funny, did they? A non-hibernating, trash-without-food attacking bear wasn't a real problem? Well, I was gonna get a picture of that trash stealing fucker, and I was gonna take it to that smug police lady, and I was gonna tell her what's what.

Camera in hand, I slowly made my way out the bedroom door. I tiptoed across the hall and down the stairs, sure that any sound I made would scare the bear off like it had two nights ago when I last tried this. I inhaled sharply as the last stair groaned loudly, stopping for a moment to feel my heart beat like a drum. I couldn't hear anything from outside. Was I already too late?

Without a sound, I made my way across the living room floor. My sofa was positioned right under the dark window that faced the backyard. The window was pitch black, but I knew what was outside it. A short lawn fenced in by a low hedge, and beyond that, a field that gave way to the dark woods. The woods where the goddamned bear lived, no doubt. I had positioned the trash can in the middle of the lawn the day before, giving me perfect vantage over where it'd be if it happened to show up again. Luckily, it did.

As quietly as possible I crawled onto the couch under the window that faced my backyard. I cupped my hands around my eyes and pressed my face to the window, hoping to catch a glimpse of the large predator that was attacking my trash so viciously.

I scanned the scene for a few seconds before movement caught my eye. A few meters out in the blackness, something was bobbing around, rifling through my trash. I strained my eyes against the dark. Was it really a bear? It was too large to be a raccoon, but it looked too small to be a bear too. And the color was off, a little too light. Could it be a mountain lion? I felt a chilly fear creep into me. The movements weren't graceful enough to be a feline, were they?

For the first time, doubt crept into me. "Honey, that's not a bear." Had they been right?

My heart pounded as I reached for the window clasp. I didn't want to remove the barrier between me and whatever was out there, but I couldn't have glass between the camera flash and the creature. And I needed to know.

The cold air hit my face, making my skin pucker in protest. I lifted the camera, pointed it in the general direction of the creature, sent a little prayer in the general direction of a god who might give a shit, and pressed the button that illuminated the whole backyard.

In the brief moment of light, I had seen a monster. Mostly hairless, crouched in a strange position, head hidden in my trash, that thing was no bear. Years of atheism and skepticism went out the window; I had just seen a real, live werewolf.

A shriek rang through the night, and I fell backwards off the couch in panic. Light thuds that could only be made by paws hitting the hard ground rapidly rang through the silent night, and a shot of adrenaline pulled me to my feet and sent me racing back up the stairs. I took the stairs two by two, and in seconds was in my bedroom. I slammed the door closed, leaned against it, and allowed myself to breathe again.

An unmistakable sharp crash sounded from downstairs, and my breath caught in my throat again.

I had left the window open. That thing was in my house.

Whatever it was moved around downstairs. Desperation pushed me to search for a weapon, an escape, fight or flight. The stark minimalism of my bedroom screamed its uselessness at me. No clutter, nothing that could be fashioned into a weapon of any kind. No phone—technology before bed is bad. No defense between me and the monster downstairs but a flimsy wooden plank of a door. Can werewolves open doors? Do they keep their hands? The fear was clawing at my gut, my breathing laboured. I bet they could knock a door down either way.

Another crash from downstairs brought one crystal clear thought up from the chaos my mind had become in the fear: I was going to die. The werewolf was going to eat me alive.

Wait, no. It couldn't be a werewolf, that was insane. Damn, I should have gone to see a shrink about the egg situation before I spiralled into full on hallucinations. But what had I seen? A mountain lion might appear furless when you expect a bear, right? A bear might be hairless if it has mange. A mangy bear, unable to hibernate, starving. It fit with the odd behaviour and the horrifying image etched in my brain. I felt brief relief at having found a rational explanation, but it soon gave way to a new tidal wave of fear. Whatever the hell that thing was downstairs, it was my demise. Hungry mountain lion, mangy bear, or straight up werewolf—did it matter? Any option would happily maul me to death.

My searching eyes finally landed on the heavy wooden dresser. That would hold off the mountain lion better than the flimsy door. I grabbed the closest end and pulled. It didn't budge. Tears filled my eyes, and I snuck around to the other side to push it. No luck. My cheeks were wet with tears and sweat, and I desperately grabbed the large leather chair in the corner, pulling at it with strength I didn't know I had. It moved, and as it did, a jarring scraping sound of wood against wood sent shivers down my spine. I froze, listening intently. No sound from downstairs. The monster had stopped too. It had heard me. It knew where I was. A soft thud, barely audible through the wooden floor signalled movement. And another. At the third soft thud the direction became painfully clear. The thing was walking towards the stairs.

A familiar loud groan of wood from below meant it was on the bottom step. The thuds increased in frequency and volume, and I whimpered as they hit the top of the stairs and continued down the hall. Closer and closer they came, until they stopped by my bedroom door.

I held my breath in the silence. A soft sound penetrated the wood. Loud breathing? Panting? No, that wasn't it. Sniffing. That thing was smelling me through the door, it knew where I was. It was going to break down the door, rip me to shreds, and chew on the pieces. I fought back another whimper.

A light scratching sound pierced the silence, and I jumped before steeling myself against the chair. I propped my legs against my bed and held with everything I had.

The push never came.

The thing scratched at the door one more time, sniffed loudly, before soft thuds disappeared down the hallway. The imminent danger lessened, I breathed in relief. It was still in my house, I was nowhere near safe, but I was also not currently being mauled by a mangy were-lion. That was something.

A loud clang sounded from my bathroom, and I jumped, heart back in my throat again. What the hell was it doing? A few more loud noises from the bathroom, followed by a strange gurgling whine. Then the thing made its way down the hall again.

It stopped outside my door and sniffed loudly again. I closed my eyes, sent a prayer in the general direction of a god I had long since stopped believing in, and waited. Seconds, minutes, or hours passed before it moved again. Thud. Thud. It was moving away from the door! Thud, thud, thud, followed by the unmistakable diminuendo of the sounds could only mean one thing. My neglected god had heard my prayers, and the monster obeyed by lazily descending the stairs, crossing the living room, and climbing back out of the window.

I sat there, waiting for it to come bounding back up the stairs and fly through the thin plywood of my door. Only when the sun shone through my window did I finally get up. My legs were still shaking.

After making sure the house was empty, I went into the kitchen to make a cup of tea, and then I called the police again.

"Definitely raccoons," I was told in a condescending tone. "You really need to accept that living close to the woods involves some critters now and then, and stop bothering us with this silliness," she added before she hung up.

Only then did I remember that I had a picture of the thing. That had been what incited the whole near-death experience, how could I have forgotten?

I turned on my camera, and pressed the button to see what I had taken the photo of.

I frowned. The shape didn't resemble a bear, and not a mountain lion either. Definitely too big to be a raccoon.

I zoomed in, and almost dropped the camera when I realized what I was seeing.

It wasn't a bear at all. The weird prints made total sense. I hadn't forged them to resemble bear prints, but someone had.

It was a man.

Crouched on all fours, naked except for furry boots and gloves that I could only assume made bear-like paw prints on the ground, he had his face buried in a pile of my trash. I felt sick as I realized what it meant. This man had been going through my trash for weeks, he had been in my house, he had scratched on my bedroom door knowing I was cowering behind it, and kept me trapped in there for hours. I felt violated.

I walked my ass all the way up Main Street to the police station and handed off the camera triumphantly. They took my statement and told me they'd look into it when they had time. With everything that has happened in town recently, I'm worried it'll be a while before they have that time.

Back home again, I collapsed onto the sofa and turned on the TV. After a few hours of vegetating, a rumbling stomach reminded me that it was time for food. I opened the door to the kitchen. For a moment I just stared at the gory scene, before I retched violently.

A half plucked, headless chicken lay on the table. The blood that had seeped out from its neck had congealed on the table, and one of the wings was half missing. In a daze I walked closer to the gruesome sight and saw that the wing had been chewed off. I leaned in closer. The bite marks were unmistakably human. On the other wing was a silky red bow, and under the bow someone had tucked a note. I reached out a shaking hand and extracted the blood-smeared piece of paper. The short message was scribbled in child-like handwriting:

"Your trash is my treasure. The one in the bathroom smells the best.

I thought my little gifts were a good trade, but if you don't like the eggs, how about you get the whole chicken (I only ate a little, I couldn't help myself). Please enjoy it.

P.S. Don't be scared like the last girl. Bears can smell fear, and we don't like it."

I stared at the chicken as the full gravity of the situation sank in. He had been coming into my house for weeks. The open window had nothing to do with anything, he had a way in. And god knows how many of his eggs I had eaten over the last months.

Serenity Falls is really not living up to its name.

HORROR STORIES TO RUIN CHRISTMAS

THE ELEVENTH DAY OF CHRISTMAS
DUG TOO DEEP

BY CHRIS THOMPSON

Dear Melissa,

 I know you *P*robably have a thousand questions for me, and I will do my best to answer them all. I *L*ove you Mel, and I need you to remember that. When I met you, I knew I wanted to spend the rest of my life with you. I came to the diner three times a day for nineteen days before I found the courage to ask you out. I remember the look you gave me before asking why I took so long to ask. Thirteen dates in and we were living together. Remember that horrible apartment?
 When I found this house, I thought we had struck gold. Perfect size, big ole yard, and cheap. I admit, that last thing was a major deciding factor in me buying the house. It was the perfect size for the two of us. So I went around and signed the contracts while you were at work and brought you home to your new house.
 26 months after I met you in the diner, we were married. As far as I was concerned, life was perfect once we got settled in to our first home. But then last month, you told me the news. We were going to be parents. I was over the moon when I heard those words come from your mouth, I knew that life really was complete. Because it had taken so long, I was close to accepting the fact that we would not have children. It hurt, but being with you was more than enough for me. You give me my reasons for living. I spent a week just making plans to renovate the house, paying special attention to give the nursery a window. One that didn't open, for your own sense of security. I never even thought of building permits until the contractor asked for them. So, I went to the courthouse to file.
 When the clerk at the courthouse gave me an *E*vil look as I turned in the applications for the permits, I shrugged it off. After *A*ll, it is a small town, chances were she lived close enough to us that the construction would cause her *S*ome aggravation. How was I to know that was the first clue to how fucked we would be? I shrugged it off, turned in the paperwork, and left. The next morning, I got a call from a blocked number. I answered only to hear, "What lies below shall remain

unknown," in an Eerily low voice. I was a little shaken, but figured it was a crank call. Big construction jobs in small neighborhoods get a lot of shit reactions from neighbors, ya Know?

When I remodeled the garage, I had to file for almost a dozen permits (I thought it was due to being in town) and during that whole thing, Every business around me complained to the courts and tried to get the permits denied. When they finally went through, I had to deal with three months of dirty looks and shit talk from Every single business around me. Even the diner, Melissa, remember when you would just glare at me? I was Pretty sure that you would hate me forever. I am elated you didn't. I cannot imagine living a life without you. Which is why I sent you away. I want you to Remember that I will always love you.

I'm glad that I was able to convince you to stay at your mother's house for the duration of the renovations. I am sorry, Unfortunately I lied to you. I didn't want you to leave because of the fumes and dust, but because we've been targeted for something, by some pretty bad people. The morning you left, I found a note stapled to the front door, written on the back of a Polaroid photo of us in bed. The Note was similar to the phone call: *"What lies below, you will not know."* That was the very moment that I panicked. That was the moment I knew we were in trouble.

I had you leave that same morning because I knew that trouble was coming, and it was bringing company. You've been gone for three days Now, and it is killing me waking up in the morning without you lying beside me. It Is killing me. Just in case I can't manage to stop these people, I'm going to tell you what's been happening. If you receive this, I'm likely dead as it is "in the cloud" on a timer awaiting me to restart the clock. If I fail to restart the clock the letter sends to your email, the fax at the diner, and to your mother's house fax. It may seem like overkill, but I want to be certain you get this message.

After the photo was discovered, and you had left for your mother's place, I went to work. Upon opening the shop door, I found something that actually managed to shake me to my core. I discovered a gutted fetal pig laying on the floor, with the blood used to paint a hasty message on the wall: *"What lies below, you shall never know."* I called the police, and they came and took pictures, Notes, and my statement. Of course there were no clues, but the video surveillance camera above my door had caught the perpetrator as he dumped the pig, and wrote his message. Unfortunately, the footage simply showed a blurry fuzzy mass of a figure. I closed the shop early that day, and went to the next town over to rent a Bobcat with a blade. I drove home to start to dig up the yard. When I pulled up to the house with the small machine on a trailer behind my truck, I noticed fresh footprints in the snow. I got out of the truck and went to inspect them. The prints went all the way around the house, and were concentrated around the windows. The problem was not the real foot prints, but the enormous ones alongside them. Like size 19 shoe prints, right beside some size 13 shoe prints, just traipsing around my fucking home, Gazing into my fucking windows. I sort of lost my shit at the sight of this, and decided to forgo the digging for a while, and got my pistol out of the glove box before entering our house to see if they had made entry. I checked everything, and even looked at the cameras I installed for the house. I told you they might come in handy one day, and boy, did they ever have something to show me.

Remember how I sprung for the better cameras for the house? Well, they have a much higher resolution than the ones for the garage. What was simply a blurry figure on the garage cameras turned out to be a guy in a ghillie suit, all black with his face painted as dark as Vantablack. Beside him was a fucking clown. I mean it, a full blown circus clown, big shoes, painted face, tiny hat, with beady eyes underneath. It was the single creepiest thing I have ever seen. Here it was broad daylight, and there was a fucking clown walking around our house, looking in the windows. The pair of them never tried to get inside the house, and eventually walked through the side yard, down the little bluff to the back street, where there was a car waiting for them. A brilliant green 1939 Lincoln Zephyr. The pair jumped in and sped off towards town.

I made a couple calls. When you build fast cars for a living, baby, you learn to make friends with some nasty people. I called them all. I told them the first to give me a solid lead on that Zephyr would get 5k dollars from the bank as soon as I stopped this insane shit. I stayed awake that night with help from No-Doz and coffee. The next morning around eight, I received a call from one of the rat bastards I had called. They found the green Zephyr.

I gathered a small arsenal and went to the location he had given me. It was a shack in the woods—well, what was left of one, anyway. It was nearly black with burn marks, and the soot on the ground meant the fire had been recent. The place had been torn apart, and there was blood and shit everywhere. I.V. poles and bodily fluids littered the floor of a subterranean cellar. The upstairs was empty save an overturned table and a couple chairs. I searched the place high and low and found absolutely nothing. That made me think, how could the rat bastard know where that car was, and know that the owners would not be with it? He had to be a part of all of this, somehow. So, first thing in the morning, I'm going to go after him. This particular rat is vulnerable, and I think I can get some fucking answers. Please, read this carefully, Melissa.

I love you, and always will.
David

HORROR STORIES TO RUIN CHRISTMAS

THE TWELFTH DAY OF CHRISTMAS ISN'T VERY FUNNY AT ALL

BY JESSE CLARK

Rob Davis and I didn't find Lou in his normal spot behind the diner. He wasn't near the liquor store either, or near the auto shop. Instead, he was sitting on the hill between Serenity Falls Elementary and the empty house south of it. He didn't look at us when we parked our patrol car behind him. He said nothing when we sat down on either side of him. And he barely noticed the bag of food I placed on the snow by his feet.

"It's cold." I said. He looked down and opened the bag and began to unpack his meal silently, studiously. I continued, "It was warm about an hour ago."

He took a bite out of his burger and chewed without a word.

"Ethan and I were looking all over town for you, Lou." Rob said. "You weren't in your usual haunts."

"Sometimes I move around." Lou took another bite and chewed silently.

"It's 26 degrees out here."

"Yeah."

I shook my head. "How is it?" I asked.

"Cold."

"Yeah." There was a brief pause before I cut to the chase. "So Lou, wondering if you knew anything about these… occurrences lately?"

He looked at me briefly, and then forward again.

"Occurrences?"

"Yeah."

"Nah."

"Nah?"

"Nah as in I don't know."

Rob asked, "You don't know about them, or you don't know if you know about them?"

"I don't know." He took another bite.

"I mean, you must've noticed, right?" I said. "We've got an attempted murder down by the falls. Some real estate freak with a knife. A missing dentist. Random flyers and phone calls around town, vanishing homeless folks. Plus all the missing medical supplies from the clinic. All happening at once. You've got your ear to the ground. Just came by to see if you, you know. Knew anything."

"Got my own issues, man."

"Okay."

"Not like y'all care."

"Lou."

"I called you last night about it, man."

Rob and I shot each other a look. Then I nodded at him, and he went back to the patrol car. "I'm sorry, Lou," I said. "Must've missed it."

"You think?"

"It's been a crazy few weeks."

"You told me that if I called y'all, y'all two would show up to help. I called. Y'all didn't show. Last few nights, Ed went missing. Then Slim. Then Crew. One at a time, yo. Someone be pickin' 'em all off."

"Who?"

"A clown?" Rob said. I turned around. He was holding our shared cell phone to his ear, listening to Lou's voicemails from last night. I looked at Lou.

"A clown, Lou?"

He took another bite. "Now y'all two is laughin' at me."

Rob sat back down on the other side of him and pocketed the phone.

"We're not laughing at you, Lou," I said. "We just want some clarification."

"A clown was chasing you down Main?" Rob asked.

"Yeah."

"What did the clown look like?"

"I don't know, man. A clown. Y'all ain't never seen a damn clown before?"

I rolled my eyes. He didn't notice. "I mean… what, red wig? Green wig? Big button nose?"

He shook his head. "Looked like one of them older clowns. Like the big collar and paint."

"Face paint?"

"Yeah."

Rob said, "Was last night the first time you saw the clown?"

Lou shook his head. "Nah, man. Been seein' his ass out in the trees south of town for days now. I'm out at the dump like always an' I look up, an' he just be walkin' around, sometimes smilin' at me with balloons." There was another pause before he added, "Recently he started like, wavin' me over."

"Into the woods?"

"Yeah."

"Did you go?"

"Fuck no, I ain't go into no damn woods with no damn clown. You serious?"

"Okay, okay. Easy. You think this clown is abducting your friends?"

"Yeah. Gotta be him, yo."

"Do you see him every night?" I asked.

"...Yeah."

I nodded. Then I said, "Lou, listen. If you see him tonight, call. I promise I'll answer."

We got the call later that same afternoon while we cruised around town.

"Lou?" I said. Rob and I looked at each other.

"He's comin,' man!"

"Wait. Who?"

"What you mean who, dude?!"

"The clown. Okay. Okay. Uh… where—where are you now?"

"He's chasin' me into town, dude. There ain't no one left. I'm goin' for the diner."

"Okay. We're coming."

The patrol car was idling behind us, illuminating the alley behind the diner. It was empty.

"I thought you said he was here," Rob said.

"He said he was 'going' for the diner. Not that he was here."

"You think he didn't make it?"

"Given the evidence I'm curious as to what the alternative could be, Rob." He snorted. I pulled out my phone. "I'm gonna try him again. Keep looking for clues."

"Ay, yo. This is Lou. Leave a message."

"Lou, it's Ethan again. We're at the diner. Please, pick up if you can."

I hung up. Then I stuffed my hands in my pockets to get them out of the cold.

"Ethan," Rob said. I turned around. "Come here. Look at this." I joined him. On the ground beneath our feet were footprints.

"Could've been anyone," I said.

"Not that."

He wasn't looking directly down. He was looking off to the side. An old flip-phone sat in the snow and mud behind a dumpster. The screen was lit up blue. '5 new voice messages.'

"Oh, shit." I walked over and picked it up and opened it. The first four digits of a phone number which matched mine were typed into the screen. I backed out, went to the voicemails, and played the most recent message.

"Lou, it's Ethan again. We're at the Diner. Please, pick up if you can."

I looked at Rob.

"Check the rest," he said. "Pictures, texts. Any kind of clue."

I did, and sure enough, we found a video on the phone. The quality of the sound and picture, taken on such an old device, was questionable at best. After a moment we recognized the place in the clip as the fields south of town, near the town dump. The cameraman was walking backwards, and up ahead and covered in shadow, a figure moved towards the screen. It wasn't walking or running. It was skipping. Dancing, even. A bizarre, jovial gait. It was impossible to make out more specific details, but that only made it more eerie. There were shallow, rapid breaths from the camera operator.

"Ay, man! You stay back, yo!" shouted Lou in the clip. He sounded equally afraid and out of breath. "I'm filming your ass. You hear me? You wanna get on TV, you keep comin'! CNN gonna be gettin' all this at first light, boy! Folks ain't gonna be fuckin' around when they see proof some clown-ass dude be stalkin' people in the woods, yo!"

The figure kept coming.

"Fuck this," Lou declared. He turned and fled. The video cut out after a few more seconds of shaking, shuffling, pounding feet, and labored breathing.

"Dammit," I said. I turned to Rob. "Now what? How do we find him now?"

He was looking up. I did too. A single balloon, too deflated to rise and too inflated to fall, floated at the far end of the alley. Rob pulled it down and turned it over to reveal the writing on the front: 'Mister Mystery's Travelling Circus and Extravaganza'

We looked at each other.

"You ever heard of that?" I asked.

Rob shook his head. "Sounds like we might find it in the woods. That's where Lou said he found the clown, anyway."

We parked the car in the snow in front of the treeline near the town dump. Even during the day the woods in front of us were impenetrably thick and foreboding. At night they were nearly demonic. I hoped to be done with this mess by evening.

Rob and I stood in front of the car, hands in our pockets, shivering.

"We're going in there, aren't we?" I asked. I could see my breath.

"We made the man a promise."

I nodded. "You think we'll find him in there?"

Rob didn't answer for a while. He just scanned the trees. Nothing of note.

"No."

We went in anyway.

By the time we saw a shack in the woods, the still-flashing lights of our cruiser, kept on to guide us back, were barely visible at all; little pinpricks of light hidden by dense forest.

"There," Rob whispered. He nodded towards the shack. It was a dilapidated wreck, covered in graffiti and old tires and heaps of trash. Scarred with scorch marks, it looked like it had recently been lit aflame, then snuffed out as an afterthought. An old car was parked nearby with no one inside.

"How do you figure?"

"It's the only thing there is to figure."

We approached the place cautiously, weapons drawn, and rolled our feet to muffle the sound of crunching snow. When we reached the wall, I did a quick sweep around the back—nothing—and returned to find Rob staring through the one window that was only partially boarded up.

"What do you see?"

"A mess."

"Is he in there?"

"Someone was. Recently, too." After a pause he added, "I think I see blood in there."

My heart pounded. "Seriously?"

"Yeah."

I stood up while he tried the knob. When it didn't give, he kicked the door open and we stepped inside.

"Police officers!" I said. The place was uninhabited. But it wasn't empty. It was filthy beyond belief, and Rob was right: there was blood here, and not a small amount of it. Above the floor dangled various bladed weapons. Axes. Knives. Saws. Rob found something else of interest while I inspected a flyer for Mister Mystery's Travelling Circus and Extravaganza.

In the center of the flyer, filled with gleeful post-Vaudeville font and matching aesthetic was a circus master: tuxedo, mustache, top hat, white gloves, and a whip. He looked proud and genial and inviting. Behind him were cages, though, and there weren't animals inside. There were people. I couldn't make out many details, but they appeared to be miserable, and disfigured.

Beneath the image was the caption: *'Come one, come all: See beasts big and small. Ride rides, eat food, see lights that glow—and make sure you visit our lovely freak show!'*

"A freak show?" I mumbled. "Seriously?"

"Ethan, look at this." I looked over: Rob had followed the trail of blood to something hidden beneath old boxes of luggage. I put the flyer down, walked over and helped him move the things, revealing a trap door. We looked at each other, and then back down. We got it open with some effort, and the stench of death and rot flew out to meet us. I wretched. Rob winced. Pulling our shirts over our noses, we peered into the darkness below. Little could be seen; our flashlights only revealed the ladder descending to the room, and the fact that the bulk of it was hidden beneath the center of the structure.

"Shoot for it to see who goes in first?" I suggested, but Rob just handed me his flashlight.

"Watch the door," he said. "Then follow me down."

He descended the ladder and vanished around the corner. Moments later, I joined him.

The place was some kind of operating room, covered in plastic sheets drenched in blood. A single, flickering bulb illuminated the place.

On the various operating tables were not only the supplies stolen from the town clinic, but multiple men, dead or dying. Mutilated. Deformed. Diseased. Mangled. Hooked up to IVs working mightily to keep them alive. Rob and I gazed around in horror, rendered speechless.

I inspected the first man. His legs had been removed and the stumps were sloppily stitched and bleeding. I felt for a pulse. Dead. On the table beside him, another man now had four legs: his own plus two spares. Where they were sewn onto his stomach, rot and infection had set in. The man breathed slowly and shallowly under a sedative.

"What... is this?" Rob said.

"Found a flyer upstairs for the travelling circus. Mentioned a freak show."

Rob stared at me.

"Go call it in," I said. "Get Weis, Hatch, Mueller. Everyone."

He ran off to make the call. When he was gone, I saw another man lying on a table in the corner of the room, behind the others. I walked over.

"Lou," I said. He was sedated, but not operated on yet. "Lou, hang on, buddy. I'm gonna get you out." I placed my hand on his stomach while I searched for a way to unbuckle the straps holding him down.

Instantly, he snapped awake. He screamed, kicked, howled. Mad with fear.

"GET AWAY FROM ME, YO! HEY! HELP ME!"

"Lou. Lou! Hey, it's me. It's Ethan. It's okay." I reassured him.

He started crying when he recognized me.

"It's okay," I said. "Hey. We're gonna get you out, okay? We're gonna get you out."

"S-strap buckles on the other side," he said through tears. His voice shook.

"Okay." I leaned over him and unfastened it. Together we pulled out the IVs in his arm; the remaining liquid dripping onto the floor. "I'm so sorry we couldn't get to you earlier. We tried."

"I know."

"Do you know where the clown went?"

He looked up at me and shook his head a single time.

"I don't—"

He hadn't finished the sentence when Rob descended the ladder in a panic, two rungs at a time. He ran over.

"What's wrong?" I said.

"Hide."

"What?"

"Hide!"

We did. All three of us shrank into the shadows of the room and made ourselves small. Lou shuddered; Rob clapped a hand over his mouth and held a finger up to his own.

After a long silence, we heard a scream. It was deafening. Ear-piercing, even, high-pitched and barely human.

"You've broken my door!" Shrieked a voice from upstairs. Lou's reaction was all I needed to identify the source. "You've broken my door. That was rude of you, hmm? That was nasty."

We heard footsteps.

"Are you... someone who has left me?"

Creaking floorboards.

"No, no," continued the voice. "The door has caved in, yes? Someone has come inside, not gone out."

Rob and I looked at each other. Slowly, quietly, we brought our weapons out.

"Someone is still in this place, yes?" said the voice. We heard the sound of a bladed weapon being taken from the wall. *Shling.* "Someone is still with us in this place, yes, yes. Someone who should not be here. Someone who wasn't invited. No."

The footsteps crept towards the trapdoor. Behind them, the sound of something heavy being dragged along.

"And this door is open too, yes?"

A long pause.

"Someone is down below," said the clown at last. "Hello in there! Hi! Hi!" He giggled and we watched silently as the shadow on the ground showed he was waving, and he began descending the ladder. "I like hiding games," he announced. "I like them very much."

A moment later, the scuff of a footstep on the floor. He was here, a post-Vaudeville jester in a black-and-white suit. No wig. No button nose. Just simple face paint, a ruffled collar and cap, and an axe from upstairs.

Lou squeezed his eyes shut. Rob continued to hold him steady. The clown turned his back to us and faced the opposite wall.

"Are you... over here?" he said. He swung his axe into the opposite corner of the room; it connected with the empty, shadow covered wall with a clang.

"No," said the clown. "Not there." He dragged the axe along to the far corner on the opposite side of the room. "No one here. Hmmm."

Slowly, Rob released Lou and motioned for him to stay quiet. Lou nodded. Then Rob looked at me, and we crept out from the corner. The clown was circling around a shelf of medical supplies. Behind that, another potential hiding place. He brought up his axe.

"Are you... in here?" he said. He swung the axe. Nothing but old shelves took the brunt of that swing, and Rob and I used the commotion to muffle the sounds of us clicking the safety on our handguns to off. As the clown moved to the table Lou had been in, Rob signalled to me to go wide to the left. I nodded, and off I went.

"Our guest is missing!" said the clown. "Where has he gone off to?!"

I crept around the room from the back while Rob approached the clown directly, still crouched and keeping his distance. Before I was in position, the Clown whirled around and saw Rob.

Instantly Rob fired his gun, but the bullet went wide. The clown screamed and swung the axe wildly. Rob tumbled over as the blade connected with the operating table above his head. Then the clown brought his boot down hard on Rob's stomach, who howled, dropping his weapon.

I stood up and fired once, twice, three times. Three misses in the dark. The clown lunged forward and brought the back end of the axe into my stomach.

"Rob!" I shouted.

"That was rude of you," said the clown. He planted his boot on my chest and brought the axe up over his head, only for it be caught by Rob. The two struggled for a moment while I kicked my way out from underneath the bastard's shoe.

I scrambled for my gun. Above and behind me, the clown grabbed Rob's neck and threw him to the ground, crashing him into the remains of the destroyed shelf. My gun was beneath a medical table now. I reached for it.

"Hang on!" Rob said. He was struggling back to his feet, but he was too far away.

The clown grabbed my hair and pulled me back. I landed against the wall of the room with a thump; my head smacked against it, and my vision swam. I saw my gun get pulled away. Rob was stumbling in my direction.

"Stay still!" the clown said. He raised the axe a final time, when—
BANG!

The bullet smacked into the wall between the clown and myself. The clown stumbled back in surprise, dropping the axe.

"Least I can throw shit," said Lou.

At that, he threw my pistol at the clown, and it connected with his nose, blood exploding outward. A moment later, Rob wrapped his arm around the clown's throat and brought him down. I piled on, followed by Lou. The clown shrieked and curled into a ball as the three of us kicked and stomped.

"STAY DOWN!" I said. Rob handcuffed the clown. I turned to Lou. "I owe you one, pal."

"Make sure the burger's at least warm this time."

"Rob, did you call Weis?"

He nodded and stood up. Then he wiped his nose of blood, and stared at his hand. "Y-yeah. They're coming. They were looking into yet another clinic break-in from earlier tonight. I guess this piece of shit ran out of supplies."

He kicked the clown a final time.

Rob and I stood in the snow and watched as the last of the clown's victims were carried out of the shack on stretchers. The available ambulances had to take them out in shifts. Behind us, Lou sat against the side of the shack and hugged his knees, watching his friends go.

A car door slammed. I looked over to see Sergeant Weis had locked the clown inside his cruiser. Rob and I walked over. Inside, the clown was handcuffed and bloodied, broken nose, black eye, but still grinning and making silly faces.

"He say anything?" I asked.

Weis stared at the clown, arms folded. "Said he works for some guy called the Ringmaster."

"The Ringmaster."

"Yeah. Guy ordered him to round up folks. Make freaks out of 'em with sick experiments."

"Flyer mentioned a freak show."

"Ayep. Settles the clinic break-ins, too." He nodded over toward two duffle bags full of stolen supplies, lying by the shack door.

"You think he'll talk?" Rob said. "Tell us who the Ringmaster is?"

Weis shook his head. "Said he wouldn't tell us even if he knew."

"There's a surprise."

"Said something else, though. Said the Ringmaster's not even the one we want."

"What do you mean?"

"Said the Ringmaster works for someone, or something else. Couldn't or wouldn't give us more than that. But I'm thinking all this madness around town's connected somehow."

Rob and I shared a look, then turned back to the clown. He met our gaze through the window, face stretched into a big, ugly grin.

I looked at Weis. He wasn't looking at the clown anymore. He was looking at the sky. The sun was setting.

Nightfall.

"C'mon," he said. "It's getting dark."

HORROR STORIES TO RUIN CHRISTMAS

ON THE THIRTEENTH DAY OF CHRISTMAS, MY LUCK RAN OUT

BY P. F. MCGRAIL

Tears streamed freely down my face, smearing the "rosy cheek" makeup and causing it to leak crimson drops onto my fluffy white beard. My fake belly shook like a bowl full of jelly as I sobbed. I tried to hold back another 'ugly cry' attack. *It* would be angry if that got in the way.

I wiped the mess from my face and beard, looked at my reflection, and forced a smile.

It didn't matter if I was dead inside.

I faked a huge grin, and the elfish visage of Santa smiled back at me.

Showtime!

The snow crunched beneath my coal-black boots as I walked across the park. I could hear the children, buzzing like bees, just out of sight behind the elm grove.

I rounded the corner. It looked like a scene right out of a Norman Rockwell painting. A light dusting of snow covered the grass. Bright-eyed children huddled close to their parents to hide from Jack Frost. Old Ms. Hoggins was sharing a platter of warm, fresh-baked apple cinnamon muffins with everyone nearby.

I saw it all just before they saw me.

And when they recognized me, the screaming was overwhelming.

"IT'S SANTA!"

If it weren't for the parents and teachers holding back the flood, I'm certain that the children of Serenity Falls Elementary would have trampled me to death.

And why shouldn't they be excited?

It was nearly December.

No one had *any fucking idea* what was in store for them over the coming month.

For the moment, they were happy and whole in a way that this town *never* would be again.

Despite it being the weekend after Thanksgiving, most of the students had shown up to school and crossed over Dairy Road *just* to meet me.

"Oof!" I groaned as a boy in a purple sweater plopped onto my lap. He grinned in the mostly innocent, partially greedy way that only eight-year-olds can get away with.

"Ho, Ho, Ho! What's your name, son?" I hoped that he couldn't hear how much I was forcing it.

"Liam!" he shouted back, flashing a gap-toothed smile. "And I want to say thank you, Santa, for coming to the tree-lighting ceremony here in Serenity Falls. I know you're busy this time of year."

He had clearly been rehearsing this speech.

I awarded him with an equally-rehearsed answer.

"And what do you want Santa to bring you for Christmas this year, Liam?"

His eyes lit up with desire. "Pokemon cards! So, I have a shiny Charizard from an old deck…"

And this is where Santa tunes out.

Because Santa isn't real, and Christmas magic wouldn't be necessary if the world weren't so fucked up.

I cut him off. "Santa can *definitely* bring you all of that, Liam," I interjected jovially as I leaned forward to make sure the microphone was in range. "Now, why don't you tell Santa *exactly* where you live, so I can bring you the Pokemon cards!"

"I'm at 1913 Elm Street!" he nearly shouted.

"Thank you, Liam," I responded, making sure to angle my voice toward the hidden mic on my shoulder. "Off you go!"

He seemed disappointed, but I had a lot of kids to get through. The next boy, who was about six years old, was clearly having an internal battle between fear and anticipation. I smiled, bent down, and scooped him up. His big brown eyes spoke of hope that his voice was unable to express.

"And what would *you* like for Christmas, special guy?" I asked in a *very* successful imitation of happiness.

For several seconds, he did not speak. When he finally found his voice, I had to lean in just to hear him.

"My daddy works hard to take care of me. Sometimes, I'm a pain in his neck, but he loves me, because my mommy is gone and there's no one else to love me. I... I think I want to ask for a new mommy, so that he can be happier and not so lonely all the time."

I quickly controlled the tear that was welling in my eye. "Well. That's very thoughtful of you. But, Santa can't bring people. They have to bring *themselves* together. So, I'll tell you what, since you're such a good boy who's always thinking about others, I'll get you your favorite thing in the whole world. Can you tell Santa what that is?"

He concentrated for a moment, and then his face lit up with pure joy.

"Ice cream!" he shouted gleefully.

I nodded. "A sweet treat for a sweet boy. Say, why don't you tell Santa where you live, so I can make sure you get all your gifts?"

He grew bolder. "I'm at 26 Edd Road, just outside of town."

I split my face with a manufactured smile. "Wonderful! And what's your name, special guy?"

He matched my grin. "My name is Carter."

I collapsed into the chair behind my desk and poured myself a plastic cup of Kirkland Signature moonshine because I just didn't give a shit anymore.

And it was even cheaper than their chartreuse.

Besides, it was after-hours at the water treatment plant. For the moment, nobody else was here.

I sighed, then detached the hidden microphone from beneath my shirt. The Santa suit had been jettisoned at the earliest possible convenience. I'm 90% certain that the teenage couple behind the counter at the costume rental place was currently using it for fetish roleplay, which was still more wholesome than my recent activities.

And their carnal anticipation at least meant that one was waiting for the other's embrace. I ran my fingers through silver hair and wondered once more what I'd be doing right now if things had gone differently after everything in high school. Yet again, I told myself that it was buried far too many years in the past to matter.

Besides, my world had become an homage to emptiness and pain. Everything would be so much harder if I weren't alone.

I helped myself to three healthy gulps of moonshine.

Then I uploaded the conversations and updated my files. Any time I felt like crying, I poured some more moonshine and got back to work.

Because I'm a damn good organizer.

Notes! Those were next on my checklist.

I had to throw out the first two drafts, because tears and snot kept falling onto the pages and ruining everything.

I swatted the plastic cup from my desk and took a huge swig from the bottle.

It burned. I was dizzy. I couldn't think straight.

That made everything easier.

With the steadiest hand I could muster, I wrote the messages. I kept them snot-free this time.

"I know."

"Leon says hi."

"Keep the tourists out; no county calls. Locals only. In case of emergency… LIE."

I was disgusted with myself. I grabbed the handcuffs from my desk and squeezed them, pulled them, twisted them around until the edges tore at my soft flesh and tiny rivulets of blood ran down my wrists.

It was the most therapeutic sight, because I *deserved* to suffer.

It was enough to keep me going.

I slipped the cuffs into my pocket, then reached over and unfolded the large map of Wisconsin. I scanned Waushara County, found Serenity Falls, and circled it three times with my highlighter. Then I folded it back up and wrote another note. *"It's the perfect place to start over,"* I penned, then I stuck both the note and the map into an envelope.

My stomach turned as I thought of what I had to write next. *"Your trash is my treasure. The one in the bathroom smells the best."*

I didn't even realize how much I had been wincing in disgust until I put the note aside and physically felt my face fall back to normal.

I quickly scribbled the next message. *"What lies below, you will not know."*

It was strange to think about it. I didn't know everything that was going on. And I wish that I could erase the things I *did* know from my memory.

I sighed, then looked around my cramped office.

We needed the bigger space. Soon. Now.

And we couldn't even *start* "recruiting" someone to work on teeth until the farm was ready.

I pulled out the candidate files and stared at them.

It was a waste of time from the get-go, in my opinion. Timothy Poole wasn't a man of strong mental fiber; he'd crack like an egg and prove himself worthless. I had no idea what Clara Davis saw in him. But Hugh Ratcliff—he had known pain. Understood *resilience* to it. Maybe that was why he chose oral surgery as a profession.

Can you imagine picking your son up from preschool, then both of you stumbling upon your wife's corpse in the front yard?

Knowing that you couldn't scream or cry, because you had to protect your child?

Realizing that you had to *leave your wife's body behind* with her leg still twitching and her head skewered on your (formerly) white picket fence?

One slip-up while hanging Christmas lights on the roof, and your widower of a husband hates the holiday forever.

But he endured. Yes, Hugh would prove valuable.

Timothy Poole?

My guess is that he'd lose his sanity faster that he'd lose his fingers.

Regardless—it was time to get a bigger place.

I opened the box of fake business cards and took one out. "Pure Serenity Reality" flashed back at me in embossed letters. I chuckled at the lie; it was the only way to avoid sobbing.

I swiveled around and started a video on my monitor. A ten-year-old girl in grimy clothes was bound tightly to a chair. Snot and drool hung from her face, but she was beyond crying.

I quickly turned away, pulled my memory stick from the computer, and stuffed it into an envelope with the fake business cards.

Unfortunately, I was raised to believe in hell. I have zero doubt that I am going to roast there when I die, wishing for all eternity that my soul had never existed.

I took another swig from the moonshine and got back to work.

"The Bad Man's Home" was a new level of darkness. I pondered this fact as I unfolded the shabbily-made flyer in front of me. The quality was poor, but such were the specifications of the request.

I ran my hands through my rapidly-thinning hair. "The Bad Man." Was that really me? Or was I "The Ringmaster"?

I looked down at the engraved name plate sitting on my desk. "Neal Coughlan, Director, Waushara County Department of Water Treatment."

Until a few weeks ago, it was the most boring title ever.

I didn't know who I was anymore.

I turned to my phone next and selected a number that I hadn't dared to match with a name. When you're dreading a phone call, it's best to dial quickly and get it over with.

A voice on the other end responded. It danced along the register between alto and tenor, and could easily have been male or female.

"He's ready, Dr. Yihowah," I said plainly. "He's returned."

I hated hearing that voice. I ended the call as quickly as I could.

Everything about this was terrible.

The funny thing is that you have *no idea* what "everything" truly is.

Not until what you had *believed* was "everything" gets torched to the ground, and then your flesh keeps right on burning without the mercy of turning to ash.

I reached forward and picked up a picture of a mugshot. John "I always orgasm as I watch them gasp for air" Doe—six feet, two inches, and 191.3 pounds of ugly—stared back at me.

I didn't know where this guy came from, and—despite painting his crime scenes with DNA evidence—neither did the cops.

Now he was *my* problem. Just one of many.

With the police incapacitated, though, even killers could be easy to spring from jail.

But John Doe was going to be one *hell* of a loose cannon.

And speaking of loose cannons…

John Doe was physically dangerous, and Frank Ramsey was *psychologically* dangerous. I didn't like using either one of them, even if they were nothing more than pawns.

But neither compared to the man who had just dropped by for a late-night visit.

I could hear his shoes marching down the hallway. I knew who he was long before he arrived.

I opened the door. The rest of the building was not lit, so he was barely visible in the darkness.

"Hello in there, Ringmaster! Hi! Hi!" I could faintly make out his black-and-white suit. No wig. No button nose. Just simple face paint, a ruffled collar and cap.

Without making eye contact, I reached over to the table and grabbed a stack of papers. "I've… observed the homeless population of Serenity Falls," I deadpanned, handing him the papers. "This is everything I've learned. Start with them. People won't notice when they're gone."

His white teeth gleamed as he smiled in the darkness.

I really fucking hate clowns.

"You have the Ringmaster's orders. You know what to do. Now leave. I have business here that cannot begin until you're gone."

A chill ran through me as he slipped into darkness. Honestly, if there's a demon in my room, I at least want to know where he is.

But I had my orders as well.

Whether I liked them or not.

I walked into the dark hallway and headed toward the plant's main engines. The constant thrumming grew louder as I passed pipes, steam valves, and pistons grinding to a steady rhythm.

It really was beautiful. Every drop of water that went into Waushara County taps ran through these pipes first.

In a way, they ran through *me*.

And without this plant, the need for Serenity Falls would have dried up and disappeared years ago.

I had believed that was beautiful, once.

As per protocol, I pulled the cuffs from my pocket, slapped one end on my wrist, then bound the other to a metal handrail with a vicious *click*.

I didn't have the key.

I was at the complete mercy of the person in the shadows.

The engines hummed softly in the darkness as I waited.

My buzz was wearing off, so I started to cry.

Step, step, step.

I didn't want to look as it approached.

Step. Step. Silence.

It was in front of me.

I looked up at the humanoid figure in the shadows. I couldn't tell anything about age, gender, height, or size.

Just like every other visit.

"I've done everything," I started, my voice cracking. "I've followed all of your written demands. Things are going to start tomorrow—Monday, the 26th, just like you told me." The tears started to flow, unbidden yet inevitable, like the final thaw after a winter freeze. "I just want one thing after doing *everything* you've asked. So many people are about to be hurt, and so many others will do the hurting. All of them used to be innocent, and no one will be once this is done." I sobbed. "But I did it, I forced them all, and I did it well. Because I understand what you've told me. I know how many people this water reaches."

I let out a wail, the tears and snot once again flowing freely. "I know that twenty thousand people will suffer if I fuck this up, *I GET IT!* Most people have NO fucking idea how many ways their water could be poisoned, or how many years they could be made to hurt without understanding how. You've found a way to break into and out of my plant that I'll never understand." I let out a rattling, shaky breath. When I spoke again, it was through the whispered husk of an utterly broken human being. "If it's what you want, I will terrorize dozens to save thousands, then accept the world's hatred when it's all over. I won't even kill myself, because I understand that you will release the poison if

I do." I took several shallow breaths, then looked up at the shadow with bloodshot eyes. "But I want this one thing."

The shadow didn't move.

"Why?" I asked in complete desperation. "Why are *so many* people going to endure so much agony? Why will so many others be coerced into becoming the instruments of pain? Why unleash killers and give them bizarre tasks to fulfill? And why turn so many thousands into the ransom of your demands? *Why?"*

The shadow took three steps forward and stopped. It leaned toward my head and spoke softly in the darkness.

"Because."

The shadow remained still for several seconds, then turned around and walked away from me.

With a *clink,* the handcuff key was tossed at my feet.

As per the rules, I waited two minutes before releasing myself.

Then I turned around, headed to my office, and got back to work.

Days later, I was holed up at the farm. All was quiet.

The bound and gagged figure at my feet was my only companion.

I knelt down on his chest and released the gag. "You can cry and whine all you want, Liam," I snarled gruffly. "But we're too far away from town. No one can hear you scream."

His eyes shone in the moonlight. The look on his face told me that he believed every word I said.

"What's going to happen to me?" he whispered. "Are you going to hurt me?"

I couldn't afford pity. It would destroy me.

"Liam, it won't make things any easier if I lie to you."

I said it in a mean voice. I had to.

He cried so quietly that I wanted to jump into the fucking river and just end things right then and there.

"But what about Christmas miracles? Daddy told me that my mommy got taken away by the angels because it was a Christmas miracle, and that's why we celebrate every year. Won't I be safe? Won't things be happy in the end?"

I could actually *feel* the dead part of my soul lingering inside of me like necrotic tissue.

I was so glad that such a big part of me was too dead to hurt.

"No," I snapped as I pressed harder on his chest. His eyes bulged in unadulterated terror as I grabbed his neck in both hands and squeezed with all the strength that my fingers could muster in the cold night air.

"There's no Christmas miracle, Liam, none. There's agony and pain on a scale that makes you wish you'd never been alive, and nothing more. You die, and that's how this story ends."

THE FIRST NIGHT OF CHRISTMAS IS FOR SPECIAL PEOPLE

BY RACHELE BOWMAN

My weakness was always power.

I don't mean that in the inspirational way that you might find in fairy tales or *The Children's Book of Virtues*. I mean it literally: I will do anything for power.

Anything.

And I did.

I suppose my attraction to power stems from my miserable start in life. There's no point describing it, so let's just say life started bleak and got bleaker as I grew older. I became bleaker too. Colder, hungrier, meaner. My only solace was my uniqueness. I knew I was different than everyone else. I thought differently, behaved differently, felt differently. I was just *different*.

Therefore, I was special.

My grandparents, who'd taken custody of me following my mother and father's respective death and incarceration, disagreed. They thought I was sick in the head, so they took me to the doctor. When all the pills and syrups proved ineffectual, they took me to the only psychiatrist in Serenity Falls.

Because of my grandparents' wildly insane work schedules, the appointments were always at night, usually after the clinic had officially closed. I always came in the back, through a small door that led directly to his office.

I saw him for three years and honestly expected to see him for many more. I was wrong.

One day, I walked into the office. Instead of the gloriously fat, reassuringly unshakeable Dr. Horner, I found myself staring at a man with a curiously blank and utterly hairless face.

"Good to meet you," he said. His voice confused the hell out of me; it danced along the register between alto and tenor, and could easily have been male or female. "I'm Dr. Yihowah. I'll be handling your therapy from now on."

"Why?"

"Dr. Horner," he continued delicately, "is deceased." He pursed his lips. "Suicide."

I was too stunned to speak.

"I met you here today to make the transition as smooth as possible, but I practice out of my home. We'll have our appointments there from now on."

He handed me a simple white card that only read:

Doctor Yihowah, MD

26 Adonneye Road

"Okay," I said.

Dr. Yihowah's house was on a tree-choked hill several miles outside town. I don't even think the road was officially named, rather than a street sign, he had a hand-painted piece of plywood announcing *Adonneye Road*.

My grandfather bitched up a storm about the drive. "Fifteen miles! Fifteen miles outside town! What did you do to Dr. Horner?" he snarled. "Chased him off, you little psycho?"

I didn't answer. There was rarely any point in answering my grandfather.

Though small, Dr. Yihowah's house was curiously grand, an old-world European style estate compressed into a half-dilapidated Midwest cottage. I loved it immediately.

Our first appointment began with pleasantries. Then Dr. Yihowah made me tea—rooibos, which I still love to this day—and we got down to business.

"Tell me about yourself," he said.

"Uh... I was born in town." My eyes wandered. There was so much to see, so many colors to drink in. Colors of the deep, cold sea: indigo and silvery blue, glassy green and black with the darkest gray. "At the clinic. The old one."

"The one by the Falls?"

"Yeah."

His gaze traveled over his desk. An array of glass bottles took pride of place. They matched the colors of the room: blue, black, gray, green. He took one and turned it slowly. Liquid sloshed within. "That building is part of the treatment plant complex now."

"Oh. Cool."

He watched me keenly for a terribly long minute. For the first time in my life, I felt anxious. Then he set the bottle down and folded one leg over the opposite thigh. "Tell me. Do you like causing pain?"

I frowned. "Do I like...hurting people?"

"Dr. Horner's notes indicated—"

"No," I answered. "But yes."

Another long pause, stretching through the air like taffy.

"I like being in charge," I clarified. "Scaring people and hurting them makes them think you're in charge. I figured that out when I was really little." My enthusiasm dimmed. "My dad says thinking that way makes you crazy. I guess that's why I'm here."

Dr. Yihowah ran a hand through his thick yellow hair. It was heavy and smooth, clipped in a pleasantly dated style that fell somewhere on the spectrum between Farrah Fawcett and Sonny Crockett. "Shall I tell you something?" His blank, sexless face practically glowed with excitement. "*Crazy* is a label weak people use to describe people who have power. People like me..."

I waited.

"...And people like you. You aren't crazy. You're just powerful."

Excitement flared and coursed through me, lighting my veins with pleasant fire. *I knew it.* "My granddad says—"

"You granddad," he snorted, "is weak. The weak resent the powerful. Do you know why I took on your case?" He crossed his other leg and leaned forward. His eyes practically blazed. Like someone in love. Or someone whose dream is coming true before his eyes.

"Why?"

"I want to make you strong. As strong as me. Or even stronger, if you're worthy." Those wild, burning eyes paralyzed me. A small smile spread over his face. "Are you?"

"I am," I answered.

He picked up the bottle again. "This," he said, "is medicine. I created it right here in Serenity Falls. It will help you reach your full potential." He slid the bottle across the desk.

I looked at it dubiously. I am a broken person, but not a stupid one. Not now, not then. I knew that all of this was wrong.

But did I care?

"How do I take it?" I asked.

"Here in my office. Twenty-six doses. One per month, for two years and two months."

"What does it do, exactly?"

The doctor smiled. "It makes you powerful. Take it."

I uncapped the bottle and drank. It was just water. Clear, clean, terribly cold water.

Part of me was furious, but part of me was intrigued. "You're not a shrink, are you?"

"I'm a specialist," he responded, "for special people. Are you special?"

I didn't answer.

After a long moment, he smiled. "Good. I have an assignment for you. Think of it as homework."

"Okay."

"Envision yourself as a powerful being, every night before bed."

"Okay."

He watched me shrewdly. "That'll do. We're done for tonight. We'll have our next session in a week's time."

I'll be honest; I soon grew to love Dr. Yihowah for his stability, understanding, acceptance...and of course, for the praise he lavished upon me.

Our sessions always followed a script. Pleasantries, rooibos, and long conversations about power, potential, and weakness. Every fourth appointment, I drank a bottle of the doctor's medicine-water, after which he would give me a homework assignment. These ranged from meditation to other, darker activities. Things like exerting power via emotional means, such as manipulation.

And of course, through physical means, as well.

It wasn't difficult. Everyone, including my grandparents, was already terrified of me. I'll spare you the details—I'd rather not share the secret of my success—but with the doctor's guidance and medicine, I whipped my grandfather into shape within days. Others followed, teachers, children, neighbors. And I almost killed a man, a sniveling, weak piece of shit named Calvin Tims. I had so much power over him, he refused to press charges.

It was phenomenal. Unreal. Intoxicating. Here I was, a scrawny little shit from the wrong side of town, controlling every interaction in my daily life with almost no effort.

I was *powerful*, thanks to a blank-faced doctor and his magic water.

After the ninth dose, Dr. Yihowah asked, "What is the most powerful thing that you can think of?"

"Being in charge of everything."

"You misunderstand. When you think of power, what comes to your mind's eye? That is to say, what is the most powerful being?"

"Uh…"

"Powerful," he repeated. "Omnipotent. Almighty."

That jogged my memory. Grandma loved going to church, and she sure loved praying to Father God Almighty to save her crazy grandson. "God, I guess."

"Yes!" Dr. Yihowah's eyes blazed again. "God is power. God is life. Life is also water!" He slammed the empty bottle onto the desk. "Water is life. Life is God. God is power. I engineered God and put Him in water. In these little bottles right now, just for you." He smiled. "One day, that will change."

"So…you're going to turn *everyone* into…" *Into me*, I thought but didn't say.

"No. *No*. Not everyone is powerful. My medicine only works on the powerful." A small, satisfied smile spread over his face. "On the deserving."

I considered this for a long while. He picked me because of my innate power. His medicine and therapy would make me more powerful. Enhance me. Perfect me. But I wasn't the only one, I wasn't actually special. There were others like me. Many others.

I didn't like it, not at all. But I had no choice. It was better to be one of the few than one of the weak.

So once again, I said, "Okay."

Perhaps the doctor sensed my deception. Perhaps he simply changed his mind. Whatever the reason, when I returned for next week's appointment, he was gone.

The house was emptied of everything but the remaining bottles, arranged in a box with a note that read:

Remember to take your medicine. Remember to be powerful.

As I stared at the bottles, the last of my excitement and my warmth, died. My bleak life grew bleaker and darker from there, reaching depths of emptiness that I could hardly comprehend.

In my mind's eye, I saw my soul as Wisconsin's winter landscape: cold, hard, and bitter, with the occasional gleam of the cold winter sun on brilliant ice.

One of those gleams was Eleanor.

I met her six months after my last dose of medicine water. I was eighteen. Our relationship was doomed from the start. I was too cold by then. Too broken, and too vacant. I was like a shark. Endlessly moving, searching, for something that might provide happiness. But I'm just like my parents. I don't feel happiness. I only take it.

I took Eleanor's.

I broke her into pieces, relishing the way the light in her eyes dimmed a little more every day. Enjoying the new, delicate lines slowly etching their way into her young face.

Waiting with bated breath for her joy and softness to melt away, revealing the cold, broken, *genuine* thing beneath.

That's something no one wants to understand. Happiness is an illusion at best, a delusion at worst. Happiness isn't real. But power is. Forcing someone to acknowledge this truth is power in and of itself. I held power over Eleanor. But it was trivial power, useless and worthless.

Boring.

So I left her.

Worthless though it was, I didn't like relinquishing my power. So, I stretched it out as long as I could by impregnating her first.

I pretended to be overjoyed. I pretended to change. I joined the military, because the military is the best prospect I had. "It's for us," I lied. "For our baby."

I waited for the light in her eyes to fully rekindle before snuffing it out for good.

"I hate you," I said. "And I hate *it*." I pointed at her stomach. She recoiled, eyes so wide she looked grotesque. "I'm doing this to get away from you. If you come after me…" I forced a carefully modulated chuckle. "Remember Calvin Tims?"

She stared at me like a tortured deer caught in headlights.

"That was nothing compared to what I'll do to you."

I fully believed Eleanor died that day. Sometimes it made me proud. Sometimes it made me feel uncertain. But mostly, I didn't think about it. The power I created and exerted over her was complete, but ultimately useless.

And compared to the power I created and enjoyed in the military, utterly forgettable.

Just as I spared the details of Dr. Yihowah's assignments, I will spare the details of my tenure in the service. Suffice it to say I found it incredibly easy to create and exert power, especially on deployments. The military is full of people who are intentionally broken down and rebuilt to follow a leader. They love leaders. They just need the right one.

I molded myself into the right one. I even managed to operate under the radar, which made my power all the sweeter.

It was ethereal. Beyond all imagining. I would have given anything for Dr. Yihowah to know how far I'd come, to see the pride in his face. Sometimes I could almost feel his medicine coursing through me, cold, clean, clear.

I could have gone on forever. And I probably would have, if it weren't for a weak link. The weakest people resent the strong.

And a very weak piece of shit brought my empire down.

Through manipulation and influence—that is, through the power and influence I so meticulously cultivated my entire career—I narrowly escaped a court martial. I received a dishonorable discharge, and drifted home.

I quickly discovered that my power in Serenity Falls had evaporated. No one remembered me. I passed Eleanor in the street a dozen times, and she didn't even recognize me.

To my chagrin, she looked happy. Tired, but fulfilled. Her smile was cautious but bright, her step light.

I hadn't snuffed her out after all.

This confounded me. I followed her around town for days. I soon realized that a child, our child, had undone all my work.

Clearly, this made me weak. Dr. Yihowah would be terribly disappointed if he knew.

This realization crushed me. I withdrew, losing myself in the frozen winter landscape within my heart. It was safe in there. Empty. Controllable. Smooth, unbroken, unfeeling ice.

Then, not very long ago, I got an email. The sender was a boy. A local student with my last name.

A boy, it turned out, who was looking for his father.

Is your mother Eleanor? I wrote back, even though I knew the answer.

Yes, he responded.

And there it was: an avenue, a plan, a means to rectify my mistake.

We exchanged emails for awhile. I pretended I'd had no idea he existed. It was simpler than the truth. Soon enough, we made plans to meet. I emailed him my phone number.

Shortly after, my telephone rang.

"Hello?" I asked, expecting my son.

Instead came a high, steady voice that danced along the register between alto and tenor. *Dr. Yihowah.* "I heard you'd come home."

The ice in my heart broke apart, revealing a volcano beneath. Confusion, joy, and love erupted, rendering me speechless. "How...?"

Dr. Yihowah chuckled. "It wasn't difficult. I've been following your accomplishments. And I'm proud. Very, very proud of you."

My heart swelled with excitement and happiness. I'd done it. I'd made him proud.

"Will you visit me?" he asked.

"Of course."

We met by the Falls near the water treatment plant.

I drove up and saw him standing on the shore, limned in cruel moonlight. He'd barely changed. Same hair, wiglike in its dated perfection. Same smooth, androgynous face.

He smiled. Tears glittered in his eyes. "You seem so powerful. Almost perfect."

That single word punctured my excitement. "Almost?"

"Almost," he repeated. "Here." He reached into his coat and extracted two identical glass bottles. They caught the moonlight and shone like silver. For a surreal moment, I was a teenager again, bemused and dreadfully curious about my new psychiatrist. "You need one more dose."

"Then why are there two?"

He pressed one into my hand. "Drink."

It was so cold it stung my mouth and made my teeth hurt. It was glorious.

When I finished, he said, "I have an assignment for you. A last bit of homework."

I watched him silently. Moonlight shafted through wind-driven clouds, dappling him with silver light and darkness.

"I need one last thing from you. Or rather, *you* need one last thing from you. A final act to establish your power. Once you've done it…" He gave the second bottle a brisk shake. "You'll get your final dose."

He explained that powerful gods, truly great gods, must spill blood. The taking of life is a great power. Transcending human bonds is another, perhaps greater, power.

"Prove to me that you're strong. Prove to me that you're worthy," the doctor said. "Take the life of your son."

Smugness and pride seethed; I'd come up with this plan on my own. Killing my son would serve a dual purpose. It would show Eleanor that I was still in control.

And it would propel me to the perfected state Dr. Yihowah had always wanted for me.

The doctor mistook my proud silence for doubt. "If he's strong, he'll survive," he promised. "If he's not strong, he won't. And would that really be a tragedy? The world doesn't need more weakness."

"Of course," I said.

I'm not heartless. I spent several hours choosing the way my son would die. I settled on drowning. The water would be painfully, paralyzingly cold this time of year, perhaps cold enough to stun him. And while drowning itself isn't pleasant, the body releases one last burst of chemicals that will put you in a state of bliss. That seemed appropriate. I could give my son joy.

With that in mind, I scheduled our reunion at the Falls. It was easy to convince him; I lied and said it was where I'd taken his mother on our first date.

He wanted to bring his mother. The ice in my heart cracked again, once more revealing that volcano. Eleanor. The first woman to feel the full force of my power.

Except she hadn't. She'd escaped with our child, so she escaped with her heart. All my work, undone.

"Of course," I said.

My son said they might be a few minutes late because of Eleanor's work schedule, so I offered to pick him up. "She can follow when her shift is over," I said.

The night that I finally met my son was frozen and beautiful. He looked like me, but smaller, with his mother's hair and nose.

We drove to the trailhead near the falls. He was too shy to look at me for long, but the few times I caught his eye, I saw hope. Bright, profound hope.

We got out of the car and hiked to the falls. They glittered under the moon, a vast, jagged palace of ice and diamond.

We stared at the frozen falls for several long minutes. Soon, my son began to shiver. I put my arm around him and drew him close. His chest hitched. I pretended not to notice. But disappointment bloomed in my gut. *Crying already?* I thought. *How weak of him.*

Once he'd gotten himself under control, I asked, "When is your mom going to be here?"

"Not for at least an hour."

My mood soured even further. "Do you want to wait in the car where it's warm?"

Trembling, he blurted: "Why did you really leave?"

Irritation swept over me. I withdrew and looked out over the falls, carefully choosing my next words. But why? I was wasting time. I was being weak. "I lied earlier," I said. "I did know you existed before today."

"Then why did you—"

"I wasn't ready. I loved your mother," I lied, "but I didn't want to have a family yet. I'm sorry."

My son shrugged. When he spoke, his voice was thick. "Were you really in the army?"

"I was."

"And a diplomat? And a doctor?"

I laughed. A diplomat? A doctor? Oh, Eleanor.

"But you really did love my mom?" he persisted.

"I still do. More than anything," I lied. "That's why I'm here. But I'm still not ready to have a kid. I don't think I'll ever be."

The brokenness in his face made me feel an entirely unique kind of power.

I put my arm around him and pulled him close. Then I stepped toward the railing. "It's only going to be cold for a minute. After that you won't even feel it. It'll be just like drifting off to sleep."

He began to struggle. "I want to go back to the car."

"Everybody wants something," I said, "but not everybody is willing to do what it takes to get it."

I threw him over the railing and into the frozen river. He hit the ice with a shudder-inducing *crack*. The ice broke under his weight and the water pulled him under.

He struggled and fought for several minutes. I willed him to give in, to experience that last burst of ecstasy and die.

After a while, he fell still. I waited another moment, just to be sure.

Then, I turned and left.

As I got into my car, I felt curiously light. Empty. Not at all godlike. Not at all powerful. In fact, with each passing minute, I grew anxious. Then afraid.

Then, for the first time in my life, I panicked.

I sped out to the doctor's house. The plywood sign had long since disappeared, but I found it anyway. It was dark, with broken windows and dry-rotted siding, but I went inside anyway.

Dr. Yihowah was waiting for me.

The relief I felt was exquisite. I envisioned the doctor's final dose, no doubt nestled in his coat. He would give it to me, and I would be complete.

I would be fully powerful.

"Is it done?" he asked.

I nodded.

"Do you feel powerful?" His face was blank, colorless porcelain in the shadows. A disembodied mask.

Fear engulfed me. My skin began to crawl even as relief coursed through me. He understood what I was feeling. "N-No."

He smiled. That smile is something I will never forget, small and prim and terribly white. "Then…I'm afraid you aren't worthy, or powerful. I was wrong. You are weak."

And with that—with his disapproval, his disappointment, the rejection by the only parent I had ever had—a lifetime of panic and terror descended upon me. It was a living nightmare, hours and hours of unimaginable horror.

When I finally came to my senses, it was morning. Frost covered my shoes and clothing.

And Dr. Yihowah was gone.

I left town quickly, but not before learning my son was alive. I hadn't killed him after all. I wasn't special. I was a failure. All that work, all those years of Dr. Yihowah's medicine and therapy…and I still failed.

I'd do anything for power. And I did. But it wasn't enough.

I suppose nothing is enough when you're as weak as I am.

HORROR STORIES TO RUIN CHRISTMAS

THE SECOND NIGHT OF CHRISTMAS IS A HUGE MISTAKE

BY BLAIR DANIELS

I CAME HOME TO A QUIET HOUSE.

Too quiet.

"Aubrey?" I called. "Where are you?" My daughter *always* greets me with a squeal of delight and a hug.

Silence.

"Aubrey?" I called, walking towards the art room. "Aubrey—"

My breath caught in my throat.

The art room was a disaster. Paint splattered everywhere, dripping down the walls in thick lines. Snapped colored pencils all over the floor. Aubrey's latest piece—a drawing of a wolf walking through the forest—was halfway torn, nearly decapitated.

Silence. Then—

A voice from upstairs. "Help me! Please, somebody, help me!"

Aubrey's voice.

I bolted out of the room, up the stairs, and into the master bedroom. "Thank God, I thought you were—"

I was staring at a laptop screen.

Aubrey sat in the center of a shadowy room, bound to a chair. Nearly unrecognizable, with tangled hair, a bruised face, and grimy clothes.

"Help me! Please, somebody, help me!" she screamed.

"Aubrey, I'm here!" I shouted, even though the webcam light was off. "Aubrey!"

The video jittered. Then she looked up at the ceiling and screamed, again: "Help me! Please, somebody, help me!"

It was playing the same 20-second clip over, and over, and over. A black thumb drive stuck out of the USB port.

I yanked it out. The video froze, contorting my little girl's face.

Then it fizzled to black.

I turned the drive over in my hands. No markings, no logos. I stuck it back into the computer and scanned the contents.

There were only two files on it: the video, and a file named README.txt. I clicked.

Les,

We need the farm on Dairy Ave. for the surgeon. The owners won't give it up. We need you to pose as a real estate agent for "Pure Serenity Realty" and get it for us.

If you don't buy the farm...

Your daughter will.

I picked up the phone and dialed 911.

"911, Leanne speaking, what's your emergency?"

"My daughter. Aubrey. She's been abducted and—"

"Okay. Slow down. Deep breaths. Can you tell us what happened?"

I told her everything. When I was finished, she gave me a vague "we'll send someone your way." before the call disconnected.

No one ever came to my address.

After an hour passed, I decided to take matters into my own hands. I glanced at the desk. A stack of *Pure Serenity Realty* business cards sat next to the laptop.

I stretched out a hand and picked one up.

The door swung open to reveal the same tired-looking, 50-something-year-old man I'd seen the last five times. "Yes?"

I sucked in a breath of air. I was desperate now. It had been five days since I last saw my daughter. All I had to remember her by was a torn drawing and a 20-second clip.

"Good morning, sir! Have you perhaps reconsidered our offer yet?"

It was a nice little farm. Rolling hills of green surrounded by patches of woods. Just beyond the treeline sat a wooden shack, its roof poking out as if watching us.

"Look, I told you the first time, I'm not selling the farm. Stop coming around here, it's not going to happen."

I walked away from the house dejected. Terrified. Reeling with thoughts of my poor little girl. I needed to get that family off of the farm. *Now.* And the carrot method, of offering a hundred thousand more than the estimate, wasn't working.

Maybe it was time for the stick.

That night, I snuck into the barn. Killed one of their sheep. Strung up its body. I figured they'd be out by noon.

I was wrong.

That evening, I pulled into the diner for dinner. I was a mess. Broken. Despondent. I'd tried the most gruesome of ways to get them out, and I'd failed.

"May I take your order?" A woman with a gold name tag that read Melissa approached me.

"Yeah. A double cheeseburger, please, and a diet coke."

As she left, my eyes caught on the TVs around the room. They were old, not flat screens, but small, boxy, heavy things held up by a cable. Some local newscaster was blathering on about the weather. *"Cold and clear in Serenity Falls tonight! Watch out, as always, for icy roads and—"*

The video feed interrupted. Static filled the screen.

And then a different video flicked on.

"Help me! Please, somebody, help me!"

I was staring at my daughter. Tied to the chair with thick rope, tears streaming down her red face.

"Help me! Please, somebody, help me!"

The clip played three times. Then it fizzled back into the newscaster. *"Bundle up, Serenity Falls! Now, on to the news in town..."* No one in the diner seemed to notice. They were all absorbed in their smartphones, their cups of watered-down coffee.

Clink.

The waitress set down the double cheeseburger and fries. I numbly stared at the plate and counted twenty-six french fries before I snapped out of it.

I ran out of the diner. Without eating, without paying. Melissa called out to me as I left, but I didn't even turn my head.

Brzt. Brzt. I felt the phone in my pocket buzz. I reached in and pulled it out. A new text, from an unknown number.

Aubrey's having fun with us! [aubrey.jpg]

An image of my daughter filled the screen. Hanging upside-down, mouth stretched open in a scream.

I broke into a run, passing the dollar store and the funeral home. Finally the water treatment plant appeared in the distance, lit dimly by a few flickering street lamps.

And that's where I saw the clown.

At first I thought it was some kind of tacky statue. Like those weird Ronald McDonald statues outside some McDonald's. But as I stared at the shadow, halfway between the sidewalk and the water treatment plant—it *moved*.

It turned its ball-tipped nose in my direction and stared at me with black eyes that sharply contrasted with the white makeup of his face.

Brzt. Brzt.

My eyes snapped away from the clown. I frantically pulled the cell phone out of my pocket to see another text from the same number.

She's crying for her daddy. How sweet.

I sprinted the rest of the way to the farm.

When I got there, I stood in the darkness, glancing around. The shack poked out of the trees as if silently egging me on. A little hen house stood off to the far right, the sheep-pen from where I'd plucked my sacrifice to the left.

Mumbled voices came from the right. From the silhouettes cast in faint porch light, it was the man I'd tried to persuade so many times before, with a young woman. Maybe his daughter.

Daughter…

My heart plummeted. I glanced from the house, to the darkened yard, to the shack. I pulled out my phone, glanced one last time at the text.

She's crying for her daddy. How sweet.

I walked towards the house, my fingers landing on the cold steel knife in my pocket.

THE THIRD NIGHT OF CHRISTMAS IS WELL-INTENTIONED

BY KYLE HARRISON

IT WAS NEVER SUPPOSED TO BE THIS WAY.

In my head, the plan had been a simple three step process: work more hours here and there, hire the cheapest babysitter money could buy, and keep Charlie distracted until Christmas Day. The reason behind this didn't have anything to do with Charlie but everything to do with his mom.

We separated about a year back over a difference in ideologies, she the big city dreamer and I the simple country boy. Though we couldn't agree on much, the one thing we always seemed to see eye-to-eye on was Charlie.

Since her move was all the way to the east bay near Milwaukee (case workers were more needed there apparently), we agreed that joint custody would probably be nearly impossible, so Charlie stayed with me until she could, quote unquote, "get her life straight." All I really wanted was for her to hurry up and sign the divorce papers I'd sent her weeks ago.

She stipulated that since she now had a bigger income he should be allowed to spend his Christmas holiday with her. That of course turned into a heated argument about the merits of her new lifestyle and how superior it was to the odd jobs I did around town. One thing led to another and well...

As stupid as it sounds, my ex wife and I made a bet about Charlie's behavior.

I felt confident that I could get him under control with discipline and tough love. She argued that Charlie knew how to push my buttons.

"I'll tell you what. If I can get him to be on good behavior for a solid month, then you'll be the one to eat crow and buy all his gifts," I told her.

Much to my surprise she agreed to the terms.

I didn't tell my ex, but I had a secret weapon up my sleeve to win this bet.

The Bad Man's Home.

It was this weird gimmicky flyer I saw one morning while grabbing a cup of joe from Mel's Diner and checking the town bulletin board for any news on the fall festival.

The premise was simple: a mysterious boogeyman designed to make kids behave better than any Santa Claus could. And while I'd always hated the idea of lying to my son, I figured the concept would work as a last resort if he did start to act out.

Charlie has attention deficit disorder, so for the most part I try to give him a wide berth and a lot of patience. Luckily, since the majority of my work is temporary, a handyman job here, a janitor gig there, I can spend the most of my time with Charlie when he isn't at school. The only time this schedule really gets out of whack is on Wednesday nights.

I managed to score a good contract with Doctor Poole to clean his dentist office once a week, wax and strip the floor, empty trash, that sort of thing. Sadly, the job is in the evening and that meant hiring a babysitter.

I thought that here in Serenity Falls with our small population, finding an eager teen ready to earn a few bucks would be easy, but after a few weeks of no shows and one hit wonders, I was beginning to realize that Charlie's behavior really was getting out of hand.

The only consistent sitter I could count on was Sarah Jennings, but with her being touted as the town's best of the bunch, my tired and stressed out brain started to worry that I would lose her too.

That was when I made the biggest mistake of my life.

Charlie was being an extra handful in the grocery store. I was praying to God that the twenty-six dollar check I'd just written wouldn't bounce as I passed it to the cashier, when I heard a clatter of cans and saw the huge mess that he had made.

I quickly jumped out of line to make sure he was okay and once I confirmed that I berated him for the stunt.

"You realize you could've gotten hurt, or hurt someone else? You could have broken an arm or a leg, snapped a femur or something! You need to be more careful!" I snapped.

Charlie only laughed in response, which only made my temper rise.

I was tempted to take my belt off right there in the store, but wisely kept my anger in check as I collected our groceries and we drove home.

I think my silence was starting to make him realize he was now in serious trouble as my brain worked to think of the appropriate punishment.

That was why, when I turned off Main Street onto Wilt Avenue and noticed the flyer again in my rear view mirror, a light bulb went off in my mind.

"Charlie... you know what will happen if you keep misbehaving. I'll have to send you away."

Now I had his full attention.

"S-s-send me away?" he stammered.

I nodded slowly as we pulled up to our driveway and gestured toward a nearby hackberry tree where another sign hung.

"The Bad Man's Home. It's a place where kids who don't listen to their parents have to go. I sure would hate to send you there."

I don't think his eyes could have possibly gotten any wider.

We walked inside and I picked up the landline. "I think I should just call them now, give them a heads up."

Charlie hastened to my side and started tugging on my pants leg.

"No, dad! Please, I'll be good! I'll be good!!"

I pretended to dial the number.

"Hello? Yes, Jake Sullivan here," I said talking to the imaginary fiend on the other end of the line. "Yes, I have my son here, and he's been rather naughty..."

Charlie was crying now.

I paused and cupped the phone, whispering to him. "Charlie, they say they can pick you up tonight. Unless you think you might want to change your tune?"

He sniveled, lip quivering, as he nodded his head fervently to show he got the point.

I smiled in satisfaction and told the imaginary caller that I would have to take a rain check before ordering Charlie to get ready for bed.

He cooperated fully with the ritual by brushing his teeth, putting away his toys and even taking his vitamins without any questions asked.

As I tucked him into bed he started to shiver. "Daddy, will you really send me away?"

"Not as long as you keep being good, bud. Looks like that Bad Man will have to go knocking on someone else's door," I replied.

The next night, my words had sunk in so well that when Sarah came for her usual babysitting gig, Charlie was on his best behavior.

The warning I'd given him had clearly made a lasting impression on his mind, and I felt bad as I watched him worriedly toss and turn in his sleep when I got home that night.

First thing in the morning, I resolved I would come clean and admit that the whole thing was a hoax and apologize to him.

That changed around 3:30 am when the landline started to ring incessantly. I stumbled out of bed and to the living room to grab the phone, thinking it was just some obnoxious telemarketer with no awareness of time zones.

"What in blazes are you doing calling this late?" I muttered as I tried to read the number.

That was when I heard a soft click on the other end followed by the sound of deep breathing.

"Hello?" I asked curiously.

An unimaginably low voice answered me back. It was enough to give me a chill.

"We're watching."

Immediately all my senses were on high alert.

"Who is this?"

The receiver went silent.

I went back to bed, confused and even more worried than before.

The phone rang again, and the same message played out. One time, it woke up Charlie and I literally screamed into the phone before slamming it down.

"Dad, what's... what's going on?" he asked.

"It's okay, bud. Nothing to be worried about. Just a prank."

"Is it the Bad Man?" he squeaked.

"No... no, bud. It's nothing. Go back to bed."

I barely slept the week after that. The calls kept coming, each one more sinister than the last.

"You've tipped the scales."

"A price will be paid."

"The time is nigh."

It was making me worried. I heard other parents talking about receiving similar calls all throughout Serenity Falls.

One night after cleaning Dr Poole's office I stopped by the bar on Elm to calm my nerves. The place was empty save for one of the day shift officers, I think his name was Yaeger or something I can't remember. By the looks of the empty glasses surrounding him on all sides, I could tell that he'd been trying to drink his own problems away well before I made it there.

"Hey Jake! Haven't seen you in here in quite a spell!"

Tony, the bartender, smiled as he cleaned a glass.

"What'll your poison be tonight, Jake?"

"Chartreuse."

The officer gave me a curious look. "Fancy stuff there, Mr. Sullivan.

Are you celebrating something?"

"Just trying to get my mind off things."

"Well, a bottle of that ought to do the trick," he agreed as he tipped his glass toward mine.

I returned the gesture. Then another idea formed in my head.

"Say, um, Officer..."

"Not on duty. Call me Ted," he corrected me.

"Right. Ted. Can I ask you a hypothetical question?"

"Shoot."

"Well... I've seen these odd posters around town see, and..."

"Let me stop you right there," Ted said with a glare.

"I take it you've, uh... you've heard about them?"

"I can't tell you how many damned calls I've gotten from folks asking us to look into the Bad Man's Home. If I find out who the son of a bitch is that made those things, I swear I might just tase their ass," Ted muttered.

"Well, what exactly are the police doing about it?"

The officer gave me a look like he thought I had half a brain.

"You're kidding, right? We're swamped right now, we've had homicides piling up and I just had to take a kid to the ICU over in Clearmount because some shithead of a dad tossed him over the falls! We don't have time to worry about some perv making prank calls."

"Good lord," Tony murmured, shaking his head. "What is happening to our town?"

"Same thing that's always happened to it. People come here; they die. Case closed. Just cause it's the holidays don't mean that crime is gonna take a vacation too," Ted said with a loud burp.

"But, sir. Don't you think that maybe the threats might be... real?" I asked, adding nervously, "I'm a single father. My son is my whole world! What if there is someone out there trying to take him from me and using this boogeyman as a front?"

"Look, I understand your concern, I do. I got two kids myself at home. But we don't have the resources to expend on a problem like this. Sorry, Jake, but those are the facts. If a crime does happen, we'll do something about it. Until then, maybe you can spread the word and tell everyone you run into to stop calling dispatch? I swear the lines are always backed up when Leanne takes a shift," Ted muttered.

I sighed and clenched my fists under the counter. It had been a mistake thinking that our small police force were going to do anything to solve this problem.

So I did what any drunken single father would do. I stormed home, dug the flyer out of the trash, and called the number again myself to handle the situation once and for all.

Three rings and thirty seconds later, the mystery caller answered.

"Early to bed." Despite my newfound conviction, the voice still gave me the creeps.

"Listen up, motherfucker. If you harm one hair on my boy's head, if you even dare to try and come near him, I swear on my mother's grave I will hunt you down, and I will kill you with my own bare hands."

I caught my breath, feeling satisfied with my response to this twisted sicko.

But their answer only made me even more afraid.

"Soon."

The line went dead. I tried to call again, but there was no number to call back to this time.

No longer in service.

Charlie was standing in the hallway, having heard my shouts, and was holding one of his action figures like a security blanket.

"Dad, what's going on?"

I got down on one knee and stroked his hair.

"It's going to be all right, bud. I promise. That Bad Man isn't coming to get you. I took care of everything."

I lifted him and we headed back to his room.

As I stepped into the darkened hallway leading to his door, I stopped short as I realized that there was someone else there in the house.

I held Charlie tighter. "Keep your eyes closed," I whispered to him.

Those words barely escaped my lips before the world went black.

I woke up to more darkness and the sound of rain. A few drops fell on my forehead as I tried to move and failed.

My wrists and ankles were tied to a chair. I felt a cloth against my mouth when I tried to scream.

I strained to look around and get some sort of sense of things when I heard footsteps coming from somewhere nearby. Charlie was nowhere to be seen.

I remember thinking that I was going to die.

From amid the shadows four figures emerged.

Three boys and a girl, all roughly a few years older than Charlie.

"He's awake," the tallest boy exclaimed.

"Get the boss."

I tried to talk, but one boy swiftly punched me in the stomach.

"Quiet! Bad Man gonna come talk to you."

From behind the group of kids I saw another figure, twice their size, standing in the shadows.

"And you're sure you weren't followed?" the newcomer asked.

I tried to pick out every detail I could. Male. Strong voice. Smelled like cigarettes and... something oily.

"Yes, sir," the kid replied, saluting smartly.

The shadowy figure tossed them a handful of coins and the kids clamored to get them as they counted up their profits and then raced off together, giggling in glee about my predicament.

"Children. They really are the reason for the season," the man said. Then I heard the distinctive sound of someone cocking the barrel of a gun.

"Since you're the first to wake up, I'm going to make this quick and easy. Do as you're told, and you'll be out of here in no time."

I nodded my head and muffled out a yes. I didn't care what the price was. I just wanted my life back.

"Smart man. Now I understand that you're an errand boy of sorts around these parts? And that you work for Timothy Poole. Is that correct?"

I muffled another reply.

"Oh, for heaven's sakes." He reached forward and removed the scarf around my mouth. I saw the glint of a badge in the dim light.

I looked up to see the familiar face of Officer Ted.

"You? What the hell? Where's Charlie? What did you do with my son?!"

"I was only ordered to get you. Someone else is taking care of Charlie... Look, you can judge me all you want later, but right now I'm the one in charge!" He slammed the gun against my head.

Fighting through the surge of pain, I managed to respond. "Okay, okay. Just talk to me, Ted. What's this all about?"

He relaxed for a moment then he stepped back and muttered, "Doctor Poole. How well do you know him?"

"His paychecks keep my lights on. I've only met the guy once, why?" I asked nervously. Something in Ted's voice sounded off.

"This is a list of chemicals that you'll need to bring to this address in two days. Do that, and you'll be home before the holidays," Ted said.

He shoved a quickly scrawled note into my hands and I stared at the items for a long moment.

"Ted. What are these for?"

"No damn questions!"

Then he left and went to somewhere else in the dark room. I heard a woman's voice.

She made a sound like her fingernails were being pulled off.

I sat there for the next six hours listening to a variety of screams and wails as the others that had been kidnapped alongside me were interrogated.

Morning came and the four kids that had tied me up splashed cold water on my face to wake me.

"Morning, sunshine. Time to get to work!" the tallest one said.

"Oh, and before we untie you, don't even think about running. We have eyes everywhere!" the girl said.

"Wouldn't dream of it," I said. I felt tired and defeated. I was out of options; I knew I had to listen to Ted's demands.

"Man. Wish the others were as amicable as you. I swear I really thought we were gonna have to give Miss Hughes a heart attack."

"What did you want her to do?" I asked.

"None of your beeswax!" the leader said.

They untied me and the second boy remarked, "Don't try going home until you finish what you were told to do. You got it, champ?"

I rubbed my wrists together and nodded, as the girl steered me toward a door and I was shoved out into the bright sun.

It took me a moment to reorient myself.

I was standing in a back alley behind an abandoned warehouse on Main Street.

I knew I could easily make it to my home in less than fifteen minutes if I went south.

Then I remembered Ted's threat. I took the alleyways down Elm all the way to Poole's office. As I got close I heard a few sirens racing my way and briefly thought maybe I'd been caught.

Instead, I soon realized that there had been a hit and run in the clinic parking lot. The whole area was blocked off.

How the hell was I supposed to get inside now?

I glanced about the nearby buildings and spotted a fire escape stairwell on the old bakery.

I used every ounce of energy I had left to pull myself up on a couple of trash cans and then leapt to it.

Once at the roof of the bakery I looked across the gap toward the clinic and took a silent gulp of air.

It had to be nearly a five foot jump across to the other building.

I held my breath this time and made a running leap for it. It was just barely enough for my upper body to land on the roof.

I scrambled and kicked my way to the top of the dentist office, pausing for my heart to stop beating out of my chest, when I heard voices in the alley below.

I couldn't make out who was talking, but it looked like a tall man speaking into a cell phone. I could barely hear his side of the conversation.

"Job's done." Those two words stuck out more than any other.

He tossed the phone and stepped into a vintage car. The bizarre green tint reminded me of my dad's old Lincoln Zephyr.

The car drove off in the opposite direction and I looked toward the front of the office, realizing that it had to be the vehicle involved in the hit and run.

I shook myself back to my present predicament and found the fire exit that led into the offices alongside Poole's.

Making my way to the supply cabinet was surprisingly easy; the simple scrawled map that Ted had given me leading me right to where the drugs were kept.

I ran into a small snafu when I realized the cabinet was locked.

I searched the darkened room until I found a fire extinguisher and used it to bash the lock apart.

The list of supplies was pretty straight forward, but as I started reading the actual medicinal purposes off the labels I took pause.

For use as pain killers and for anesthesia.

These were tools meant for a murder. Or something far worse.

As I was gathering the supplies, I heard a low rumble and voices from the office floor below and froze.

Officers were searching the property.

I hunkered down and listened as they moved about. The walls and floors in Poole's office have always been pretty thin, so I got the opportunity to be privy to their conversation.

"I don't care what Hatch says, I think Poole is dirty."

"Yeah? And Holmes, too? What about Mr. Sullivan?"

I felt my heart beat faster when I heard my own name.

"Beats me. But something sinister is happening in this town. I don't think we've been this busy in years."

"Not since the factory shut down. Man, that was a clusterfuck."

"Well. Doesn't look like there's anything here. The office is clean. Poole must have made a run for it."

"No shit, Sherlock. We're here to find those files, remember?"

"What do you think they want them for anyway?"

"Above my pay grade."

They were getting close to where I was hiding. I quickly ducked inside a closet to stay out of sight.

"You would think for someone with bizarre fetishes Poole would have, like... extreme OCD or something," the first officer said.

"Hey Weis, check this out," the second man called.

He shone a flashlight over where I had broken open the cabinet.

"Looks like we've got ourselves a burglary, maybe that hit and run was a distraction?"

"The way things are happening so often around here, I get the feeling everything is just distracting us from the bigger picture," Weis said.

"Oh, here we go again," the second man muttered.

"What? It's obvious."

"And I suppose next you're going to tell me that the Ghost of Serenity Falls is behind it all? Man, you buy into all that conspiracy crap," he laughed.

Weis was about to respond when they got a call on their walkie-talkie.

"Dispatch to 014 and 012, we have a reported suicide over near the cemetery, can you please respond?"

"Damn it, Cary-Anne, we're over here at the Poole place!" the second man responded.

"We're spread thin and you're the only two not on patrol at the moment," came the dispatcher's reply.

Weis and the second man didn't argue with that and left the office, complaining the whole way.

I waited several minutes before sliding out of the closet, noticing that they hadn't taken any files with them. I decided to go ahead and grab a few, just in case they were important, and left the dentist's office the same way I had entered.

I knew only one place I could go to lay low for the next few days—the same abandoned warehouse where Ted had kept me hostage.

I started thinking immediately of a way out of this mess, first by reviewing the files that the two cops had tried to steal.

It was just a bunch of pictures of the same kids that had accosted me, taken all throughout Serenity Falls, but that gave me an idea.

That next evening, I went back to the alley behind the clinic where the mystery man in the Zephyr had tossed his burner cell. I made a phone call to the one person I thought might be able to help me.

"Hello? Who is this?"

"Hey. It's me." I told my ex.

"Jake? What's going on? It's late. Did something happen to Charlie?"

"No, no, nothing like that. Well, see, I wanted to ask a favor of you," I explained.

"Must be a good one if you're calling me this late."

"Charlie and I met some kids the other day near the old church, pretty decent bunch of kiddos if you ask me. They don't have parents to speak of, and well, Charlie thought it would be a great idea to buy them all a simple Christmas gift," I explained.

She paused.

"And how do I fit in?"

"Well I got the kid's pictures, but no actual addresses or names. I thought maybe they might be in the system and you could figure out where these kids stay?"

She paused, trying to think of a logical reason she couldn't do it. I knew that my lie was a good one; she had such a hard time saying no to Charlie.

"Yeah. It might take a little time, but I'll see what I can do," she answered. I sent the pics in immediately.

Six hours later, she gave me all the details I needed.

As I expected, the group of malevolent children all had a record of some sort.

"Not so sure that these kids deserve anything short of coal in their stocking. We should call CPS," my ex said.

"Let's not do anything rash yet. But I might just tell Charlie we can't afford it," I replied hastily.

"Jake... is everything else okay? You sound stressed. You already bought Charlie his gifts, right?"

I knew she was really trying to see if she had won the bet.

I made another lame excuse and ended the phone call. The kids were back to check on me and make sure I hadn't called the cops.

"Less than twenty-four hours and you'll get your old life back, Mister," the girl said.

"Funny. I was about to tell you the same thing... Bridgette," I countered.

The girl froze, and gave me an odd look as I turned to the boys and explained, "Yeah. I found out who you are. And now you're going to do just what I say, or your names are going straight to the police and Child Protective Services."

They all looked at each other nervously.

"You would pick on a bunch of runaways?" the tall one asked.

"You started this when you agreed to help a dirty cop make a few bucks," I pointed out. The second girl kicked a rock at the ground.

"What is it you want us to do?" she asked sourly.

The address in question for the drop-off was down Edd road, well past the the water treatment plant. I could hear the roar of the falls as I waited for Ted to show up.

I walked over to the waterfront and skipped a few stones.

The air felt heavy as I saw his patrol car roll up, and he hopped out waving his gun for me to move away from the side of the waterfront.

"Where's Charlie?" I asked him.

"Looks like you pulled it off after all, Mr. Sullivan. Well done."

He tossed me a dark hood. "Put that on. We're going for a ride."

"I'm not going anywhere until you tell me where my son is," I warned him as I revealed the drugs I'd brought along with me.

"If you don't cooperate, I'll dump this out right here and now," I said.

Ted laughed.

"You got some moxie, Jake. Look, I don't want this any more than you do. We're both at the end of our ropes here. And you're out of options. If you don't come with me right now, your son will die," he said evenly.

I swallowed hard. It had to be a bluff. It had to be.

But this was my son. I had only one card left to play.

"Guess I won't get to eat any cherry pie this year after all," I said loudly.

Ted was about to make another smart remark when a rock was flown across the field and straight at his forehead, narrowly missing.

He was briefly distracted as another came from the opposite direction. "What the hell?"

The kids had pulled through and given me the chance I needed.

I rushed him, pushing him down to the grass.

I punched the living daylights out of him again and again as we rolled around at the edge of the water.

Ted was strong though. His police training kicked in and in less than a minute he'd gotten the upper hand.

He grabbed my arm and twisted it as he slammed me on the ground.

"That was a big mistake, Jake." he reached for his taser.

A gunshot rang out across the empty air.

Ted flinched and looked at his right arm where the bullet had passed through, before falling to the side of me in agonizing pain as I tried to see where the shot had come from.

Behind his patrol car I saw a familiar figure moving forward in the early morning mist. No taller than the Lost Boys I had hired.

"Charlie?! What are you doing here?" I asked in shock.

My seven-year-old son came out of the fog nervously clenching a gun.

I heard the squeal of tires off in the distance.

"I got him, dad. I got the bad man!" Charlie said excitedly as he looked toward Ted.

I nodded weakly and was about to move toward him when Ted lunged at me again.

This time, he took out a knife and held it straight at my neck as he pointed a finger at Charlie.

"Put that weapon down, son. Nobody needs to get hurt here. Tell him, Jake."

Charlie was crying and shaking, still pointing the gun in our direction. I flinched and nodded, trying to fake a calm I didn't feel.

"Listen to him, Charlie. You know the police are on our side, buddy. Remember?"

"Why were you trying to hurt my dad?" Charlie asked.

"Just playing, kid. Put that gun down or you'll regret it for the rest of your life," Ted said.

The kids I had asked to help me were moving out of the tall grass. Charlie nervously fired a warning shot.

"Stay away!" he yelled.

Bridgette and the others hunkered down.

"Go get help!" Ted snarled.

"Don't move! Don't move or I'll shoot him! He can't hurt my dad!" Charlie yelled.

It was a standoff. The tension was so thick, I had no idea what would happen next. Then I heard the sound of a twig snap behind Charlie.

My son turned and fired into the fog. I heard the sound of gurgled surprise followed by the clatter of something heavy.

Ted let go of me in shock as the fog cleared. Charlie dropped the gun when he saw who it was.

"Mom? Mom!!"

He sobbed and we both rushed to her side. The pool of blood around her was growing rapidly, and I realized the bullet had connected straight with her chest.

I noticed that she had brought a present, something to surprise Charlie with.

"Dad! Dad, is she going to be okay?"

"Ted, call an ambulance!" I exclaimed frantically as my ex wife gasped for breath. Instead, I once again heard the cock of a gun.

"I can't do that, Jake. You know that."

"Ted... don't do this. Whatever they're paying you, it's not worth it!" I told him.

"Paying me? They're blackmailing me, you idiot. Do you think I wanted to do any of this? I'm not a dirty cop. Hell... why the hell did I ever make that damned trip to Clearmount." He was rambling and confused. I thought for sure I could talk him down.

"Ted, whatever happened, we can get it straightened out if you come clean..." I stood up and gestured toward my shattered family.

"She needs help. If we don't get it soon, she's going to die," I begged him.

Charlie was still weeping. I heard some of the orphans try to make another run for it.

"God damn it!" Ted said as he realized that they were running to find help.

"It's over, Ted. But you can make this right. Do the right thing." I pleaded.

He was sweating profusely despite the chill in the air.

He took a step back toward the waterfront.

"Who'd have thought that damn pudding would be my last meal?" he asked, dream-like, to no one in particular. Then he snapped his focus back to me. "Tell Mary I'm sorry," Ted said as he took the gun and put it in his mouth.

Charlie screamed as we watched the man blow his head off, his body collapsing onto the frozen stream.

I held my wife's head up as she coughed up blood. Charlie was crying over her, shaking and wailing with grief and shock. His present lay forgotten, stained with his mother's blood.

The paramedics arrived in nineteen minutes. She died on the way to the clinic thirteen minutes later.

After we got cleaned up, I was asked to go down to the precinct to give a statement. I called Sarah to come to the clinic and watch Charlie.

"Hey, it looks like he got a new video game system!" she said excitedly when she saw the gift. I didn't have the energy to tell her the circumstances behind it.

Instead, I saved my spill for the sheriff, told the police everything I knew about Ted and the other odd events that I'd been witness to during my time with the Serenity Falls irregulars.

Sergeant Weis escorted Charlie and I home. On the way, I clutched the stained gift wrapping and saw that his mom had thought to buy him a new superhero action figure along with the 3DS. Charlie was half asleep as I checked the card she had attached to it.

Hey buddy,

Santa swung by my house a few nights ago and told me that you've been super good, so I wanted to get you something extra special before Christmas rolls around! Thanks for being such a champ for your dad and I while we work through our stuff. You're always number one in my book, Charlie. Don't tell Dad, but I got him something special too!

Love,
Mom

With a horrible ache in my stomach, I shoved the note in my pocket as we pulled into the driveway. There was a package out beside my mailbox. I knew it had to be the one that she'd left for me.

Weis escorted Charlie inside while I walked to the box like a zombie. I reached down to pick up the package and saw a familiar flyer stuck underneath it.

The Bad Man's Home sign.

On the back of it she'd written a note for me as well.

I took it all inside and thanked the sergeant. Charlie was already fast asleep, the mild sedative that the doctors had given him in effect to provide a full night's rest.

I sat on the side of his bed and turned the flyer over to read my wife's note while I stroked my sons hair.

Jake,

I know that things have been hard, and that I haven't been the best mother or wife I can be. I wanted to give you both what you've been asking for. I hope it's a step forward for our whole family. Please accept this gift as a token of my apology. Merry Christmas.

    I opened the package and felt tears well up in my eyes.
    Inside were divorce papers.

THE FOURTH NIGHT OF CHRISTMAS IS FULL OF REGRET

BY EDYTH PAX-BOYR

I'M SORRY. PLEASE TELL EVERYONE I'M SORRY... I CAN'T FIX what I've already broken, but I also can't go on knowing how much worse everything has been because of me.

If there's a rhyme or reason behind all the suffering that's happened in Serenity Falls this past winter, I don't know what it is. All I do know is that I played a part in it, and for that... well, there's a place reserved for people like me, where the fires burn bright and eternal; where I can maybe start to pay for all the things I've done (and failed to do); as a sister, as a public servant, and as a person.

It all started with a note on my desk when I came on shift a few weeks back.

Cary-Anne Peterson, my day-time counterpart, was a vision in white. Her pale blonde hair was set in soft curls, her makeup light with a subtle shimmer, and her icy blue eyes shone like beacons in the station's dim light. She looked like some kind of modern snow fairy, and I was under her spell.

She gave me a smile radiant enough that my legs threatened to fail, and I struggled to smile back in any way that looked natural.

"Hey, beautiful," she said, handing me a fresh cup of coffee in a paper travel cup with a hand-drawn sunflower on the side. My cheeks burned as I realized she must have had Merry deliver after hours and I was suddenly grateful the night crew preferred keeping the lights low— low enough to conveniently hide my blushing, I hoped.

"Ah, haha," I laughed, wishing there was any bone in my body capable of being cool. "Hey, Cary-Anne. What's the buzz? Tell me what's-a happening..." I hid my awkwardness behind a long draught of coffee just a degree or two shy of too hot.

"Oh my gosh," she said, her smile dissolving instantly. "You wouldn't believe it. A kid fell in the river. Right at the base of the Falls."

"A what? You're kidding!" I barely remembered to stop drinking in order to speak, and hid behind one hand as I smeared the dribbling coffee from my chin.

"Not even remotely. Worst part is," she said, leaning closer to whisper conspiratorially—as if no one else in the station knew about it. "He said his dad did it to him. I mean, that's what the EMTs said about it. The kid was pretty deep in hypothermia at that point, so who knows what he was really saying."

"Jesus, though…"

Cary-Anne nodded, staring through the floor with wide, pensive eyes. Eyes the same shade as light passing through exposed glaciers, that shade trapped between tropical turquoise and searing white…

God, she was gorgeous.

"Oh," she said, snapping me back to reality and out of her unintentional charm. "You have a note." She pointed to our shared desk where a plain white square sat between the computer monitors and the keyboard. I could just make out my name neatly printed on top.

"Aw, Cary-Anne, you know you can tell me anything. You don't have to leave me notes." I grinned at her, hoping I didn't come across as too corny.

She rewarded me with a sly smile and a playful finger wag. "Trust me, if I'm going to leave you a note, it will either be on personalized stationery, or thirteen-dozen Post-It notes; there is no in between!"

We laughed at that, and for a second I forgot to be uncomfortable in my own skin. But my shift was calling me, and a bottle of wine and her Netflix account were waiting for her, so we parted ways with a playful wink and my thanks for the coffee.

I thought nothing much of the note as I sat down at the desk and waved Cary-Anne out the door, but it was unavoidable the second I looked down. It was just a blank folded square of white cardstock with my name printed in crisp black ink that didn't look anything like Cary-Anne's looping script. The disappointment was real, but I also hadn't really expected it to be from her. Not really.

I had hoped, though.

I flipped the note open and read.

I know.

That's all it said, with a web address scribbled underneath in the same neat but unfamiliar hand that had addressed me. Cryptic and forgettable, I threw it away.

I don't like games. I thrive on clear, direct communication—it's why I became a police dispatcher in the first place and why I love my job; there's a code for everything and everyone speaks the same language.

Miscommunication is rare this way, and I'm bad enough at social communication. There's just too much subtext, and I'm awful at subtext.

But police dispatch? Infallible.

Any friendships I've ever maintained have been through no fault of my own. My brother was the one with all the social skills. He'd had friends in every grade, every clique and niche. I didn't have the mind or temperament for social games. That included cryptic notes, so if someone really wanted to communicate with me, they were going to have to talk to me like everyone else, not through mysterious notes and digital scavenger hunts.

Besides, I wasn't going to be responsible for downloading a virus to the department's computers.

So, I threw it away and moved on with my night. By the time Beverly came by to drop off some of her famous five cheese macaroni I'd forgotten all about the note.

And no one could have blamed me. How could I have thought of anything else when a plate of the best damn comfort food this side of the Mason-Dixon was waiting in the break room?

By 0300 hours, my world had become the exact size and shape of an old Corelle plate piled high with gooey gold. The note never crossed my mind again.

Two days later, though, the note was back, and it brought a friend.

My name stared up at me from the blank cardstock. "*Read me,*" taunted from the second.

I wasn't happy about the escalation—notes? Plural. Really? Was I back in college with a passive aggressive roommate again? I was reluctant to play along, but someone was going through a lot of effort to reach me.

I fiddled with the keys on the keyboard in front of me, tapping them lightly in indecision as I chewed at the inside of my lip. I thought about all the people I had helped since joining the force, and all the people I had failed. How some people couldn't reach out to ask for help through the usual channels. How some people were trapped... unable to call. And I started to worry that this might be one of those cases.

Guilt won the battle, and I opened the new note and froze.

Leon says hi.

I actually felt the blood drain from my face. I blinked dumbly through a wave of nausea and vertigo, and my heart seized as the cold flames of panic licked at my senses, narrowing them to a single point, the note in my hands. I scanned the room in a daze, looking for some sign this was all just a supremely uncanny joke, but no one was laughing. The station was nearly empty except for me, Officer Taylor, Sergeant Weis, and Sheriff VanLanen. Lieutenant Bartelt was on break, and everyone else was on patrol. No one present paid me any kind of attention.

Did one of them know?

But, how could they…?

I slid the first note closer and typed in the web address. It opened to a satellite image of a river cutting through sparse woods surrounding a small smattering of buildings with a string of coordinates attached to a single dot on the north bank, just behind the treeline.

"Oh my god, no."

"You okay, Leanne?" Taylor's voice gave me a start. I must have looked as horrified as I felt, because he was watching me with concern. My cheeks burned the second I realized I'd unintentionally said something out loud and drawn attention to myself.

I closed the browser tab and made some excuse about finding an article capitalizing on the latest mass shooting and how disgusting that was. I don't remember what, if anything, I said after that. My brain was stuck in this jagged white panic that annihilated any thought other than "*How in the **fuck** do they know?*" But if Lee wasn't convinced, he still let it go.

My heart lurched when a call came in, reminding me I had a job to do. I quickly put on my business voice, hoping there was no trace of uncertainty or fear coming through; that was the last thing anyone needed to hear in an emergency, after all.

"911, Leanne speaking, what's your emergency?"

A man's panicked breathing exploded in my ear.

"My daughter. Aubrey," he said, his voice shrill and tight. "She's been abducted and—"

"Okay. Slow down," I said, stopping him as I tried to pull up the incident entry screen. "Deep breaths. Can you tell us what happened?"

I attempted to listen as my computer went through bouts of freezing and program crashes, choosing at just the best possible time to suffer several major digital seizures. Eventually I resorted to scribbling his information on my notepad. I'd have to log it in the computer later, but the important part was getting our guys out to him.

"We'll send someone your way," I offered in an attempt to reassure him, but before I could say more—*click*—the call disconnected.

I was jarred by how a man so distraught over his daughter's kidnapping could be so curt to someone trying to help, but my computer screen caught my attention by opening up a notepad of its own. *On* its own.

I watched in horror as words typed themselves into existence.

Leon would prefer if you pretended that call never happened.

Burn the notebook.

I looked around the room, sickly fear crawling up the back of my neck as I realized whoever this was could see me in real time.

But none of my coworkers paid me any more attention.

Well, there was Lee. He didn't even glance at me as he asked what the call was about, though. I guess I was taking too long to actually dispatch.

"Prank," I said feebly, clearing my throat as I settled back in my seat and deleted the note on my screen. Then I emptied the recycling bin on the desktop. "Just a local kid trying to prank the cops. Probably wanted to show off for a girl," I said, forcing a laugh.

Lee looked at me then with a twinkle in his eye. "Yeah, I bet you can identify with that."

He wasn't wrong, and I smiled in what I hoped was an accurate imitation of a "You got me there" face.

I'm ashamed to say I did what the note said. I pretended there had been no call. I sent no one to help that desperate man. No one to find that poor little girl. And I took my notepad home and burned it in the fireplace until only ashes remained.

And I sat with jagged shards of dread digging into my heart for almost a week before another note appeared.

I'd just come on shift, so it was maybe 11:05 pm when I got a chance to sit down with my coffee and catch myself up on the day's events.

A postcard sat on my desk, face down. No return address.

Needles of fear prickled against my neck, crawling over my scalp and down my arms. I licked my lips nervously before reaching out to slide it close enough to read.

Keep the tourists out; no county calls.

Locals only.

In case of emergency… LIE.

Locals? Serenity Falls didn't have any local police. Just the cops Waushara county dispatched to the town. None of us at the station even lived here. Technically every emergency call was a county call, it just went through the local dispatch (me or Cary-Anne) first. Did the note mean local dispatch only?

I flipped the postcard, chewing my lip as I chewed on that thought, idly hoping there might be some kernel of clarification on the other side.

It was an idyllic shot taken from the woods around the Tam river, some twenty or thirty miles outside town. Scrawled in red permanent marker were the words *"Wish you were here."*

"How...?" I gasped, suddenly struggling for breath as the room spun out of control around me. I gripped the desk for support, anchoring myself against the turbulent sea of my own bewildered shock. How could they possibly know where he was buried?? No one knew where—

A call came in, cutting my thoughts short. I surprised myself with how easily I slid back into a professional tone, belying nothing of my inner turmoil as I took down the emergency's details. It reminded me of that misty morning so many years ago, when police found me on the northern bank of the Tam, cold and shivering—alone—and I managed to convince them I had been that way all night; that I had no idea where my brother had been. Where he still was.

As I terminated the call, my eyes slid to the postcard, certain the timing could not be coincidental.

Double homicide. In Serenity Falls.

I reached for the radio with numb fingers.

No county calls.

Who would I call?

My mind clattered around stiff mental gears, struggling to re-engage as the postcard taunted me from the desk, still in sight, and still full of malicious secrets; *my* malicious secrets.

Locals only.

Only one name came to mind as I slowly swam back to the present.

"Dispatch to 26 alpha," I called out, and waited.

The seconds ticked by painfully as I worried at the inside of my cheek.

"26 alpha, go ahead," the radio crackled with Julia's familiar voice.

"Please respond to [address redacted]. I've got two possible one-eight-sevens. Be advised, suspect may still be on the premises and is considered armed and dangerous."

"Jesus, a double? 10-4. En route."

I left my post after that. Not for long, I just ... I needed a minute. Or ten.

The station coffee wasn't as good as Merry Hoggins's, but I didn't really need "good." I needed "strong." And if I added a little whiskey to take the edge off, it was no one's business but my own. As I thought the fate of my brother had been, up until a few weeks ago.

I shredded the postcard when I got back to my desk. It was cryptic, and now I understood why—if anyone found it, they'd have a hard time pointing any steady fingers at anything—but I still didn't want anything that could lead back to November 1991.

About forty minutes later the radio crackled to life with Julia's voice again.

"26 alpha to Dispatch."

My heart flipped preemptively. I hadn't done anything wrong ... per se, and as far as I knew the murders had nothing to do with me, but I still had to take a swig of "strong" coffee before I felt calm enough to pick up the handset and respond.

"Dispatch. Go ahead, 26 alpha."

"Leanne, I'm going to need backup out here."

I glanced at the fragmented remnants of the postcard peeking up at me from the trash can beside my desk, and sent the locals.

That's when things really started going wrong, though. That one double homicide was unusual for Serenity Falls on its own, but it brought with it a rash of missing parents just a few days later. I sent Officers Taylor, Jansen, and Koehler to deal with that mess; each to different homes, each within blocks of each other.

Every call was like that going forward. I kept it local. Kept it quiet. Every emergency call—and there were many all of a sudden. I didn't call the county for backup. I deflected when asked up front—"Oh, I knew we could handle it," or "It's nothing we haven't seen before; you know how strange these small towns can be." Every call, from 11:00 pm to 7:00 am, I stopped from reaching the county department.

I did it.

I'm why we've been alone. As murders, and attempted murders, and strings of abductions, and disappearances, and whatever the *fuck* was going on with the dentist ... while the town has been torn apart by violence and insanity, I'm why no one has come to do a damn thing about it.

And the other night ... I found a new note.

Printed on the inside of a picture of my family, neatly folded in half to hide its message from prying eyes. On the outside I saw my parents, my brother Leon and me; all dressed up for Christmas. I knew the picture well, since it had lived on my mother's mantle since the day it was developed. So he could "still join us for the holidays" she said. It was the last holiday card my mother had made us sit for, and she never sent it out, because Leon was gone by Thanksgiving. To find it here meant whoever was pulling my strings had gotten into my mother's house and either stolen the picture or somehow managed to charm it off her. Either way, it served its purpose; to let me know they had access.

I flipped the picture over and found the address of an abandoned house outside town printed on the back along with something resembling actual instructions.

0200
Send Hatch.
Report lights and possible break-in.
No fire department!
In case of emergency... LIE.
Leon can't wait to see you again.

My stomach protested, churning fitfully around a stone of dread.

I was done wondering "how". How no longer mattered. What mattered now was that they knew. Somehow they knew, and the threat was implied; do this or your family will know what you did, too.

I was still reading and re-reading the note when my fist closed around it in cold resignation, crushing one of the last pictures taken of my brother before he "disappeared".

It was 1:46 am; 0146 hours. In just fourteen minutes I was going to make a call to Julia to send her on a fake B-and-E, and why?

To protect myself.

There was no way my mother would ever forgive me for leaving him in that old root cellar in the woods, and there was no reason she should, but I didn't want to lose everything I had built for myself since then because I let my brother die when I was six, and the law never forgets.

I stared at the crumpled photo in my hand, willing it to disappear as a migraine gnawed on the right half of my skull, listening to the thin cadence of the clock ticking ... ticking ... ticking down down the minutes until 0200 hours.

This was wrong.

Everything was wrong.

Everything I had done was wrong.

But what choice did I have?

As 0200 hours came, I hesitated, my hand hovering over the radio at the pivotal point between two diverging realities; one where I accepted my fate and paid for my sins, both past and present, and one where I made the call and continued to dance to my fiddler's tune.

0204 hours. I was out of time.

"Dispatch to 26 alpha..." I said, cutting myself off from any hope of redemption, ever.

For a brief, tingling second, I thought maybe Julia wouldn't respond. I hoped and dreaded with no idea which would be worse; the consequences of her not answering the call, or the consequences of intentionally backing down.

I didn't have long to think about it, though, as the radio crackled to life.

"26 alpha, go ahead."

Damn.

Resolve settled uneasily in my stomach, and I leaned into the grim reality I'd built for myself.

"Please respond to [address redacted]," I said, resting my forehead against my palm. "Caller stated that they saw someone enter the abandoned residence and could see them use a flashlight throughout the house."

I hated myself then, but it was a quiet hatred. The kind of hatred that exists within the fabric of life, part of you every day without ever raising its voice. The kind of hatred that lurks in the back of your eyes, too weary to even be disgusted.

"10-4. Does the caller want to be seen?"

I coughed out a dry, empty laugh to myself. *What caller?*

"Negative," I said. "Caller was anonymous." It was almost like not lying at all.

After that, it was done. And I sat alone with the knowledge that I had done something terrible to someone I admired.

And not ten minutes later, the calls started rolling in.

Fire.

First it was one or two, but it quickly became an avalanche. I guess half the town could see the angry light burning on the horizon.

Sergeant Weis commented after the very first call. He'd been milling about with a plate of Beverly's finest, shooting the breeze with Schwartz when the call came in.

In case of emergency... LIE.

I told him it was a false alarm, because what else was I supposed to do? I told him I'd already radioed Julia to confirm and she told me to disregard. I told him she said there was no fire.

But when one call became a flood, it was impossible to pretend there wasn't some truth to the first report.

It was significantly harder to keep Weis from calling in county help at that point, but I managed. Some bullshit about distance, and road conditions, and "Serenity Falls has an emergency civilian fire crew specifically for these situations." And, while that's all true and valid, I still only said it to cover my own ass. I had no investment in which was the better option for the situation; only what was best for me.

Julia survived. She broke her leg and has some new titanium parts. The doctor is keeping an eye on her for any lingering lung damage, and Weis stuck her on desk duty, but she's alive.

No thanks to me.

And there are plenty of people who *can* thank me for their current conditions—lost, trapped, abducted, or worse.

I don't know why—why Serenity Falls; why me—but I know I'll never be able to fix what I helped break in this town, including my family.

So, tell everyone I'm sorry. I was selfish, and weak, and so, so stupid. And I know that won't fix anything, but maybe knowing the truth will help someone bring an end to the suffering in Serenity Falls.

As for me, I've decided whoever wrote me those notes might have had one thing right in the end, despite all the wrong they made me do.

I think maybe it *is* time I went to join my big brother.

After all, he's been waiting twenty-seven years.

THE FIFTH NIGHT OF CHRISTMAS IS FOR THE SOCIOPATH

BY JACOB MANDEVILLE

I FIRST SAW HER AT THE MECHANIC'S PLACE AS I WAS BEING released from the jail. She was a radiant beam of light that permeated through the bleak shadows on the intersection of Elm and Main in this little shit-house town, Serenity Falls. I walked out the door, bail posted, and felt the weight of the pending trials I would probably have to face unless my stupid public defender managed a sweet plea deal.

Her beauty captivated me. I instantly froze before awkwardly stumbling down a few steps and regaining my composure, ending up erect with my gut sucked in. She didn't notice, not at all. Of course not, she was across the road, focused on her phone. She smiled deeply at it, then tapped on the screen feverishly, and beamed with the effervescence of newly found love.

I waited. She waited. She typed and smiled, smiled and typed, and I was smitten. Infatuated. I had to have her. After an eternity, or maybe twenty-five or twenty-six minutes, she was approached by the grease monkey working on her car. She entered the office and talked to the service writer. The monkey, all filthy and fucking gross, slipped into her car, pulled it around and parked it next to the door. He lingered in the car, then stepped out oddly, dipping his head low as he crawled out. It looked as if he sniffed the seat as he left.

She left the office and hopped in her running car. It was then that I panicked and knew I had to figure out how to get her attention, or I'd lose her forever. I froze in indecision as she pulled out onto Elm, then turned left on Main. I raced to the intersection and memorized the license plate as she rolled away. I jaywalked the intersection and ran to chase her, and then, much to my sweet surprise, she parked the car on the shoulder by the thrift store. I slowed my sprint to an awkward jog, feeling the lactic acid release in my underused muscles. I walked into the store and found a perch to set my trap near the dressing rooms.

"Yes, ma'am, my name is Matt. I'm a friend of Ally's. Is she home?" I heard the greasy little punk responding to Ally's mom. I thought to myself, *"Nope, ya dumb fuck, she's already with you,"* and chuckled lightly. She struggled against the silk ties I'd lashed her hands with as she tried to grunt and make noise, but the angles of the porch were perfect enough that he couldn't hear over the whine of the water treatment plant.

I carried her past the adjoining yard and headed to the woods near the Falls, beyond the row of houses and apartments. I had her. I could smell her fear. I took her deep into the forest there, to my usual killing floor. Oh, I haven't mentioned? Yes, I kill people, and the stupid Serenity Falls PD has no clue. They had me in their cells just earlier today before Neal Coughlan pulled some strings! No idea why the head water department schmuck would wanna do that, but hey, thanks, pal. Anyways, I'm getting ahead of myself.

I hovered near the men's used clothes rack, faking a selection of some jeans and polos to try on, when she walked over to the dressing rooms, a small pile of clothes in hand. She was talking on the phone, and I overheard her saying something about, "He's going to move here!" and "I can't wait to meet him in person." I heard her giggle and tap away on her screen in the room. Young love. How disgusting. She set her purse on the floor outside the door, and I knew right then that this was my chance.

I walked over with my clothes in hand and softly kicked her purse away from the door and toward the one across the way. It wasn't as smooth as I'd hoped, but it was effective enough. She was distracted by her incessant annoying humming—I think it was Fools Rush In—so she didn't hear the shuffled kick of her purse. I reached in, found her phone, luckily still unlocked, and entered the dressing stall. I quickly searched her phone and found the text tree with "Matt." What a joke. Tinder? Really? Desperate. I'll be able to take advantage of this chick easily.

It only took a few minutes for me to gather enough information to assemble her identity. I knew her address, her boy-toy's name, and tons of other great tidbits. I opened and exited my stall, shuffling her purse back to the door. I left the pile of clothes there. Not my problem.

I strung her up to the tree I usually use, and stripped her down to her emotional bareness. She openly wept, sobbing and choking on her own tears and phlegm. Her phone kept vibrating and vibrating, but whatever. I had her tied up, and I had all the time in the world. She continued crying as I secured the knots.

"Hi! I'm Matt!" I said to the older lady who answered the door. She wore a faded blue-striped shirt that made her hazel eyes look sunken and sad.

"Matt! Oh my gosh, in the flesh?" She beamed. Of course she knew Matt. Apparently I looked similar enough to the punk to pass the mom test. "Yes, Ally is home, she just got back from the store." She bent closer and started to whisper: "I think she got some new clothes just for you."

"I can't wait to see her. Tell her I'm here, please?" I politely requested in my best imitation of a sincere gentleman.

"Matt's here?" I heard bellowed from the hallway. Her mom turned around and yelled an enthusiastic, "Yes, he is! Come get him!"

I heard rushing steps stomping down the stairs as she quickly left her room upstairs. "I just knew you'd come, I knew it!" She giggled as she ran. I stepped sideways out the door and she rushed out and right into my arms. I pressed my face against hers and kissed her, throwing her off her guard in an instant. She hadn't had the time to see I wasn't actually him.

Her mom let out an audible sigh, set the door ajar, and walked back into the house. I really enjoyed how Ally tasted, her lips sweet with a flavored lip balm, and her minty breath fresh from a newer stick of gum. She slowly pulled away, and as she did, she opened her eyes. Shock, fear, and disgust registered in her eyes all at once. She opened her mouth to say something, but I already had the stone in my hand swinging hard at her temple.

I started my hobby nineteen months ago, and this victim has thankfully allowed me to hit the coveted bakers dozen. Look it up, it's a thing. She grunts and chokes and wiggles, grasping to the last moments of life I've left to her. I kick the bucket she was teetering on from under her feet and she drops the six inches of slack I left onto her neck. She gasps as I lay under her, letting her bare feet tickle my abdomen.

I grabbed her phone and reached up, pushing her fingers to the button. Stupid iPhones. It unlocks and I read the flurry of messages and calls missed while I strung her up. It was at this moment that I had a delicious idea: I'm gonna kill him too. I'll use her little catchphrase to lure him to me. I pulled her up with the slack rope so she's way high up in the tree and I clean up the mess. I'll head to the old hunting shack and shower, then bring back my wheelbarrow and tools. I'm not too worried about anyone finding a body here; no one has found the previous twelve.

Showered and prepped for some nasty mutilation work—I hate this part, but Dexter Morgan showed me it was important—I assemble the saws and blades for dismemberment when the phone chimes again. I grab her finger—I forgot to tell you, I bit it off—and open the phone. Desperate Matt again. I decide it's time to lure him in.

"Where are you now?"

A minute passes. Then another. No reply.

"Where are you now?" I send again. Still no response. Whatever, I've got a body to clean and store in the meat fridge. Steaks tonight!

I didn't plan this event like normal. That's where it went wrong. As I stroll back the kill site, sirens and lights fill the forest ahead of me. *Shit.* They found her, they found my kill site. I freeze, dusk settling its blanket of darkness over me, amplifying the red and blue flashing lights. I watch them carelessly haul her into the back of an ambulance. Now that my spot is contaminated, I've got to get away, find a new one. I spin around, ditching the supplies and sprinting towards the shack. I've got to burn it. It's an old hunting shack, no one will miss it. *Shit.* Did I refill the kerosene?

I hit the door with my body and open it, crashing to the floor. I look up to see Matt standing there, holding Ally's phone in his hand. My bloody clothes are piled in the corner, and my knife collection is hanging on the wall, but a few are already missing.

"You sick motherfucker…" he trails off, shedding a tear. It's now I notice Ally's mom in the corner near me. She has a bat, and she winds up to hit me. I lunge-crawl towards Matt as she swings for me, screaming, "You stole my baby!" I barely dodge the blow, letting it glance off my back. Her swing is mismanaged, and she smacks Matt in the jaw. He goes down, and I jump up, grabbing the 18" machete propped on the wall. Instead of tending to Matt like I assumed a doting mother would, she winds up and swings again. Her blow knocks me in the chest, crushing the wind out of me. I hear an audible crack as my ribs pop under the pressure of the strike. Mom must have played softball.

I'm lifted backwards and upwards slightly by the blow, but use the repositioning to my advantage. I make a large slash and strike her in the shoulder. The blade cracks through collarbone and ribs as it slides down towards her breast. I pull it out with a tug, grateful for the serrations sawing even more bones, and swing again, this time at her head, and hear another crack as it connects with her skull.

I swing around, jerking the blade out, pulling bits of skin and hair with it. The red and brunette matter sprays across the walls as I recenter myself to kill Matt. He's ready for me, holding another blade of mine in his hand.

We stare each other down.

"Why?" he chokes out through stifled tears.

"Because," I answer, smiling. I give a chuckle, but the adrenaline rush has faded a bit, and I feel the broken ribs poke my lungs as I chortle.

"I love her, and you hurt her, you animal! Why! Why HER?!" he screams, thrusting the knife at me in exasperation.

"You *loved* her," I correct, smiling and chuckling again, despite the pain. "Can't love the dead, Matt."

I jump at him, thrusting the machete into his lower abdomen, gaining purchase as it slides through the soft meat. His eyes open wide, and he gasps in shock. I smile and bow my face close to his and kiss his cheek. I don't feel his stab into my neck until after the peck.

I hear the police coming now. I'm dying, I know it. So much blood has spilled out of me already. Matt stares at me in disbelief. He's bleeding out too, but he's still hanging on. I can't breathe anymore thanks to the cracked ribs, and am forced to watch as Matt slowly drags Ally's mom outside. She's alive, even with the head wound. Her blood makes the floor slippery and slick, but Matt manages to find the kerosene can and lighter before he falls to the floor, weak with his own blood loss. I forgot to fill it, but there's still enough to set this shack ablaze. I watch Matt light the small amount of fluid he spills onto the porch, and see the flames start dancing in his eyes. He smiles with a moral victory, but shudders with a physical defeat all at once. He reaches the door, kicks it closed, and I am left in here to burn to death.

The fire spreads slowly, working its tickling fingers towards my pale and bloody legs. That dang stab in my neck went deep. I hear the sirens closer now. I use the last of my strength, the last of adrenaline, and scoot towards the window as the heat urges me to escape. I manage to pull myself up and lean heavily against the pane. It's getting dark and dizzy in here. I slap the window with the last of the energy I can muster, and it weakly cracks against the old, rotting wood it's perched in. One more slap and the small window falls outward. Fresh air on my face, scorching heat on my back. I fill my lungs and pull myself out, but not in the 'nick of time'. I am burned badly all over my backside. I scrape myself across the ground away from the shack and watch it plume to the heavens.

If I survive, I am gonna leave Serenity Falls. Gotta set up a new kill site somewhere else. I need to get my story straight—Matt did this, he did all of this. I'm just the victim. Ally loved me.

THE SIXTH NIGHT OF CHRISTMAS IS FOR ALL THE SWEET BOYS

BY H. G. GRAVY

SIGNING THE MASTER PROMISSORY NOTE, I DIDN'T REALIZE it would damn me for the rest of my life. It's an appropriate name, honestly. They are my masters now and I promised to become their slave for the rest of my life in exchange for college tuition.

Need some cash? We've got plenty! Don't worry about how much you are borrowing. You can pay us back later with a little interest on top. Don't you know a college degree guarantees you'll get a life-affirming job with incredible benefits, a pension, and an amazingly high salary after you graduate? All you have to do is pull yourself up by your bootstraps, work hard, put in the time, and you'll get promoted to CEO. You'll pay us off in ten years!

The lie was sold to an entire generation and we did what we were told. Our parents, the high school guidance counselors, and society all said a college degree, *any college degree*, would be the most valuable tool we'd have for the rest of our lives.

What a crock of shit.

You'd think taking out $80,000 in student loans would have been the worst mistake I ever made in my life, right?

Sadly, it isn't.

Fast forward two years after graduation and I'm right back where it all began, living in my parents' basement in Serenity Falls. It hurts to think that I tried so hard to escape this godforsaken hell hole of middle-American minutiae and failed. Living in New York City for four years, I realized I never wanted to return to Serenity Falls. Why bother? There's nothing here for anyone. It's a tiny little town in the middle of nowhere that no one gives a shit about. I didn't want to get stuck here like Merry Hoggins, who's been here her entire life. Or at least that's what people said. She always seems so damned happy though. Maybe she bakes a little weed into her brownies.

Coming back to Serenity Falls put the nails in my financial coffin. There isn't anywhere in town to work where I could make enough money to support myself and pay off those student loans. There are a few low-level business establishments like Lucky's Tavern, the pharmacy, or the failing liquor store, but those aren't jobs I could take.

I'm jobless, have no prospects, and am completely and utterly defeated. Not being able to find a job, I've fallen behind on my student loan payments. My heart rate jumps when the cell phone rings. On the one hand, I think it might be a potential employer. On the other, it could be Navient, Nelnet, or any of the assortment of debt collection agencies calling to inquire about my financial situation, wanting to know when they're going to start receiving their payments.

There are days when I'm too fucking depressed to answer the phone. Then I kick my own ass for fear I missed a phone call from a potential employer. Other days when I'm feeling in the mood for a laugh, I'll answer the phone and ask the representative if they're hiring or pretend to not speak English, gibbering away some nonsense until they get sick of asking if Henry Greenwald is available and hang up.

It was early evening a couple of days ago. I was home alone and firing off my resume into the abyss of online job sites when a call from an unknown number came through on my cell phone. I hesitated to answer with the dreadful prospect of it being another debt collector. Those bastards didn't give up, even during the holiday season. Then again, I'd been applying for jobs and it could have been someone looking to set up an interview.

Looking back on it now, I remember feeling like the universe was going to change my fortunes. Things had to go in my direction at some point. Plus, I figured if it were a debt collector, the old gibberish routine would get me through. I took a deep breath, readied myself for either outcome and hit answer.

"Hello, my name is Edgar Rodriguez and I'm a financial counselor at Serenity Falls Debt Solutions Group. Is Mr. Greenwald available?"

Serenity Falls Debt Solutions Group wasn't familiar to me. I hadn't financed any loans through them and I hadn't applied for any job with them either. At least I didn't think I had. Sending out resumes on a daily basis for hours at a time didn't exactly leave me with much memory of the companies I'd been applying to.

"What is this in reference to?" I asked attempting to sound pleasant.

"Mr. Greenwald, I'm calling to notify you that Serenity Falls Debt Solutions Group has purchased all your outstanding student loan debts and will now be collecting. We have made several attempts to discuss payment of your defaulted account balances and could not reach you. We will need you to make a payment today over the phone," Edgar explained.

I sighed as hope drained out of me. The only thing which stopped me from hanging up the phone was Edgar's pleasant demeanor. I didn't want to be rude considering he was merely doing his job.

"Edgar, let's cut right to the chase. I haven't been employed since high school. My last job was working at the dollar store. That was close to six years ago. I don't have a cent to my name. I don't own a car. I live in my parent's basement. I can't pay you money I don't have," I explained.

"Well, Mr. Greenwald, that simply is not acceptable," Edgar replied.

His voice was pleasant, if not even a little saccharine, yet beneath it was an undercurrent of menace. It rubbed me the wrong way immediately. Considering I was already accustomed to the strong-arm tactics and threats other collections agencies used to get me to pay them, I knew how to handle the situation.

Many tried being nice to me and understanding my situation wasn't ideal but insisted I still needed to pay. Others tried appealing to my morality and telling me I owed the taxpayers back the money they loaned me for my education. Others jumped straight into wage garnishments and lawsuits, warning me it was easier to cooperate with them now rather than get lawyers involved.

To each one the answer was the same:

"Listen, Edgar, I can't pay. I understand you have to collect on what I owe, but you also have to understand I have rights. Money doesn't grow on trees. If it did, I'd have a ton more Christmas trees. How the heck do you want me to pay you when I don't have any money at all?"

"Mr. Greenwald, please allow me to explain the situation," Edgar said dropping any semblance of a pleasant tone. "If you would please look out at the street to the right from your front door, there is a black sport-utility vehicle parked across the street. This is one of our field representatives and they are listening in on this phone call right now. Say hello," Edgar explained.

Static burst through the phone and a modulated voice said *Hello.*

"Think of them as our quality assurance department. To prove I am not lying, I will now have our field representative sound the horn of his car. Go ahead."

A car horn blared from the front of my house. I hustled upstairs from the basement to the first floor and yanked open the blinds from the window in my living room. Across the street, as Edgar said, there was a black SUV with tinted windows.

An overwhelming feeling of anxiety overcame me. My hands began to tremble and I was breathing hard, trying to catch my breath, all while trying to make sense of the situation. I almost dropped my phone but held it close when I heard Edgar's voice.

"Mr. Greenwald, are you still there? I hope you are because if you hang up on me. Well… you *don't* want to hang up on me."

"Yeah," I choked out. "I'm still here."

"Please keep in mind, if you hang up, call the police, or take any action other than what I tell you to do, I will close your case, and have our representative fulfill the terms and conditions to which you agreed upon in your Master Promissory Note," Edgar stated.

"What?" I asked, unable to focus on what he was saying. I continued staring out the window at the black SUV. It shifted a little from side to side, further proving someone was inside, even if I couldn't see them with the tinted windows.

"As I said earlier, Serenity Falls Debt Solutions Group has purchased your outstanding student loans. The total amount owed is $260,000 after capitalization, interest, fees, and an assortment of other penalties applied to your delinquent and defaulted status. As per your Master Promissory Note, you have agreed to pay these loans back in full, unless you meet the criteria for discharge."

"What are the criteria for discharge?" I stuttered. I couldn't keep my voice steady. I kept looking at the black SUV and wondering if this person was watching me back. How long had they been there? Who was it?

"The criteria for discharge is being rendered completely disabled or the death of the loan holder," Edgar answered. "Our field representative is fully prepared to enforce discharge proceedings if we do not come to an understanding before the end of this phone call."

Nausea soured the back of my throat. My insides were twisted up and my lunch threatened to make a reappearance.

"Mr. Greenwald, are you still there? I can hear you whimpering," Edgar asked, sounding gleeful at my suffering.

"Yes, I'm here. I'm listening."

"Great, Mr. Greenwald. If I remember correctly, you mentioned earlier you had rights. I'd like to go over them with you right now. I think you'll find them quite favorable to your situation," Edgar said.

I gave him a weak *"a-huh"*.

"Serenity Falls Debt Solutions acknowledges these are tough economic times. Not everyone is able to find stable and secure employment. Unfortunately, unemployment will not exempt you from your obligations," Edgar said as if reading from a script.

"Serenity Falls Debt Solutions does not wish to further complicate the debtor's quality of life; therefore, we have capped your outstanding balance at $260,000. You will no longer accrue interest. Isn't that nice, Mr. Greenwald? You cannot owe more than you already do!" Edgar asked as if he was doing me a solid favor.

"I can't pay the money. What part of that don't you understand?" I pleaded with Edgar, feeling the tears pooling in my eyes.

"Mr. Greenwald, I'm getting to that," Edgar replied sharply. The annoyance in his voice cut through me. He cleared his throat and continued:

"Serenity Falls Debt Solutions Group offers several repayment options you may find beneficial to you. As I said earlier, you have the discharge option: total disability, or death. We can also place you on a standard repayment plan of twelve-monthly payments over ten years totaling to a bunch of money you'll never actually have. If you miss a payment under this plan, our arrangement is voided, and our field representative will pay you a visit to *discharge* your loan," Edgar explained.

"Your final repayment option is through Serenity Falls Debt Solutions Group's most innovative solution for delinquent debtors much like yourself who seem to have trouble finding work opportunities. Through our Indentured Servitude plan, you will become an individual "contractor" for Serenity Falls Debt Solutions Group. You'll be assigned several tasks to complete. Once the task is completed, your account will be credited, and you will not have to worry about making the payments. These credits will be applied to your outstanding balance," Edgar explained.

"And what if—"

"If you do not complete the assigned task, you have the option of paying the standard rate, or our field representative will have the unpleasant task of having to discharge your loans," Edgar answered before I could ask. "And trust me, our representatives don't like to leave loose ends."

Listening to Edgar and watching the black SUV, I was dumbstruck. I questioned if this was really happening. The room felt like it was spinning. I kept thinking to myself, *this isn't normal. It's not supposed to work like this.* This thought repeated over and over again in my mind to convince myself it was not real despite the obvious. Someone was sitting in a car outside my house ready to come in and kill me if I didn't cooperate.

"I... I need time to think about it. Can I have time?" I asked Edgar.

"Really? You need time?" Edgar asked, almost flabbergasted at the question.

"I need to call my parents to see if they can help me. They're in Las Vegas for the holidays," I explained.

"You better hope they hit the jackpot, Mr. Greenwald," Edgar replied. "You have until tomorrow night. See if you can get mommy and daddy to bail you out of this one. Don't even think about telling them about this phone call. Don't dare call the police. Don't think about fleeing to another country either. We're a multinational group with field representatives across the globe."

"Okay, should I call you or—" I began before Edgar interrupted.

"I will be calling you at exactly 10 o'clock in the evening. Please be sure your phone is charged, the ringer is on, and you better pick up the first time I call or... well, you already know. Our field representative will remain outside your home until we speak again. Do not attempt to make contact, have the car towed, or something insanely unadvisable. If anything happens to our field representative, even if it is an act of God such as a heart attack, a meteor crashing down upon him from the heavens, or the dead rising from the grave and consuming his brains for brunch, *you* will suffer the consequences, as will your family. If you don't have any more questions, have a good night, and Serenity Falls Debt Solutions Group appreciates your business," Edgar said before the call disconnected.

    Sleep did not come easy that night. After getting off the phone, I checked my accounts online with the Department of Education, Navient, and Nelnet and saw what Edgar said was the truth. All my statements were at a $0 balance and the descriptions said they'd been moved into collections.

    I couldn't stop looking out the window at the black SUV. It was there the whole night, through the morning and afternoon, and heading into the evening. The SUV sat coldly where it was parked. Not once did I see the lights on or see exhaust fumes in the air behind it. Whoever was inside must have been freezing, hungry, and in serious need of a bathroom, unless they were prepared for the stakeout. For the sake of my own sanity, I imagined the person sitting there having to shit and piss into a container and sit with it overnight. I laughed aloud and my laughter sounded foreign to me.

    As 9 p.m. rolled in, I came to the conclusion I had no other choice but to accept the Indentured Servitude plan. Asking my parents for money was out of the question. When they were actually home together, they would always end up arguing about money. Mom's hours at the hospital were cut. To help make ends meet, she took night shifts at a hospital over an hour and a half away from Serenity Falls. Dad was only around on the weekends since he'd gotten a job as a long-haul truck driver after losing his old position a few years ago.

    For a little while, my parents were worried we would need to abandon the house to foreclosure or short-sale, but somehow they were able to keep us afloat. Since coming back to Serenity Falls, I felt like dead weight in the family. I couldn't contribute a damned thing to the monthly expenses. I made up for it by cooking, cleaning, and taking care of all the miscellaneous chores around the house. In addition to not having any money to spare for me, I didn't want them to worry. Plus, I'm an adult now. I needed to handle the situation myself. I was already relying too much on mommy and daddy as it was.

    At 10 p.m., my phone was in my hands and I waited for the call to come through. I made a fist to keep my hands from shaking so much but the nerves wracked through my entire body. My heart pumped like

I'd run a marathon. My teeth were clicking together and I felt nothing but cold despite the sweatshirt I wore.

At 10:01, I got worried. Edgar didn't seem like the type to miss his deadline.

At 10:05, I went into full panic. I paced back and forth in the house checking all the windows and doors and watching the black SUV. I waited for someone to step out. The darkness of the night seemed to encase the vehicle in an ominous shadow. Or at least, that's how it felt at the time.

At 10:15 p.m., I was close to giving up on Edgar. It was a horrible prank. Someone back in New York must have set it up as a joke. It wouldn't have been hard to pull off. Nothing but hiring a person to sit outside in a car and make the three-way phone call. The loans in collections made total sense since I never paid them. All the companies calling me could have been selling them to each other over time and it's become lost in the constant resale shuffle. Plus, anyone familiar with my situation knew I hadn't been paying for years now. It was an easy prank to pull. I thought about who would go to such great lengths to mess with me and couldn't come up with a name.

At 10:26 p.m., I tried calling the number Edgar had called from. The phone number was out of service. I tried calling a few more times hoping it would get through but I got nothing. I stopped calling and assumed it was a prepaid phone someone had used to call and fuck with me. If it wasn't, I hoped Edgar hadn't been calling while I was busy trying to call him.

10:28 p.m. rolled in and I was about to hit the ceiling with anxiety when the phone screamed to life ringing and vibrating.

"Hello," I answered immediately.

"So, what's your decision?" Edgar asked skipping the formalities.

"Indentured Servitude," I replied to keep it as short as he did.

"Excellent. Your first task begins tonight. You will go to the abandoned warehouse on Elm Street next to the police station at 11 o'clock and await further instructions when I call you. Make sure you answer. Understand?"

"Yes, abandoned warehouse, 11 o'clock," I replied.

"Oh yeah, before I forget, please do not leave your bedroom until you hear the sound of your front door closing. Mr. Representative, please let Mr. Greenwald know how good you are at your job," Edgar said before the line died.

An explosive bang hit against the bedroom door like someone swung a hammer into it. I jumped back into the corner of my bedroom and searched for a weapon I could use to defend myself. Then I heard heavy footsteps walking away from the door as they descended down the stairs. There were a few moments of silence before the front door slammed shut, startling me enough to release a cry. I charged toward the window with the hope of catching a glimpse of who had been inside my house without me realizing it. I watched the street waiting for him to go across and jump into the black SUV but to my bewilderment, the lights of the vehicle turned on. It pulled away from the curb and disappeared down the street.

Before leaving the house, I stopped in the kitchen and debated taking one of the knives with me. It wouldn't be much of a weapon considering the resources the collection agency likely had, but it was better than nothing. I swallowed hard and placed a knife inside my jacket. Luckily, I didn't need to use it.

Serenity Falls was fully in the Christmas spirit with lights decorating all the homes and businesses. Beverly's Bed and Breakfast and the Sunflower Bakery seemed to be competing with each other over who could be the gaudiest with their decorations. The empty building next door looked like a corpse compared to its lively neighbors. A few cars were parked across the street at the diner. I couldn't imagine anyone wanting to bother eating there. The few times I'd gone there, I thought the food tasted a little funny.

Walking across the front of the police station, I was tempted to go inside and tell them everything. Seeking out help was natural. Maybe Sheriff VanLanen was available and could help me sort out this nightmare. I'd taken down the license plate of the black SUV and could probably get them going in the right direction with it.

Of course, I didn't do this. What the hell was a small-town police department going to do against a multinational debt collection agency? I had no reason to doubt Edgar's threats. Everything he'd said to me had come true. Everything. Therefore, I could also assume if I cooperated, I might actually be able to put a dent in the loans. Seeing how Edgar said I'd be credited for each task I completed for them, I was being given

$2167 per assignment. I'd never be able to make a payment like that in my life. I'd be stuck paying the loans forever. Perhaps it wasn't such a bad thing to have gotten a call from the Serenity Falls debt collectors.

Ultimately, I decided against it and continued onward to the abandoned warehouse next door. I checked my phone and saw I'd made it there with five minutes to spare. There was nothing else to do but wait it out. I checked the perimeter of the building to see if I could get a look inside. Even with broken windows, I couldn't see anything. They were all covered with plywood nailed on from the inside. Then the phone rang, interrupting my thoughts.

"Mr. Greenwald, I'm glad to see you are taking this seriously," Edgar said as I answered.

"What the fuck else am I supposed to do?"

"You could have easily gone into the police station and made the worst decision of your life," Edgar replied. "I saw you standing outside like you were considering it."

"How the hell are you watching me?" I asked looking all around me to see if I could spot someone on the phone. The street was desolate. There was no one around as far as I could see.

"Don't worry about how I am watching. Just know that I am at all times. Before you continue, toss that knife across the street." Edgar commanded.

I tossed the knife across the street. It clanged as it hit the cement.

"Thank you. You won't be needing it tonight. Should I ever require you to be armed for a task, I will provide the armaments. Now please make your way to the Serenity Motors parking lot and search for an ice cream truck. It will be hard to miss. You will find a set of keys beneath the driver side front tire. Enter the vehicle, place the headset over your ears, and then turn the engine over. Once this is accomplished, sit in the driver's seat until you receive my phone call. You will have fifteen minutes to do this. Go," Edgar said and the connection broke.

"Son of a bitch," I uttered. I put my phone into my pocket and headed toward of the auto repair shop. Entering the lot, I spotted the ice cream truck immediately and followed the directions Edgar gave until I was sitting in the driver's seat with the headset on. I put my phone on the dashboard and waited for him to call.

"Mr. Greenwald, if you've followed my instructions correctly, you are hearing my voice right now. Please nod your head if you can hear me." Edgar said through the headset. I jumped in my chair the moment I heard it. I nodded while searching for the camera he was watching me through.

"Good. Very good. Now for your first task, you are to drive this ice cream truck around Serenity Falls. Plain and simple. Easy-peasy. Got it? Now, hit the button on the left side of the console and go," Edgar said.

At Edgar's command, I hit the button, heard a muted melody start playing, and headed out into Serenity Falls.

Make a right on Main Street.

Make a left onto Dairy Road.

Left on Dahmer Street.

Left on Elm Street.

Edgar continued with the directions over the headset taking me all over Serenity Falls until we were on the outskirts of town. He was silent aside from his commands, and I didn't seek out any conversation either.

Turn onto Edd Road.

Now turn into the driveway on your left.

Now stop.

Edgar stopped me in front of a house. The illumination of the headlights filtered into it like a spotlight. Whoever was inside must have awakened because I could see someone standing in the living room. We stood there staring at each other for a while. I doubt he could see me considering the brightness of the lights.

Turn the button on the left three clicks. You'll feel them in your fingers.

Doing as I was told, I turned the dial and felt it click in my fingers like Edgar had said. It was then I noticed a child joined the person standing in the living room. After a few moments, the child left and a man came outside into the cold night in a coat and pajama bottoms. I tensed up immediately and wanted to leave. It was obviously scaring them, but Edgar hadn't told me to move yet. The man approached cautiously, staring at the ice cream truck like it was a sleeping dragon.

Get out of there now!

I dropped the ice cream truck into reverse and it peeled out backwards. I spun the wheel and righted the truck, then headed back down Edd Road.

That'll be all for tonight. Return the ice cream truck to the auto shop and leave the keys where you found them. Tomorrow afternoon, I will be giving you a call. Congratulations, Mr. Greenwald. You've earned one credit payment.

The line went dead.

The next afternoon, Edgar's phone call came in and the request this time was a strange one. Once again, it was nothing too crazy or extreme, but at the same time, I could only imagine how fucking weird it must be for this man and his son to have an ice cream truck outside their house in the middle of the night. Now, I had to leave a bowl of different flavors of ice cream on the front steps with a note for the man that said "For Carter, A Sweet Treat for A Sweet Boy."

"Come on, Edgar. That's fucking weird in a real uncomfortably pedophilic way," I complained.

"Mr. Greenwald, I didn't ask for your opinion nor do I care for it. Do as you are told or suffer the consequences," Edgar replied and hung up.

Once again, I set out toward the auto shop. As I entered the lot, I saw David Holmes watching me closely. We made eye contact yet he didn't stop me from walking onto his property and taking the ice cream truck again. It took me a few minutes to figure out how to get to the house on Edd Road again. In the middle of the daytime, driving the ice cream truck around felt like I was calling more attention to myself than at night with the music blaring. It was like being exposed except for the fact that the windows on the ice cream truck were tinted. It was something I hadn't noticed the night before. Considering how freaked out and unnerved I was, I could have driven past a Christmas parade and wouldn't have noticed.

This time around, I figured I could accomplish my task without being seen. Instead of driving down Edd Road, I took a turn into the park. I killed the engine, went into the back of the truck, and scooped a bunch of different flavors of ice cream into a white bowl. Then I left the truck and traversed the woods leading back to Edd Road. While I wasn't the best navigator, I managed to find the house again. I remembered the gravel driveway and the front of the house. God knows I sat staring at it for a while like a fucking creep.

Coming up to the porch, I took the creepy note out of my jacket pocket and placed both the note and the ice cream bowl on the welcome mat. It was difficult to think in that moment, I was worried about figuring out if Edgar wanted me to leave a spoon along with the bowl and the note. He never mentioned a spoon, so maybe it wasn't required. Then again, he might have just assumed I would have thought to include a spoon with the bowl of ice cream.

Realizing I was standing on the porch in broad daylight, I decided it didn't matter and ran off back into the woods until I found the ice cream truck again. As soon as I turned the engine over, the music started blasting over the loudspeaker. I smacked the volume dial in a panic and turned it up even louder. With my gloves on, it was difficult to grab the switch, but eventually, I turned it off.

Another task completed, I took the damned ice cream truck back to the auto shop and hoped my next job wouldn't involve this family anymore.

Unfortunately for me, this wasn't the case.

Later in the evening, I received another phone call from Edgar.

Tomorrow at eleven o'clock, you will go to the cobbler's place across the street from the diner and pick up a package. Leave the package in the back of the ice cream truck. Then drop the truck off at the market across the street from the elementary school. Leave the keys underneath the driver's side front tire and go home. You won't hear from me for a few days but rest assured, I will be watching. I'll call you again when I need you.

"What's a cobbler?" I asked.

Edgar hung up.

As you can imagine, I followed Edgar's directions to the letter. At eleven o'clock, I made it to the tailor/shoe repair shop which was empty. I called out a *Hello,* hoping someone would answer. I got no response. It felt weird being inside the shop with no one there to attend me. It felt like I didn't belong. I was sweating despite the cold inside the shop. If there were no one to give me the package, I wouldn't know what the heck I was supposed to bring to the ice cream truck. Then I saw it in the middle of the shop with a note on the front of it which said: "Greenwald."

A mannequin outfitted in an old-fashioned ice cream truck driver uniform. It was an all-white button-up shirt and white pants to match. A red bowtie was tied around the collar. A classic captain's hat rested atop the mannequin's head. I grabbed all the pieces of the uniform and stuffed them into a bag I found behind the counter. Then after checking out the rest of the shop, I went out the front door, and ran to the auto shop again.

David Holmes was there again. We saw each other and neither of us acknowledged the other's presence. Something in my gut told me Edgar was giving David instructions as well. I thought about approaching him and speaking about it but then thought against it. Edgar could be watching. I didn't want to mess up whatever arrangement David had with Edgar, if he did have one. I also didn't wish to ruin mine. To what end, anyway? We find out we're both being manipulated by the same person and then what? We continue our duties until we're finished.

Taking the ice cream truck again, the drive wasn't too far. The market was right on Main Street. The elementary school was right across the road. Pulling into the market, I felt my bowels about to release when I saw the black SUV in the parking lot. The tinted window came down and a black-gloved hand waved me over to the spot next to it. Following their direction, I parked the ice cream truck and left the bag with the ice cream man uniform in the back as instructed.

With my last remaining nerve, I checked to make sure no one else was around before flipping my hood over my head and covering my face. I got out of the truck, left the keys under the tire, and started to walk home. I felt the person's eyes watching me as I walked. After getting a couple of blocks down Main Street, I felt a wave of relief to be done with Edgar's tasks, if only for a little while. I didn't like what I was doing and God knows what else was coming in the future. However, I didn't have much of a choice now that I was in their pocket.

Later that night, my parents returned from their trip to Vegas. It was nice to have them back again. The house seemed so empty by myself. Considering how much things had changed, it felt like they were gone for a month and not only a week.

Greeting them as they entered, I took my Mom's bag and asked, "How was the trip?"

"It was fun. We gambled a bit and won some money. We saw the Grand Canyon. But mostly we just enjoyed each other's company. It's something we haven't done for a while, so it was nice to reconnect," my mother explained.

"Dad?" I asked.

"Gimme a minute," he replied with a frown. He went into the kitchen and checked the patio door was locked and placed a piece of wood along the track so it wouldn't open. He went to the windows in the living room and checked them too.

"What's going on?" I asked as I followed him through the house.

"You haven't heard?" Mom replied.

"Heard what?" I asked as rock seemed to form in my stomach.

"Some children went missing today at the elementary school," Dad said as he continued checking all the entry points in the house.

My heart skipped a beat and I almost collapsed. No one seemed to notice and Mom continued.

"Yeah, there's a checkpoint outside of town and they're checking all vehicles for the missing children. They're searching for someone dressed like an ice cream man and some ice cream truck that's been seen driving around town in the middle of the night. You wouldn't happen to have seen it?" Mom asked.

"I saw it," I said. "But I never saw a man."

"Okay. Just make sure to lock all the doors when we're home. Day and night," Mom said heading into the bathroom.

"What a world we live in these days. Not even Serenity Falls is safe anymore," Dad muttered, grabbing his luggage and heading up the stairs to his bedroom.

I could only nod and plaster a fake smile across my face until he left. Then I couldn't stand it anymore. I ran upstairs into my bathroom and vomited. My thoughts were scrambled. I couldn't believe I was an accomplice in a kidnapping. If anyone had seen me driving the truck around, I'd be the main suspect. David Holmes had certainly seen me. If he wasn't part of the plan, he was only a stone's throw away from the police station.

I wanted to scream and cry and lash out. Now that my parents were home, I couldn't do it without looking suspicious or crazy. I had to endure and hope nothing would come of my actions.

As I finished brushing my teeth, my phone rang and my heart stopped. I pulled it out and saw the familiar "Unknown Caller" pop-up on the screen.

"Shit," I said before before hitting the answer button.

"Mr. Greenwald, I see mommy and daddy have returned. I'm glad to see you won't be alone for the holidays. Remember, Serenity Falls Debt Solutions Group is always watching. Right, Mr. Representative?"

I let out a whimper at the sound of the static crackling over the phone. The modulated voice said something which sounded like "Yes" and a laugh followed behind it.

"Mr. Greenwald, I have another task for you to complete."

THE SEVENTH NIGHT OF CHRISTMAS IS EMPTY

BY RONA VASELAAR

I'M A MONSTER, AND IT'S TIME EVERYONE KNOWS IT.

If I tried to tell you—if I stopped you on the street and said, "Please, something's wrong with me, something inside me is broken"—you wouldn't believe me. Nobody would. But once you've read this, once you understand what I've done…

There will be no denying it.

I never thought I'd come back here. After college and grad school, I figured I would be done with this town for good. It'd be a blip in the plot of my life story, more of a footnote, really, and I had no intention of looking at it ever again.

And then, during the last semester of my coursework, I discovered something and knew I needed to come back. I called up my mom and asked if I could have my old room in the basement back. If I could stay with her for just a little while and work on something. She agreed and didn't ask any questions. That's what I like about her. She may be kind of a shit mother but she doesn't usually stick her nose where it doesn't belong.

So I came home. A bed and breakfast isn't an ideal place to set up a lab, but the basement was large. I would just have to be quiet to avoid suspicion. Besides, it presented me with certain… opportunities that I wouldn't fail to take advantage of.

Before I'd been home more than a few days, I'd managed to turn the basement into my own personal haven. My research took up nearly every inch of my bedroom floor. My lab equipment—that which I purchased, and that which I acquired by other means—was meticulously arranged so that everything would be ready when I was.

Next to my bed, I kept an old National Geographic, dog-eared and wrinkled, dated November 2014. I'd found it sitting among other outdated journals in my Biology professor's office. Once I peered inside, I couldn't stop myself from stealing it. It was what started it all, what sparked this experiment.

Within two weeks, I was ready to begin. I had read everything that had already been published, I'd come up with a million ideas, none of them workable... and then. *And then.* I'd been struck with inspiration, stayed up for twenty-six hours coming up with the process, the hypothesis, checking all my boxes. I spent the next three days reading my work over and over and over looking for the flaw, the loophole, the missing piece. There was none.

It was perfect. *My idea was perfect.*

There was only one thing missing at that point—a test subject.

I could have found myself a lab rat somewhere. Serenity Falls doesn't have a pet shop, but I could've driven an hour or two and found one. If truly necessary, I could have looked for a stray dog or a cat or something, but there are limits to animal testing. First of all, it's cruel. No animal deserves to be put through scientific experimentation like that. They're helpless, innocent. They can't process what's happening to them.

Secondly, for my research to be truly revolutionary, I needed something that could *communicate.* I wanted to hear the thoughts, feelings, fears of my subject. I didn't need a dog or a cat or a rat.

I needed a human.

I got my chance only two days after all the preparations had been made. A healthy middle-aged man, no known spouse or other family ties. Lived alone, somewhat awkward, not a lot of social contact. He was perfect.

I grabbed his bags for him when he came in the door. My mom eyed me suspiciously—I stay out of her way when she has guests if I can help it—but didn't say anything.

"I'm real excited to be here, Beverly," said the man with an awkward smile. "Couldn't believe my luck when I won the gift certificate in the town raffle. I've always wanted to stay here!" Then he looked at me and held out his hand. "You must be Blake! I heard you've got your Master's in Biology. We're all very proud of you, young man!"

I took his hand somewhat reluctantly. I didn't want to get too close to my subject, of course. "It's good to see you again, Dr. Poole."

"Please, call me Timothy. It's been so long since I've had you in the office, you must have been ten the last time I saw you! But now that you're home I'm sure I'll be seeing you again."

I mumbled my assent and brought his bag to his room, rummaging through the pockets and grabbing something before I walked back downstairs. He and mom kept chatting, giving me ample time to slip back down to the basement unnoticed. I didn't reappear until it was time for supper.

Mom had made one of her favorite dishes, some goopy pile of mac 'n' cheese that was probably a heart attack waiting to happen. I offered to help her set the table and she finally couldn't help herself.

"What on earth are you up to, Blake? Thought you were too good for all this. Isn't that why you went off to school four states away?"

I'd been expecting this question all day, so I was prepared with a chagrined look as I answered, "I just feel bad that I'm imposing on you while I look for a job. Not paying rent and all. I thought helping out was the least I could do."

She let it drop for the moment, but I knew what she was thinking. *You've never felt bad about lazing around before, why start now?* Luckily for me, she didn't ask.

I got lucky a second time when she stepped outside to call the cat in—can you believe a bed and breakfast has a *cat?*—and I was left alone for just a few moments.

Long enough for me to slip a little something into Dr. Poole's glass of water.

Looking back, it's not surprising that I was able to do it without being caught. But at the time, I felt like someone was going to burst in the kitchen at any moment, apprehend me and put me away for good. I had a horrible, certain gut feeling that I was going to be caught red-handed.

But I wasn't.

Instead, we had a lovely dinner together. Dr. Poole and my mother dominated most of the conversation, which was fine by me. I sat back and watched him slowly, God, *so* slowly, drink down every last drop of water in his glass.

My work was finished. Or, rather, the fun part was just beginning.

He went to bed and I went downstairs, scribbling furiously in my notebook. Dates, times, everything I could think of that would be useful to the experiment. I wished I could do some closer monitoring—take his blood pressure, listen to his pulse, that sort of thing—but then he would have to know what I was doing, and that would jeopardize the entire process. I held back.

The virus acted faster than I had expected. When Dr. Poole came down for breakfast that morning, he was pale and already had his bag in hand.

"I'm sorry Beverly, Blake, but I'm going to head home a little early. I'm not feeling so well this morning, it seems I've developed a bit of a fever."

A bit? How much is a bit? 99 degrees? 104?

"Oh, Dr. Poole, I'm sorry. Is there anything I can do for you?"

Dr. Poole assured my mother that he was going to be fine, just needed to get back into his own bed, and practically ran out the door.

If it was acting that quickly, I would need to accelerate my plans as well.

I waited one full day before I took the wallet I'd grabbed from his bag and placed it on a random side table in the living room. My mother found it a few minutes after I'd put it down.

"Oh no. Dr. Poole must have left his wallet." I happened (coincidentally, of course) to be in the room when she found it, so I was able to respond.

"Why don't I take it to him? He lives down on Dahmer Street, doesn't he? I can walk down there and be back in ten minutes."

She agreed, but seemed uneasy. She's a smart woman, unfortunately. I took the wallet before she could change her mind and started off down the street.

Five minutes later, I was knocking on Dr. Poole's door.

It took him a long time to answer. So much so that I wondered if my experiment had been *too* hasty, if I'd miscalculated something and he'd died before—

And then there he was, the door opening to reveal a very haggard face.

"Dr. Poole, you forgot your wallet at our place. Mom sent me down to give it to you."

He looked at me for a moment, his eyes unblinking. His cheeks were bright red and he looked dazed.

"Ah. Yes. Thank you. I... was wondering where I'd..."

His voice trailed off and he continued to stare at me.

"This sure is a nice place, Dr. Poole!" I said, in order to get him out of his stupor. And, of course, to prompt him into inviting me inside.

Instead of taking the obvious bait, he grabbed his wallet and slammed the door in my face.

I swore to myself. I was hoping to get a layout of the house. I'd have to do my best from the outside.

I looked around, made sure nobody was watching, and then started to walk the perimeter of his home. There wasn't much to go on, a tightly-secured back door, a few small windows covered by curtains, one large window that offered a glimpse into the living room.

But—there. On the right side of the house, there was a window that opened into a bedroom. There was a crack in the curtains and I could see Poole walking inside and sitting heavily on the bed.

Bingo.

I observed him for a while, but he just laid down and went to sleep. No matter. I could always come back later.

And I did. Every night, I came back to see what Poole would do. The first few nights, nothing much. He stayed in bed, he watched some TV. He was clearly feeling very ill, based on how much medication he was taking. I knew it wouldn't do him any good, but it's good to let people hope, isn't it?

The fourth night, that's when he finally got interesting.

He was sitting in his bed again, but this time he had a set of pliers. Strange, you'd think a dentist would use something a little more... professional, considering what I saw him do next. I mean, really, it was downright ironic.

He lifted the pliers to his mouth.

I watched, fascinated, horrified, as he attached it to his front tooth and YANKED.

There was no hesitation. His gaze didn't even flicker before he did it. It came out quickly—he made it look easy. But the scream he let out told me it was anything but. Blood was pouring from his lips as he looked down at his tooth, still held between the pliers.

I ran.

I was sure his scream would attract the attention of the neighbors, so I didn't get to see what happened in the aftermath, but that was all right. I had enough information to know that the virus was working exactly the way I hoped it would. So far.

Now it was just a matter of waiting more. And watching. I was always, always watching.

He made his move two days later. I didn't get to see it, despite my best efforts. But I heard about it. Word travels fast in small towns, you know? Apparently, he tried to feed his tooth to a patient without her noticing. They had to cut it out of her throat.

I was delighted. I was overjoyed. *It was working. My experiment was working.*

All I'd had to do was recode the virus, so to speak. Teach it to do something new. It was already capable of hijacking its host, taking over the brain. It's what it did with the host *after* it had control that mattered.

Things accelerated quickly after that.

It wasn't just his teeth, though that was where he started. He began to remove other pieces as well. It started small. I watched him snip off his own earlobe—he used anesthesia that time, I noticed; he was getting smarter—and rip off his toenails.

But then it got bigger.

The first time that I realized I was no longer in control of the situation was date night. Not for me, of course, I don't date, but for Poole. He had someone over who was way out of his league, if you ask me. I'd had to sneak around the other side of the house to watch them in the living room eating dinner together. The date wasn't going well from what I saw. The woman was clearly concerned over him, trying to ask him what was wrong, I think. He didn't answer, just kept indicating to the food, trying to get her to eat.

She did. But she spit it out right away and began shrieking.

"What is this? What the fuck did you put in here?" I could hear every word clearly, even through the glass.

"It's me, Clara. It's a part of me. I want you to have it. I want you to *eat* it."

"Good God, what is *wrong* with you, you... freak!"

She didn't stay to scream anything else. She stumbled out the door onto the porch, vomiting as she did, leaving a mess in his doorway. She practically flew to her car, racing down the street as though her toothless boyfriend was following her.

Poole just sat there at the table, staring at her empty seat. He got up and went to bed an hour later.

I went home that night, troubled.

Poole was harder to track after that. He wasn't coming home as often, and he seemed to be carrying out his operations elsewhere. As the days went on, each time I caught a glimpse of him, when I managed to find him at all, he looked worse and worse. He was losing more pieces of himself. Fingers, part of his nose, an eye. I could tell he'd put something in the eye socket to try to cover up what he'd done but, still, his original eye was completely gone.

I was shocked and confused. You must understand, this was supposed to take *months*. It was supposed to happen gradually so that I could control it, take measurements, find out what was going on in his head somehow. That was the plan. But that was proving impossible, we were running out of time.

I had to put a stop to it. I'm not as cruel as I sound. This wasn't how I wanted things to happen.

So I did what anyone would do in that situation. I broke into his house.

I hoped he had some sort of alarm system that would alert him to the fact that someone was there, but I didn't notice one. So I just sat and waited and hoped beyond hope that he would show up. I didn't have much of a plan, but I was sure if I could just reason with him, I could stop this. I would strap him down and find a way to… to… stop it. I didn't know how, all right? But I wouldn't let him continue walking around town, living his life looking like *that*. People would start to talk, more than they had already. They'd notice something was wrong.

And someone would figure out it was me.

Poole came home about seven hours after I broke into his house, long after the sun had set. I heard him out back, yanking on the door in the sun room. I opened it and ushered him inside, hoping nobody had seen us.

"You... Blake... kid... what the fuck are you doing here?" he asked, his voice hoarse.

"Dr. Poole, I know it's hard to explain, but I know what's happening to you. And I can help you, I know I can."

"You know..." he shook his head, cutting himself off. "I have to do it. I *have* to. It's... there's so much emptiness and I have to make it full and... I can't explain..."

"You don't have to," I said in a soothing voice, coming closer to him. "You don't have to explain anything, I already know, let's get out of here."

"I understand," he said, suddenly fixing his good eye on me. He staggered past me and lunged for the kitchen. I followed on his heels, but not quickly enough to stop him from getting the knife.

"You need it too, don't you? Of course you do. You're like me, you need what I have. I can give it to you, I *want* to give it to you. Will you let me give it to you?"

It happened so fast I couldn't stop it. In a moment, his false eye was out of his head and I was able to see. *God.* The socket was a mess of blood and gore and I could see that he'd never actually gotten the eye out. It was still in there, stuck inside and mangled and barely recognizable as an eye anymore.

He cut it out of himself with methodical precision. He didn't even seem to notice the pain anymore as he practically gutted it out with the knife. Then he turned to me, a fluid mass in his palm.

"Your turn," he mumbled, thrusting his eyeball-filled hand at me.

I shrieked and ran for the back door. I'd fucked up and I couldn't fix it, I didn't know how. I got outside and managed to throw myself in the bushes in his backyard. He didn't have a hope of seeing me, of finding me. I watched as he returned to the house, coming back a few seconds later with a bandage thrown hastily over his gorey eye socket. The whole interaction between us had taken less than five minutes, but I knew I would be living in that horrible moment for the rest of my life.

He picked up his phone. He was... talking to it. Was he recording something? Had he recorded *me?*

He walked into the backyard, past my hiding place in the bushes. As he was leaving, I heard him mutter something. I can't be sure but it sounded like he said, *"Who gets to eat you, I wonder?"*

And then he was gone. Off into the night, and I was too terrified to follow.

I hid in my basement for the next couple of days. I wouldn't speak to anyone, not even my own mother. I'd known when I took control of that virus, I'd known what it would eventually force the host to do. I thought I was prepared for it. But the reality of it... I made a mistake. I know that now. I understand.

But it's too late to fix it.

Because just about two weeks ago, what little was left of Poole's body was found in the back of Mel's Place, a diner down on Main Street. The rumor is some cop found Poole's severed finger in his pudding. They say that there were pieces of his body found in all the meals the diner had been preparing when the cops burst in the kitchen looking for the source of the body part.

There's something about this virus you should know.

I got it into Poole's system through water, yes. But it's resilient. It's highly contagious.

And it spreads very quickly through blood transmission.

I'm packing a bag, I'm getting out of here. I don't know how long the town has until everyone is infected. But Clara, Poole's date, is already missing and I can well imagine what she's doing right about now. I heard that cop was hospitalized, and that other people are getting sick.

It's too late, the damage is done. I have to get out of here.

I'm sorry. I know I'm a monster. I'm a monster that created something equally monstrous... and sometimes, we cannot control the terrible things we choose to create.

HORROR STORIES TO RUIN CHRISTMAS

THE EIGHTH NIGHT OF CHRISTMAS IS CLANDESTINE

BY KELLY CHILDRESS

I RIFLED THROUGH THE FILES, EACH LABELED NEATLY WITH a name and location, unsure of which to choose. Who would please my God the most?

Brenda Sheehan: Deer Crossing Lane (the old Mueller place)

Bobo: Homeless. Frequents the clinic, thrift shop, church, liquor store

Nathan Price: Serenity Falls Cemetery

I could tell without looking that Gillian was shifting in her chair. The floorboards creaked underneath her, betraying her nerves. I tried not to lean in too close. She'd come in reeking of gin and sour vomit for the third time in a week. I'd known she was fond of the bottle from the first moment I met her, but I let her think she was fooling me. It was kinder.

Plus, God's cause needed Gillian. She might have been fired from the Waushara County Times, but the woman was still a journalist at heart; she knew how to get answers when properly motivated.

I tapped the second name on the list. "He's out. I'm not going through the fuss of tracking down another homeless guy." When Gillian opened her mouth to protest, I interrupted. "I know it pays off at the back end because nobody asks questions, but I'm not interested in doing that this time. It's too much initial legwork for us right now. We need to go simple—simple and careful."

I skipped over Brenda Sheehan's name as well. We'd done light surveillance on her and repeatedly found bear prints around her trash cans, which (in my view) made her a sub-optimal choice.

I thought about my options. I thought about Nathan, Bobo… and Gillian, sweet Gillian, our newest member. An idea bloomed in my mind. She might be useful to us in a way I hadn't previously considered.

I tapped a finger lightly on one of the files. "Nathan Price."

"Are you sure, Frank? He's clean, no skeletons as far as I could find. And he serves an important function in the community. People will notice."

The words danced on my lips, but I didn't say them.

"It's important that it's him this time. But that isn't all, Gillian. *You* have to be the one to send him home. You made it. You are finally ready to prove your commitment to God." I slid a dagger across my desk.

Gillian blanched, but recovered. "Y-you're sure? You…" She trailed off into bewildered silence.

Finally, she said quietly, "Me?"

"Don't worry," I responded, unbothered by her reluctance. "If Nathan doesn't pan out, Bobo can be our backup."

Taking care to meet her bloodshot eyes squarely, I drawled, "After all, nobody misses a drunk."

All my life I've been great at getting people to follow me. In grade school, I once convinced half the class that it wouldn't hurt to jump off the top of the slide into the hedges. In high school, I got elected class president without formally running. People like me, and people like to do what I say. It's one of the reasons I went into seminary once I turned 18. I felt my talents were best suited to spreading the word of God.

And although it was one of the hardest decisions I've ever made, I left without getting my M.Div. Those men were shortsighted, noncommittal—they were soft, weak, unwilling to do the work God demanded. They wanted to save souls with words, with ineffectual mewling from the pulpit on Sundays.

Me? I wanted to save them all, and it was irrelevant whether they wanted or understood the saving. Treading lightly helps no one when it's your soul that might go plummeting into the abyss.

God's work has led me down paths I never thought I would go. It's all for Him, though. Everything I do is for Him. Even the bad things, and there's been a fair share of those. Like my last church. Well, all of them, actually.

I thought I'd finally done it with that last church. Surprise, surprise, everyone, God exists, and I'd brought Him to Oroville, California! I really thought I'd accomplished my life's work, only six months and two weeks into the entire endeavor. God works in mysterious ways, though, and that's how I ended up alone on a red-eye flight to Wisconsin, of my former congregants' savings stuffed in a suitcase. I thank the Lord for bearer bonds.

This one, though, the one in Serenity Falls, it has to be the right one. It has to. Why else did God send me that map at the time when I needed His guidance the most?

I received His message while I was on the west coast. My predictions for the end of the world had failed, again, and my followers were beginning to lose faith. Everyone was infected with suspicion. The air was thick and ripe, ready to rupture, like a cyst. And there it arrived in the mail one day—a map with Serenity Falls circled on it, and a note telling me that it was a great place to start over.

It felt like an answer. It felt like God telling me what He wanted me to do.

It wasn't easy, but I'm glad I abandoned them. I've gotten very good at stuffing things into the back of my mind, very good at responding "unless it's for God" when my conscious cries out that it's wrong to steal, wrong to lie, wrong to murder. God has burdened me with some of the most difficult tasks, but I trust He has a good reason. As long as I trust in Him, my soul is safe.

I didn't even wait for our services that night. Didn't spike the water with rohypnol to buy myself some time. I had to leave immediately; I couldn't risk them stopping God's vision from happening.

Serenity Falls is a lot colder than Oroville, but the reception was much warmer. It's one of the reasons I'm so sure this will be my last church. Once we act out God's plan, we'll all be saved.

And the souls we take will be saved, too.

Night came swiftly, as it does in the winter months. I liked this. It made it much easier for us to prepare the cemetery for Nathan's glorious sacrifice.

With everybody working, we had the grave dug and the dais constructed by exactly 7:13 PM. Exactly on schedule. I'm not ashamed to say tears welled up in my eyes when I saw our relics hanging from the trees—some red and green, others crudely carved from wood, to remind of God's humble beginnings.

As I surveyed the quiet, frosty darkness, I almost envied Nathan, that he would get to go home to God on this night. He would suffer, yes, but he would be saved.

The knife glittered on the dais, reminding me that salvation was never easy.

When the poor fool finally wandered into our midst, flashlight in hand, I did my best to keep my voice calm, to quell the excitement jostling through my veins.

"Welcome," I said dryly. My heart pounded as I saw a dark figure cross behind Nathan. Shortly after, his flashlight clicked off, restoring the gorgeous night. I couldn't help but grin as the cold air wrapped itself around me.

I felt God at that moment, in the darkness, hiding like a spider. I began chanting the sacred words.

When the words were spoken, I ventured closer to my quarry. He didn't know me, but we knew a lot about him.

"How's business? I imagine *your* business is going quite well recently." I paused, wanting my next word to cut like the knife on the dais. "Fortunately."

I went through the process as I had many times before, but this time, with an extra eddy of anticipation in my belly. I took a step towards Nathan.

Then, all of a sudden, there was a flurry of limbs. I heard "SHIT" erupt from Gillian's throat, just before she hit the frosted grass.

Nathan Price was running across the cemetery like the devil was on his heels, and then he was gone.

I chuckled to myself—even my own foresight surprises me sometimes. "We'll see you again one day soon, Nathan," I called after him, mockingly. He was still on our short list, after all.

My amusement at my own shrewdness faded as my eyes fell on Gillian, who was groaning and attempting to get back to her feet.

It was always disappointing to be let down by one of your own. I approached my former follower, joy dissipating every second, heart growing heavier with each step. It was never easy sending someone to God.

But I'd tested her, and she'd failed the test.

The knife handle was still warm when I plucked it from the grass.

"Gillian Snyder. During the ceremony itself, you will experience more pain than you ever thought imaginable. But you'll still be alive when we bury you. We'll be sure of that."

Hours later, steam still rising from her raw, stripped flesh into the cool air, she didn't have the energy to stop us as we shut the casket and lowered her into the earth.

THE NINTH NIGHT OF CHRISTMAS IS LIKE PULLING TEETH

BY M. M. KELLEY

"Michaela's still alive though, right?" I asked into my phone, watching our new hire pluck the teeth from cadaver after cadaver.

"You said her dad was cooperating, so… yeah. We don't break promises. The fact that you can still ask that should be proof enough."

I powered off my phone and walked back over toward Hugh. He'd been instructed to keep his phone off and in his car. My metal detector sweep confirmed his compliance.

"I'm sorry we had to snatch Liam and Michaela," I said casually, looking into the toothless maw of the poor sap reclined in the hot seat.

"Sure." Hugh replied curtly. "Grab me the next one. You said I wouldn't be moving bodies."

I whistled for one of the grunts to come swap them out.

"You know, they took my kid, too."

"So, why'd you take mine?"

"They're not lying about the positive points of the job. It's just sensitive and they want to ensure a clean operation. I can promise you that Michaela's fine."

"Yeah," he grunted, voice dripping with frustration and pain as he haphazardly ripped the teeth out of one of the missing parents.

"You know," he said, pointing a bloody incisor at me, "you could just use lye and dissolve all of the body."

"We need the flesh." I shrugged.

"What the fuck for?"

"I just do what the big boss tells me. He wants a mound of flesh, he gets it. I get a safe kid and a life of comfort after this is all over."

I nudged him. "That blood is appetizing though, isn't it?"

The color drained from his face. I laughed hard enough to cause his patient to shake.

"I'm just fucking with you, Hugh. I don't do anything but manage and deliver."

"Why are these people dead?" he demanded.

"Simple, they're the parents that called about the "Bad Man's Home" flyer. We were coming for you anyway, but Liam and Michaela going out and taking the flyers, well, that was just serendipity."

I went to the secured office in the rear of the barn and turned my phone back on.

"Dispose of him when he's done."

"But he's being perfectly obedient." I reasoned.

"He's a nasty man," the big boss hissed from the receiver. "Check the security camera."

There he was. His instruments were down and his tool was up as he fondled a dead breast. "Son of a bitch," I complained.

"You know what you need to do."

"Maybe he has an explanation."

"Need I remind you what's at stake if you don't follow directions?" came the impatient growl.

"Just let me question him first."

"Fine, put your earpiece in and go, but I'm still the judge of what happens."

I synced my earpiece and stashed my phone in my pocket. I snuck up on Hugh purposely.

"What the fuck, man? A dead girl?"

He stumbled. I think he nearly ripped his own dick off from the startle.

"She used to be a patient," he stammered, "I guess it was one last time for a send-off."

"Ask if she knew what was happening when she was his patient," my boss whispered in my ear.

"So, she came in to be put under and fondled?" I asked incredulously, genuinely wanting to understand what was happening.

His eyes darted all over, as if searching for the right answer, "Well, not exactly…"

"Jesus Christ. Just do your goddamn job, or Michaela goes in the fuckin' river." I snarled before walking away.

"I told you that miscreant should be part of the freak show," my boss's voice scolded me.

"I'll start breaking down what we have after; I'd like to let him finish the job. Teeth give me the heebie jeebies."

I began slicing sections off the toothless corpses after hanging them from the hooks and chains that dangled from the rafters. I used a scalpel to remove the pieces as cleanly as possible, hiding the disgust I felt from Hugh. I needed him to be afraid. Ice bins housed the parts until the delivery crew came to pick them up. A bucket of ice and middle fingers unnerves most people.

He kept his hands to himself, but he'd mostly stopped working to watch me.

"Keep moving. I don't want to be here all night, and you don't want to piss off the boss any more than you already have."

"Just deal with him. You can pull teeth yourself, it doesn't have to be a neat job. We hired him for parts." came the response in my ear.

"Not yet!" I shouted, waving the scalpel at the body hanging in front of me menacingly.

I watched Hugh fidget anxiously. Like he was going to make a run for it.

"Hey... I'll come finish tomorrow," he called to me in a hushed voice.

"Hah, just a joke, man," I said nervously, the buzz of my boss demanding Hugh's blood spilled humming in my ear.

I walked over with a disarming smile, and once I got close enough to shake Hugh's hand, I reached up and rammed my scalpel into the center of his throat. Too fucking bad the guy turned out to be such a pervert. I really would've preferred help pulling out the teeth until the parts were harvested. I don't mind butchering, but I hate, hate teeth. At least I didn't have to dodge more questions about his kids now though.

"Ok boss, he's down. I've got the rest of this on my own."

"Good job."

Right. Good job. It's always up to me to do a job if I want it done right. So I should be squared up by the end of the night. All I have to do is pull the pervert's teeth and break him down into pieces like the rest of the bad seeds. Take my delivery to the shack for the boss and by this time tomorrow night, my boy and I should be nowhere near this shithole of a town.

"Do you think you'll have enough pieces for your art?" I asked into my earpiece.

"I think I can make do with twenty-six of each limb."

ON THE TENTH NIGHT OF CHRISTMAS, T'WAS TOO MUCH TO BEAR

BY CHRISTINE DRUGA

When Brenda Sheehan reported a bear rummaging through her trash, we laughed it off as a city girl not knowing what she got herself into when she moved to a small town. Everyone knows bears aren't any trouble in the winter. We figured she had a raccoon problem that she didn't recognize or know how to handle.

When she brought us the picture of Chris Sutherland, buck naked other than bear-paw gloves and boots and nose-deep in her garbage can, we took her a bit more seriously. There'd been some weird shit happening in Serenity Falls over the last few weeks, and the town pharmacist stripping down to his birthday suit and terrorizing a resident by pretending to be a bear was near the top of the "what the fuck" list.

Still, we had bigger fish to fry, so it wasn't exactly a priority.

When Miss Sheehan called us out to show us the mangled chicken corpse and a relatively threatening note that appeared to be left in her kitchen by Dr. Sutherland, we decided to bump her case up on the list of things that needed to be dealt with now.

I went to Sutherland's house first. After knocking on the door at 26 Piper Lane for a good ten minutes and getting no answer, I started looking in the windows. When I peered through the living room window and saw that the place was ransacked, I called for backup. We kicked the door in and searched the place, but Sutherland was nowhere to be found.

In any other case, I would have seen the overturned furniture and holes in the walls and assumed that there was a struggle. Since we had photographic proof that Sutherland was currently off his rocker, we figured he had somehow snapped and that this scene, along with his behavior at Miss Sheehan's place, proved he was totally unhinged and potentially dangerous.

I left a couple officers at the house to sort through the mayhem for any clues about what happened to Sutherland or where he might be, and set out to talk to some folks who knew him well enough to notice if he had been acting weird lately.

Sutherland's colleagues—well, those that I was able to talk to—

couldn't tell me anything other than that they hadn't spoken to him in a few weeks. His coworkers at the pharmacy said he left a message informing them that he might not be in for a while, so they weren't concerned by his absence. They seemed a bit annoyed that they had to cover for him, but they figured he just didn't want to share his reasons for being gone. Lou accepted the food I brought when I questioned him, but didn't have anything to give me in return.

A visit to Lucky's Tavern, next door to Sutherland's Pharmacy, finally turned up something useful. The bartender had noticed Sutherland acting a bit odd after closing one night. She was taking the garbage out as he was leaving, and said he nearly jumped out of his skin when she called out to tell him goodnight.

"He was real shook up, like he'd seen a ghost or somethin'. Didn't say a word, either. He just got into his car and took off."

Her interaction with Sutherland appeared to be the night before he left the message about his absence at work.

I knew *something* had to have happened that night to set him off, but what was it?

Some more investigative work led to me discovering that the eggs appearing in Miss Sheehan's fridge and the chicken "gift" had been stolen from one of the farms on the edge of town. The farmer had assumed that it was the handiwork of a wild animal, though *he* didn't think the tracks in the snow were from a bear. He sure as hell didn't think they were human, either.

I was heading to the diner for some lunch when I got the call from Officer Palmer to head back to Sutherland's house ASAP.

"We found a note. It's... well, get over here. We have a problem."

"We have a lot of problems, kid. I'm on my way."

I was nearly there when I got another call. This one was from Cary-Anne. Sutherland's note would have to wait until we finished dealing with Sutherland himself.

I rushed to the park, where I was met by a small crowd of people trying to stretch their necks to get a look at the reason for the ambulance and cop cars. I ignored their questions and followed Lieutenant Westphal to the edge of the tree line. There, lying face down on the ground, was Christopher Sutherland.

He was just as Miss Sutherland's photo had captured him: completely naked, wearing only gloves and boots that resembled bear paws. The difference was that, while he seemed to be unharmed in her photo, the skin of his back before me resembled ground meat that had gone rotten and his arms and legs were covered in cuts and scrapes.

"What the hell happened to him?" I asked one of the EMTs crouched over the body.

"I have no idea. He was dead when we got here. His skin's cold, so he might've been here for a while before he was found."

"Hey! Look at this!" Westphal called out from about twenty yards away. "Come check out this tree."

"Is that blood?" I asked.

"And skin," Westphal answered. "Looks like he took the bear thing a little too far, maybe. I mean, I've seen bears rub their backs against a tree pretty hard to scratch an itch, but I don't know how he could have gone that far. Had to have hurt like a son of a bitch."

I walked back to the body as the EMTs were loading it onto a stretcher. Sutherland's eyes were wide open, almost bulging out of their sockets. His mouth was agape enough to see that he had broken some teeth, and there was white residue at the corner of it, down to his chin. It looked to me like he had been foaming at the mouth, and the foam had dried when he passed.

I was staring at the ground where Sutherland had been discovered when my phone rang. It was Palmer, wondering where I was and demanding that I meet him at Sutherland's house.

When I got there, I was ushered to the deceased's office, where Palmer awaited me.

"Look at this shit," he exclaimed as I entered the room.

Sitting on the desk, next to a small empty glass bottle, was the note:

To whom it may concern,

I am writing this so that, should any harm befall me, my loved ones may have some closure.

As I closed up the pharmacy last night, a man stepped out from the shadows. I don't know how he got in or how long he had been waiting. I believed the store to be empty when I locked the front door at closing time. His face was covered and I didn't recognize his voice, so I don't know who he was.

The man had a proposition for me: see to it that the liquid in the small bottle he held was ingested by Miss Brenda Sheehan, or my life would be made a living hell. I won't go into the ways he planned to ensure my action, but you should know that the threat was effective.

I was prepared to follow through with my task. Miss Sheehan's home was isolated and easy enough to enter undetected. However, while I stood there—bottle uncorked with its mouth hovering over the opened bottle of milk—my conscience screamed at me to stop.

I couldn't do this to another human being.

I left Miss Sheehan's home and went back to my own, where I battled with myself for hours. One part of me said that I do not know this woman, so possibly harming her in order to protect myself shouldn't cause me any major grief. The other part of me said that I couldn't possibly harm another person. I became a pharmacist to *help* people, how could I stray so far from my ambitions?

I was stuck between a rock and a hard place. I could poison this woman that I've never even spoken to and attempt to live with the guilt, or I could refuse and have my own life ruined in ways that I didn't even want to consider.

You should know that I'm a coward, and that my good reputation among the residents of Serenity Falls is not entirely deserved. However, you should also know that I am not a monster.

I don't know what this liquid will do when I drink it, but I have a feeling that it will be infinitely better than what that man has in store for me when he finds out that it wasn't delivered to Ms. Sheehan as intended.

Godspeed,
Christopher Robert Sutherland

THE ELEVENTH NIGHT OF CHRISTMAS KEEPS BAD COMPANY

BY MR. MICHAEL SQUID

A POUNDING HEADACHE MORE PAINFUL THAN I'D THOUGHT possible woke me up with a gasp. My eyelids were stuck together, and a coppery taste filled my throat as I choked trying to breathe. An unbearable pressure flared from behind my clogged nose. My palate burned and pushed against my skull from the inside of my mouth. The pain was excruciating. I yelled out and opened my eyelids wide. It felt as if my brain would burst. My vision was blurry and every breath felt like fire, I felt drugged. The last thing I remembered was walking back from Lucky's Tavern. My vision focused on the black, scrawling letters painted on the ceiling above me.

GET UP SLOW

DEVICE IS ARMED

LOOK ON THE COUNTER

Device? What device? The metallic taste wasn't just from the blood, collecting and congealing in the corners of my mouth and oozing from my pained sinuses. My tongue fumbled around something cold and metal lodged in the roof of my mouth. The pressure was not going away. I sat up, horrified and confused. I was in my bed, sticky with dried blood. My drug-hazed eyes tried to make sense of my black fibrous arms and legs. Inky dark pom-poms covered them like some sasquatch costume.

A prank, right? I tried to convince myself of that, but the pain was sobering and all too real. The tears streaming down my face were real and the blood coagulating around my molars was real. I saw a strange reflection in the mirror. My eyes blinked from the dark tangle of charcoal-colored cord. I was covered in a ghillie suit like snipers wear to camouflage themselves, black paint on my face that showed only my wide, scared eyes above my swollen jowls. Something was inside my skull.

"Dear God," I choked through the tears caused by the pain in my aching mouth.

I saw the note on the counter folded in half, written in black letters. I picked it up with a shaky hand covered in tendrils of onyx synthetic fibers like a Black Komondor dog. I unfolded the note with trembling fingers and read, fighting my chemically-addled vision to focus on the words.

FOLLOW THE INSTRUCTIONS

WE CAN SEE YOU

WE CAN HEAR YOU

WE CAN KILL YOU

GO TO THE KITCHEN

LET HIM IN

Why me? What the fuck had they put in me, and WHY ME? I sobbed, but the pain in the roof of my mouth quickly caused me to wince. My tongue felt lightly around the large, metal device screwed in and I grunted in horror. What had they put in me? I flicked the lights on, revealing the medical refuse: Bloody gauze, velcro straps, expended syringes and empty glass vials of local anesthetics lay scattered on the floor near the bed, which was smeared and flecked with my blood. I found fragments of what I believe to be my skull and six of my pulled teeth by an empty blood pack. A transfusion had taken place to keep me alive.

I felt queasy; the coiling in my throat intensified and my eyes shed fresh tears. I walked to the mirror, watching the swamp creature of black, mop-like tassels staring back.

How long was I out? What did they do to me?

I leaned close and opened my mouth to see the device, and breathed heavily to prevent from fainting. A brass disc was lodged into the roof of my mouth, held in place with a steel bar with some supporting beam screwed into the exposed white of bone in my palate. Only 26 teeth remained in my stinging jaws, shredded sockets of red jelly stared back at me from where both my upper premolars and molars had been torn out to make room for a metal bar supporting some coin-sized, brass disc. I leaned closer to the mirror and read what was imprinted into it with a shiver: '12 GAUGE'.

It was a shotgun shell, shoved into the open cavity that had been drilled through the roof of my mouth, inside my sinuses and pointed at the bottom of my brain. A steel hammer hovered just millimeters from the primer. It trailed down thin, insulated black wires that led from my mouth to weave throughout the frayed, fabric costume. A shiny black orb of a camera lens gazed coldly from under the tousled, messy cord of the black camo suit.

I winced as I shuffled as quickly as the agony would allow, finally reaching the stairs into my kitchen. That's when I saw the crinkled note on the table. I unfolded and read it as tears streamed down my face.

DAVID HOLMES

42 DAIRY ROAD

YOU WILL STOP HIM

FROM DIGGING

A photograph of a man and a woman posing with wide, genuine smiles was inside. I recognized Melissa from the diner on Main. I read the note again, confused and terrified. I jumped when the doorbell rang, and walked over to look out the window. A face looked back just inches from mine, thick white makeup cracked over a strange grin, under wide eyes peering in. A clown, reminiscent of Lon Chaney as Tito from "Laugh, Clown, Laugh" stood there, unsettling in any scenario, this being the worst.

"Hi! Hi! Are you… here?" an odd, high voice warbled through the door with a fake innocence that was truly unsettling. "Better open up!" he squeaked. I saw the remote control trigger in his gloved hands, and I opened the door as my heart sank. Muddy, oversized shoes stepped inside. White cotton-gloved fingers reached up and touched my face, gently at first before pressing hard into the skin, sending waves of pain stabbing through my temples and jaw. "Open up! The cheerful voice implored as that dead gaze looked into me like I was a defiant meal.

"Ghah!" I cried and widened my throbbing jaws, revealing the mangled roof of my mouth and the device that would surely end me.

"Mmm hmm," he said comically, pressing a gloved finger onto his chin. "Good thing you didn't try to take it off, good thing!" he said, trudging his filthy clown shoes on my carpet. He pointed a white finger, now streaked with rusty red from my dried blood, at the photo of my brother and nephew on the counter. "He's next on the chopping block if you misbehave, kids chop easy!" the clown said gleefully. With no introduction or explanation, he dialed a number on an old flip phone and handed it to me along with the script on a wrinkled piece of loose-leaf paper.

"Hello?" he answered.

I read the scribbled words on the paper in my hands. "What lies below shall remain unknown," I struggled to enunciate through my swollen, butchered mouth. The pain of speaking pushed tears down my black painted cheeks. The confused man asked some questions but the clown signaled for me to hang up with a pinky and thumb pressed into his other palm. That was only the beginning.

I was ordered to spy on and threaten David over the course of the next few days as the clown stuck close by. He waited in a flashy, vintage car that looked out of a car show, a shapely green Zephyr model from the '30s. Impossible to miss. The clown would drive me to David's home or his shop. He'd march behind me, jiggling the detonating device as if I'll somehow forget there was a live round inside my skull. He'd speak to someone on the phone on occasion but only when I was out of hearing range.

I could tell they wanted him and that car to be seen, but as to why, I was in the dark. I crept into David and Melissa's house after they'd fallen asleep and the clown waited outside. I spotted the permit plans and even the maternity pamphlets on the counter, before taking photos as ordered of them asleep in each other's arms.

That clown watched as I stapled the photo of David and his wife in bed to the front door. Next, he forced me to break into the auto repair shop and leave a fetal pig. Tears streamed as I wrote a warning on the shop's wall with the blood as instructed, fighting off the urge to vomit. I tried to imagine a scenario where my skull remained intact each time we drove in silence on the way back to my home on the edge of Serenity Falls. I think that's why they picked me.

Tonight, when the clown rushed out in a hurry, I realized something was wrong. "Yes! He's here," the frowning face studied me, cocking his head as he listened. "OK, then I'll come back for him in one hour, one hour, yes!" He hung up and marched those comically long shoes out the door. He leered back with a smile that melted into a grimace before his painted head turned away. He walked in the snowy grass over to that toxic-green car and drove off. A gust of winter air rippled in and cooled my filthy, costumed body as I watched the tail lights disappear behind the trees. With a tired whimper, I sunk into the couch and wept.

An hour stretched into two, then three. I waited in the kitchen, sorting out my modest will. I'm pretty glad I got it out of the way. Something seems to have gone wrong, and I have a pretty strong premonition this is the end of it.

It's been five hours now, but the rhythmic ticking I feel in my jaws started only 20 minutes ago. As to what exactly that nightmarish clown's confirmation protocol entailed, I have no idea. All I know is I'm sure he hasn't performed it, whether he's dead, asleep, or arrested. I've angled the camera so they can't see what I'm typing, but I think it's too late to even worry about that now. That's my will in the printer tray. Tell the Holmes folks I'm so sorry.

THE TWELFTH NIGHT OF CHRISTMAS IS JUST PRETEND

BY MATT DYMERSKI

Thanks to my best friend Ralph, I'd seen some horror movies. I wasn't really a fan because I couldn't stand anything gory, but at his insistence I'd seen enough horrifying scenarios to keep sane and focused when I was taken.

If you're reading this, then you're likely someone investigating the aftermath of Serenity Falls. Let me be blunt: they were hardly the first. The only special significance Serenity Falls holds now is that they were the largest so far.

My town was remote, and had a population barely over three hundred. We all knew each other.

Imagine my surprise when the blindfold was torn off and I found myself seated in Shane Haley's barn facing twenty-six of my neighbors. Like me, they were bound to chairs, gagged, and wide-eyed with terror. Hearing more to my left, I realized I was at the end of another line of twenty-six. The fifty-two of us had been separated into two lines and set up to face each other. I was about to curse Shane Haley through my gag, but then I saw him toward the other end. He wasn't part of it. They'd simply taken his barn for this purpose.

They were wearing black, and peered at us through narrow-eyed white theater visages as they moved down the lines checking ropes and ripping off blindfolds. The men handling the other line wore masks with grins; those attending us wore masks with frowns.

A grinner and a frowner held old lady Eaton, untied and terrified, far down at the other end. Standing shakily between the two lines of bound men and women, she lifted a note and began to read it quietly. "Citizens... township..." The frowner holding her right arm squeezed, and she grew louder. "Citizens... you are about to take part in... something special." She looked to someone she knew. "I'm so sorry, Fred, I—"

She screamed briefly as the frowner squeezed harder.

"...something special. Each of you will have a turn. Those of you sitting... in the happy row... will have a choice." She turned her head toward the grinner holding her left arm. "What does that mean?"

He just stared back at her.

She returned to reading. "Those of you sitting in the sad row will..." She turned her head to the frowner. "No!"

From their aggressive stance, I thought the frowner was going to hurt her again, but instead she was released, and he pushed her toward the open darkness out the opposite end of the barn. Timidly, she walked off into the night, looking this way and that at every masked kidnapper on the way.

No one made a move to stop her. Were they just letting her go? What if she walked right to the nearest payphone and called the cops?

Multiple scenarios ran through my head as the other fifty-one townsfolk in attendance squealed and groaned and shouted from behind their gags. One, this might all be over before she could get authorities here. Two, they might have cut the phone lines.

Or, three: old lady Eaton didn't matter because the authorities *were already here.*

I stared up at the frowner nearest me, trying to match his build and eyes to any of the police in town, but I didn't have enough time to think. The first choice was being offered at the other end.

I couldn't hear what they were saying, but Lloyd Alston's gag had been removed, and he was crying and apologizing. Who was he paired with? I could hear someone male making anxious noises, but—

Oh, God.

Eyes widened all around me as the sound of a handheld saw revving up reached us.

There was screaming—out and out wails from Lloyd, and muffled cries from everyone else—but I was silent. Something hit me in that moment, and I knew I had to do anything I could to survive. This wasn't a joke, this wasn't a game, and nobody was coming to save us.

Strangely, the faces of my neighbors relaxed somewhat after a moment. There was a sound of someone gasping at the other end, and I realized they'd ungagged the person that had just been hurt. At the very least, that meant he was still alive. In fact, he was managing to talk, although I couldn't hear the words.

I couldn't hear what was going on, but I could see Lloyd's reaction.

Lloyd Alston was shaking his head and crying and protesting twice as loudly as before.

What were they...?

A frowner walked into sight gripping a startingly-bloody handheld saw.

Lloyd struggled against his bonds, and I looked away.

The high whine of the saw rose to a shrieking pitch—and then dimmed as it met resistance.

My neighbors were all screaming as best they could, but I felt nothing but total and absolute calm.

I'd seen some horror movies. Ralph had made sure of that. He was away on an oil rig this season, so he was safe. He wasn't here. I had to believe that. There was no way these sick monsters had gotten their hands on him. You had to have a special permit to even get on the helicopter out to the rig... Ralph was safe.

And his favorite movies were playing in my head. Monsters lurked in the dark corners of my thoughts. Serial killers chased college kids across the back alleys of my mind. How do victims behave? What makes one person survive while another dies? No man, even a killer, is without motivations. The key is to not fit into their plan. The key is to stand out.

It wasn't always a saw. Did the happy row get to choose the instrument? Earl Donovan said something that caused a frowner to bring out a power drill, though I couldn't see what was being done with it until the victim was given *their* choice and Earl...

I couldn't watch. I looked away until the screaming stopped. Earl was slumped forward in his ropes, leaking blood from his forehead.

Shane Haley refused to answer. *Good, Shane. Good. Don't fit into their plan.*

Nope.

A frowner pulled out a pistol, showed it to us like some demented Jeopardy model, and simply shot both Shane and the person he was supposed to make a choice for.

The gunshots rang in my ears for several seconds, hitting home the lesson: there would be no easy moral path out of this. Refusing to make a choice would get both people killed outright.

Who was directly to my left? I strained against my ropes.

Carla Atkins.

She was forty-five, and owned a small clothing shop. She didn't deserve this, but I was glad that *someone* was there, because hers would be the only choice I would be able to fully witness. I had to understand what was happening if I had any chance of surviving. Until then, all I could do was wait and listen to the screeches, gurgling, and whines of various power tools.

The most disturbing thing about a mass slaughter is how quiet it gets. It starts out as cacophony of dozens of people screaming. There's hope. There's confusion. Each act of violence is an agonizing indication that this is really happening. There's one, then another, then another. Slowly, there's less screaming, both as people begin to die, and as people begin to lose hope.

It was totally silent as a grinner removed Jo Blackburn's gag and asked her to make a choice for Carla Atkins.

Jo looked at me.

I hadn't expected that.

In fact, I hadn't even looked directly across from my own seat the entire time. Kent Murphy sat there, wild-eyed, staring at me. He'd probably been trying to get my attention for the last twenty minutes, but I was still in a trance.

Kent looked at Carla, then at me.

I looked at Jo.

Jo looked at Carla, or perhaps at the table of power tools that had been rolled up behind her. Shaking and red-faced, Jo said quietly, "The... hedge clippers... one finger."

Jo's grinner shook their head.

She hesitated, then tried, "One hand?"

The grinner shook their head a second time, and I saw Carla's frowner reach for its pistol menacingly.

"Look," Jo said frantically. "Just listen! Her hand—take her hand—because she owns a clothing store. She sews all the stuff herself. She loves that store! If she loses a hand, she can't sew, and she'll go bankrupt, and it'll ruin her!"

The grinner tilted their head for a moment in a twisted mockery of concentration, and then looked up in askance at the darkness to my right. It hadn't even occurred to me that someone might be standing silently beyond me, waiting, watching… approving.

The grinner and the frowner seemed to take an unheard cue, and accepted Jo's choice.

Carla Atkins didn't let loose a single scream. She just glared back at Jo with a rage so fierce I thought she might actually burn through her bindings. The choice might have saved her life, but it had been a very personal and injurious one.

Blood splattered across me, but I still didn't flinch. I watched and listened as Carla's gag was removed and she was given her own choice.

The tool couldn't be changed, but the location could. Carla chose *heart*.

I closed my eyes until Jo's screaming stopped. It only took a moment, and a single squishy cracking sound followed as her ribs broke.

When I opened my eyes again, Kent was being offered a choice, and I finally had a plan.

Behind my gag, I did my best approximation of a smile.

Taken aback, Kent blinked. I was certain he wasn't sure what to make of my expression. Hesitantly, he looked past me and said, "Pliers." At further prompting, he added, "Teeth?"

The grinner shook their head.

"Uh… eyes?"

The grinner shook their head a second time, clearly implying that these options weren't nearly devastating enough.

But a different voice broke in from the shadows to my right. "No, go with the teeth. This one's smiling. Don't you see? It's perfect."

My heart was racing in my chest, but I was more than glad. Teeth could be replaced. Extensive pricey dental work was a small cost to pay for surviving this.

The frowner came up behind me with the pliers and removed my gag.

At that moment, I was hit with a stroke of brilliance. Finally able to talk, I turned my head the half-inch toward the right I could manage and said excitedly, "Hi! Hi! Can I do it?"

The unknown voice of authority was intrigued. "To yourself?"

I needed to sound crazier. I needed to do something no horror movie victim had ever done. I giggled like a maniac, and then replied, "To both of us. I've always wanted to do something like this."

Kent was horrified, sure, but I had an inkling that this was the only way out for me. All of the happy row members were dead, and most of the sad row members had been grievously wounded and left to bleed out. I figured there was no chance these masked men were going to rush us to a hospital.

At some unseen nod, the frowner untied me and handed me the pliers.

It hurt less than I thought to pull some of my own teeth out, but maybe that's because the pain was combined with the hope of survival.

Then... *I'm so sorry, Kent, but I want to live.* If pretending's what I have to do, then pretend I shall.

When it was over, that voice in the darkness sounded pleased. "You've got a quality about you," I was told. "I am your Ringmaster now." To the masked men, it commanded, "Fetch him a disguise. Or rather, a... costume."

I stood there with a broken grin, accepting this as my only way out. I had to pretend like my life depended on it, because it did.

Thing is, that was seven years ago. I've been pretending ever since. I've seen the labyrinthine mind-games the Ringmaster plays. I live every moment terrified I'll be found out as a pretender. Six months ago, I carved up my best friend Ralph, and I didn't even bat an eye. I've been playing the role for so long that I'm not sure what normal even is anymore.

So why am I writing this now, then, after seven years?

Because not two hours ago, on this, the eve of nightmare for Serenity Falls, the Ringmaster whispered in my ear, "*I know you're pretending.*"

Pressing a small vial of liquid into my palm, he continued. *"You'll drink this without question now."*

After nearly a decade of sadistic stalking, torture, murder, and ghastly experiments, I could only ask, "Why? Why did you let me live for so long?"

The answer was simple. "Because every Ringmaster needs a clown."

THE THIRTEENTH NIGHT OF CHRISTMAS WAS MERRY

BY E. Z. MORGAN

Sunflower Bakery sat next to the abandoned warehouse in downtown Serenity Falls. It stood out amongst the other buildings due to the bright white of its exterior and its two welcoming sunshine yellow doors. There was no sign indicating its wares. Instead, a large colorful sunflower was painted on the shop's face, right above the doors, taking up any space not occupied by windows. The sunflower bloomed against the paint, reaching for the light with twenty-six pointed petals.

The owner of the bakery was a woman named Merry Hoggins. Merry was a short, plump, older woman with a head of light gray curls. In her youth her hair had been a dazzling strawberry blond, but as Merry said, "Age takes what it wants." Merry was known around town as the kindest, most loving soul one could ever meet. She knew everyone's name and favorite pastry. She always seemed to have whatever her customers craved. Her shop was the first stop for many patrons before starting their day.

On this Christmas Eve, Merry was as busy as ever. Almost every resident of Serenity Falls had passed through her bakery, picking up their fruit cakes, cinnamon buns, cookies, or whatever delicious treat their hearts desired. By 3PM Merry had served her final pastry and closed the shop down. She let out a long contented sigh.

The real work was done. It was time for fun.

Merry wrapped her bright red coat around her and donned a Santa hat. The hat had belonged to her father. He wore it almost satirically. This man was no present-bearing joy bringer. He was as cruel as cruel could get. Merry was never smart enough or thin enough for him. Her mother left when she was young and Merry bore the brunt of that betrayal. She could remember when she was fifteen, and first told her father to his face that he was abusive. To be more accurate, she called him *an abusive fuck*. In response, he laughed. Merry had grown to hate that hollow laughter. He leaned in close, her chin gripped painfully in his hand, and said, "I'd be much more abusive if you were pretty enough to fuck."

As Merry got into her car, she tried to get her father's image out of her mind. She had places to go. First she drove past Dr. Yihowah's office. Yihowah wasn't his real name, obviously. The psychopath had chosen his new moniker after God in a show of hubris. His real name was Dustin Chimneys; much too simple for such a megalomaniac. Merry chuckled as she pictured his pinched face drinking her coffee over and over, unable to get enough. What an addict.

Next she drove a bit out of town to the old Hickory farm. Only the father and son were left after a brutal double murder. The caution tape was still up, blinding and garish against the dullness of the abandoned farm. It reminded Merry of the farm she grew up on. Her mother and father used to raise sheep and miniature ponies. What a lovely picture that must bring to most people. By the time Merry had been accepted to college and moved out, all of the ponies had died and the sheep had scattered. Not even animals wanted to live near her father.

Merry grew into a brilliant chemical engineer. She was applauded for her fortitude and dedication to the craft. In the male-dominated field, she'd made a name for herself creating things unimaginable to most. Concepts like love and family were far from her thoughts. Instead, she enjoyed her science. It was the only thing she could count on.

The next stop on Merry's tour was the Sullivan household. What a tragedy, yet such an opportunity—a single father, doing whatever he could for his child. Merry sneered. Fathers do not really love their children. They only use them to get what they want. Jake might pretend, but Merry had seen who he really was, and like all bad men, he got what was coming to him.

Merry rolled past the house, noticing a cop car across the street. Cops were helpful, in a way, each one acting like superheroes until their precious lives were threatened. Just the other week Ted killed himself for no discernable reason. Perhaps he couldn't live with the responsibility and guilt of controlling other people's lives. Then there was that annoying Hatch girl; she certainly wasn't the angel she was made out to be.

Merry spotted Gregory on the street. She put on a fake smile and waved to him. He nodded in response. Merry despised this man. He didn't understand human decency. She knew he had killed that young woman Ally, who hadn't done a thing wrong other than trust in a man. It was all a part of this Christmas, Merry knew that, but it didn't change her opinion. She wouldn't be surprised if Gregory was a father too, though she knew most women he spent time with weren't around long enough to conceive.

Merry's own father didn't contact her for nearly twenty years after she had left. It was a blessing. She could pretend that he didn't exist at all. But when she turned forty she got the dreaded call. Her father was dying. That fact wasn't the bad news, of course. The bad news was that he had no money and no one to take care of him. Merry offered to pay for his care but he refused. He was adamant—she owed him. He had raised her, given her food and shelter (and little else). Despite everything inside of her, Merry agreed to go back to Serenity Falls and watch this man die.

Death was a funny thing. It brought people together and yet it made people feel so alone. She thought about Jose, whose son had been murdered. His tears had been so big. Little Carter just wanted ice cream. Maybe if Jose had been a better father he could've saved him. Merry scoffed at the thought. No father could save his children. Secretly, she knew Jose was glad it was his son and not him. What a waste of air. A waste of tears.

As Merry drove back into town she was reminded of the dentist, Timothy Poole. Rumor was he'd fed pieces of himself to his patients. He lost his mind and, eventually, his life. It would almost be a pity, but like all, he created victims. He was deserving of the pain he suffered. Merry rubbed her tongue along her teeth. He did do a great dental cleaning though.

The cemetery crept up on the left. Towards the back was a simple stone with her father's name on it. She lived with that miserable dying wretch for ten years before he finally passed. It was as though he was holding on just to torture her. She opened the bakery after the first year, needing something to get her out of the house. She dreaded going home. Every time she walked in the door she was greeted with the stench of piss and a barrage of cruelty from the old man. Slumped in a wheelchair, porn on the TV behind him, her father assaulted her with words. Every night Merry would pray to whatever god would listen to make him stop, to just kill the bastard already.

But there was more in that cemetery than her rotting father. Many new souls had been buried there. Nathan Price must be rich now that the town was dying out. Not that he would be able to enjoy it for much longer.

Little Carter lay beneath that soil. Soon little Liam would as well. Two sleeping boys who would never get the chance to grow up. Who will never become fathers and continue the cycle of disappointment and violence. Merry didn't revel in the deaths of children, but she could appreciate that less boys meant less fathers, and less evil.

Finally, Merry pulled up to the water treatment plant. The building was huge and derelict. It wasn't a place often visited, simply unattractive background scenery before the falls. Merry fixed the hat on her head and pulled a duffel bag out of her car trunk. She walked slowly to the side door and pushed it open, a brief smile flickering on her face. Finally, the fun could begin.

Inside, the plant was quiet. No one was supposed to be working. Merry moved silently through the halls, knowing exactly where she was headed. She had walked these corridors before. The concrete was overwhelming, a sea of dirty gray and tan. *Could use some holly*, Merry thought mockingly.

As she walked she began to hear the sounds of weeping. She rolled her eyes as she entered the central chamber. Inside was a round room with a well of rolling water. The sound of the crashing liquid was comforting when compared to the desperate silence of the rest of the plant. On the opposite wall sat Neal—poor, pathetic Neal—sobbing into his arms. He looked so tiny and insignificant compared to the high ceiling.

Merry closed the door behind her and set the bag down. Neal looked up, his face twisted and red. "Hello, *Ringmaster*," Merry said with a sneer.

He was tired. That much was clear. He bore the marks of a month's hard work. The bags beneath his eyes were darker than his black shoes. He wore a complete Santa suit that was growing moist with tears. He sniveled. "Merry? What are you doing here?"

She ignored him. "No need for the handcuffs this time."

He wiped his face. "Merry, you've got to get out of here. It's dangerous. I know you were probably forced into coming, but it's not worth it."

Merry removed the contents of her bag. There was a large container filled with a yellow substance that she placed on a nearby ledge. She also brought out a small purple vial. Finally, she removed a photograph taken many years ago.

"Neal, do you remember when we were kids?"

Neal slowly stood up, leaning against the wall. "Please, Merry. Go home."

She persisted. "We were just playing around, weren't we? Anything to get away from my father. I wanted to watch movies or play board games. Do things normal kids did. But you only wanted one thing." She lifted the container of yellow liquid and strode confidently towards him.

Neal was clearly confused. "Merry, are you talking about when we slept together as teenagers? I thought you and I were good friends, just experimenting."

"It was an experiment for you. For me, it was different." She now stood directly above the well, leaning over it and watching the water below. "You used me like I was a tube sock. Like I was nothing."

"Merry, what are you doing?" The concern in his voice was growing. "It was consensual! You said you liked it!"

"I did," she replied, unscrewing the container and tossing the lid on the ground. "The sex was fun. It's so interesting how brain chemicals make all the difference between fun and torture."

"What's in the bottle?" Neal whined.

"But you never think of what comes after. What does sex get you, Neal? And what did you do for me?"

He paused. The dots must have been connecting in his mind. "Is this about the abortion?"

"No, you miscreant. It's about the fact that you made me believe that a father could be warm, gentle. That a good person could be a father. And then you showed your true colors. They all do. You couldn't even love a child before it was born. You were just like him."

"Merry, put the bottle down!"

"Oh, this?" She stretched her arm over the well. "You don't want me to put it in the water? The water that every resident drinks?"

Neal staggered. "It was you... all along, it was you."

Merry grinned. Seeing him squirm was delightful. "Yes, Neal. Who else could have come up with a serum so effective? Who could create a poison that would wipe out an entire town? Or did you forget that I specialize in hazardous chemicals? You forget so much."

"Don't do it! Please! There are innocent people out there!"

Merry's arm wavered. "You know what, you're right." With a swift motion she tossed the container to the floor. It shattered and the contents spilled out in a spiral.

Neal sighed heavily with relief. "Thank you, Merry. You are truly an angel."

"No," she whispered. "Not an angel." Without warning she charged at Neal, who collapsed backward in surprise. Merry stood over him, her face alight with something akin to madness. "Did you know I spent almost a decade watching my father die? First it was his legs. Then his bowels. Sick bastard couldn't even hold in his shit. Then his lungs started to go. I would listen to the rattle, revelling in the pain he felt with each breath. The doctor wanted to visit him, but I said no. I said he wanted to die at home." She laughed. "And he did, Neal. That twisted fuck died in my childhood home, covered in his own piss and shit, begging for his life. And do you know what I felt?"

Neal shook his head in fear.

Merry leaned in closer. "I felt like God."

Neal was trapped between the wall and Merry. Sweat began to pour down his brow. "Please," he whispered.

"*Please?* That's all you have to say in the presence of a goddamn *god*?!" She turned her back on him in disgust. "I bet you sound just like David Holmes before Gunther killed him. You know Gunther—our friend who enjoys the clown costume. David was going to be a father as well, but we disposed of him before his unborn child could face a lifetime of disappointment and cruelty." She reached for the purple vial and photograph still sitting on the ledge.

"Just let me go, I won't tell anyone you've been behind everything," Neal begged.

"Shut up," she snapped. "You should have figured this out weeks ago. Hell, the plan has been in motion for years! You have no idea how far it reaches." She flung the photo at him. "What do you see?"

He stared at it. "It's you, right? As a girl."

"And what is behind me?"

He paused. "Is that your dad?"

"That *was* my father. He was always over my shoulder, tainting every day with a different form of abuse. Fathers are a zit on the ass of society. All of this, every single thing we've done together, has been to punish the fathers of Serenity Falls. And the others? They were collateral. None of them stopped my father as he slowly and painfully ruined my life. None of them cared about me! They will all face my wrath soon enough.

"And you, Neal. You will be the first to try a new serum I made. Much stronger than the one I snuck into Blake's 'laboratory.' Can you believe that fool child didn't realize that I switched my creation with his useless garbage? This is stronger than anything Yihowah could have dreamed of, stronger than any of the ones I used in the towns I practiced on before here. Would you be surprised to know you aren't the first 'Ringmaster'?

"Think of this as my one act of kindness. You will not have to face the horrors waiting outside this building." She shoved the vial into his hands. "Now drink."

"And if I don't?" He tried to look brave but failed miserably.

"Have it your way. But I guarantee you the citizens of this town will be much harsher than I am."

"What do you mean? You decided not to poison the water…"

Merry took her hat off and ran a hand through her hair. "Not the water, no. It never would have worked. Too much outside fluid would have weakened the serum's potency. The same serum that made Christopher Sutherland into a madman. Did you hear he rubbed his skin off on a tree? He thought he was a bear, the lunatic." She smiled. "I couldn't risk diluting such a strong chemical entity."

Neal's hand quivered, the bottle shaking along with it.

Merry beamed. "So you know what I did, Neal? Do you know what I did?! It's genius, really. I baked the serum right into my goods. In all the cakes and pastries and buns, in every single thing I sold today. Baking is really just chemistry, if you break it down. And you know what? I sold out." She giggled, childlike. "Every single person in this town had a hearty dose of my creation. And even if a few slipped through the cracks, they'll get to experience the joys of a world in chaos. Because this serum—this Christmas miracle—turns ordinary people into monsters. They lose all sense of right and wrong and do whatever their evil inner desires tell them to. For some, like Christopher, it makes them into animals. Others, like Gunther, turn into psychopaths, thriving on the pain they rain on others. What do you think will happen to this place in a few hours, Neal? Do you really want to leave this building and face the madness outside?"

Neal shook his head as tears slid steadily down his face. He lifted the vial.

"Drink it, Neal. Or I will make sure your death is far slower and merciless."

He sobbed as he uncorked the container. The liquid smelled of fear. Closing his eyes, Neal downed the entire thing and hurled the bottle away from him, shattering the glass.

Merry beamed as the serum instantly took hold of Neal. He had no more than swallowed it when his body began to convulse. Merry approached him and pulled the shirt off his torso. He was only wearing his huge red Santa pants now. His skin looked like it was beginning to boil, pink bubbles growing large, stretching, and popping. He could not even scream as his largest organ melted onto the floor. He looked like an ice cream cone in the sun. Huge pieces sloughed off, revealing muscle and bone. His intestines flopped around like hungry caterpillars. And all the while the man was awake, feeling every second of excruciating pain. Finally, after an eye had fallen into his mouth and the majority of his skin had bubbled across the concrete, Neal died. The whole process took twenty-six minutes.

Merry didn't say a word as she left the building, got back in her car, and drove to the bakery. The roads were quiet, for now. She climbed the back stairs to the roof of her shop. And there she sat, serene, watching the town below. Surveying like the god she had become.

Within an hour the police sirens were raging. People in the streets were screaming with either glee or pain. Blood spilled across the roads. Children were playing with the disembodied heads of their parents. Naked women rubbed against each other until their skin scraped off. And in all this madness, no one thought to look up. To wonder what infallible deity had created this world for them.

And on this last night, Merry rested, content that her work was done.

ABOUT THE AUTHORS

Ground zero for our work is Reddit's NoSleep community at www.reddit.com/r/nosleep. You can find individual authors all over the place. Here is where some of them hide:

blair-daniels.com

jspeziale.com

kbprinceo.com

thejesseclark.com

humangravy.com

kellyachildress.wixsite.com/professionalsuccubus

strangehorrors.com

nightterrorsblog.tumblr.com

michaelsquid.com

mattdymerski.com

m.facebook.com/EZmisery

facebook.com/pocketoxfordwrites

tobiaswade.com

sfbarkley.com

www.humangravy.com

facebook.com/porschephiliac

www.reddit.com/r/HouseofHorrors

www.reddit.com/r/ByfelsDisciple

Made in the USA
Middletown, DE
18 December 2020